AN INCIDENTAL DEATH

ALEX HOWARD was born in London and educated at St Peter's College, Oxford and Edinburgh University where he studied Arabic and Islamic History. He worked in adult education for the British Council and other institutions in the Middle East and London. He is married with two children. Find out more at *www.alexhowardcrime.com*

Also by Alex Howard

TIME TO DIE

COLD REVENGE

A HARD WOMAN TO KILL

AN INCIDENTAL DEATH

Alex Howard

First published in the UK in 2016 by Head of Zeus Ltd

This paperback edition first published in the UK in 2017
by Head of Zeus Ltd

9 7 5 3 1 2 4 6 8

A catalogue record for this book is available from
the British Library.

ISBN (PB) 9781784971366
ISBN (E) 9781784971076

Typeset by Adrian McLaughlin

Printed and bound in Great Britain by
CPI Group (UK) Ltd, Croydon CR0 4YY

Head of Zeus Ltd
First Floor East
5–8 Hardwick Street
London EC1R 4RG

WWW.HEADOFZEUS.COM

AN
INCIDENTAL
DEATH

PROLOGUE

Melinda Huss was dying. She wasn't in any pain, the local anaesthetic in her side had taken care of that, all she could feel as the blood trickled out from her right side was a faint tickling sensation as it flowed down her skin and a spreading warmth as it pooled underneath her body.

She was lying on her back on a massage table in the spa and treatment centre of the luxury hotel's lodge. The room was small and clinical, its only decoration three severe black and white Robert Mapplethorpe photographs of flowers, their curled foliage like organs from a human body. They had an ethereal, fleshy, beauty all of their own.

There was a table with a laptop on it and two charts on the wall – one featuring traditional Chinese medicine meridian lines where chi was said to flow, another, brightly coloured, indeed almost the only other colour in the room, showed the main chakra positions from Indian yoga.

The other source of colour in the room was the enormous red stain that spread out across the white sheet covering Huss's torso.

She was quite calm, tranquil almost, but she could feel herself becoming light-headed. She wondered how much blood she had actually lost. She felt another warm trickle down her body. It seemed to be leaving her body in irregular bursts. It wasn't unpleasant. In fact, if you had to choose a way to die, bleeding out like this was not a bad way to go at all.

She lifted her head and looked down at the Velcro straps that secured her arms and legs. She had tried before to break her bonds or wriggle free. She had been unsuccessful. She wasn't going to try again.

She could feel her will, and her strength, draining away.

She thought of Enver Demirel, her fiancé. She thought of Hanlon. Her fierce, attractive face, and she thought of the long road that had led here.

To this place.

To this death.

CHAPTER ONE

Kriminalkommissar Claudia Meyer of the Baden Württemberg *Landeskriminalamt* strode out of the foyer of the baroque building just off Karlplatz in the historic Alt centre of Heidelberg.

It was incredibly noisy. Horns were beeping in the narrow mediaeval streets where traffic had backed up. Sirens wailed, police were shouting commands at a vociferous crowd that had gathered.

The red sandstone castle on the hill above looked down on the small, picturesque town below. The scene that she had just witnessed in the first floor drawing room was as gruesome as any the castle had seen in its long history. There had been an eye-opening amount of blood.

There were a couple of blue and silver VW squad cars from the cop shop on Eppelheimer Strasse parked on the narrow cobbled street outside, and the front door of the large, detached town house had been sealed off. The blue uniformed police on the door watched her as she passed. She nodded at the driver of the van that she recognized as belonging to Forensics which was pulled up on the pavement.

The street where all this commotion was occurring was in one of Heidelberg's most fashionable quarters. It was university land, but the house she had just left was startlingly expensive, even by Stuttgart standards. Prices had risen steeply in latter times. It was the kind of place that only fairly recently had become gentrified and was now increasingly being colonized by non-German investors. It lay in the heart of the city, near the exclusive Hauptstrasse. It wasn't the kind of place you associated with violent death; more expensive shopping and a *Kaffee* and a slice of *Sachertorte*.

A sign of the times, she thought. Her father would be angry, as usual. 'What is this country coming to, Claudia!'

Mind you, she thought, women in the police force made him angry too. Global warming, GM crops, refugees, transsexuals, Austrians, it was a long list that encompassed practically everything modern.

'Hey, DI Meyer!'

She groaned. So the papers in the form of *Bild*, the bestselling national red-top, were already here.

Jurgen Flur, biggest sleazebag in the Rhein-Neckar area, and face to match. Late forties with long, stringy, greying hair and industrial-size pouches under his eyes, resembling an over-the-hill porn actor. He was accompanied by a tough-looking photographer in a leather jacket.

'Is it true that's Gunther Hart up there with his throat cut?' His voice was eager. He so wanted it to be true, thought Meyer.

The photographer shot several images of her.

'No comment, Jurgen.'

'Then it is true.' She rolled her eyes. She could really do without the press intrusion from *Bild*.

'And it was Muslim extremists; they say the concierge is missing, and he's a Turk. Is it true he's the main suspect?'

A crowd had gathered to watch what was going on. Soon more TV stations would be arriving. Gunther Hart was a prominent member of the community. His murder by Muslim terrorists would make headlines on national news, and this at a time when racial tensions were heightened by the refugee debate.

'Go away, Jurgen.'

'Is it the work of Al-Ansaar al-Akhdaar?' This new terrorist group had recently posted a death list of Germans online. Prominent amongst them had been Gunther Hart.

'Oh, for heaven's sake.'

'It is, isn't it?' His voice was eager, insistent, he waved his phone in front of her face, recording her voice, probably her image as well, whilst the cameraman clicked away. She turned her back to them and moved away.

She reached her police car, a 220 Mercedes, and got in, careful of the positioning of her legs. She was wearing a skirt and any second now, she suspected, Jurgen would fling himself on the floor and try to photograph up it. She'd known him a long time. He'd done it before.

She slammed the door shut. Lucas, her sergeant, started the car.

Jurgen Flur banged on the car's roof and pressed his face up against the window.

'What about Wolf Schneider? Our readers love him, or does Berlin want him dead?'

'Drive,' she growled to Lucas. Jurgen Flur was tapping on the window, the camera behind him was poised. She could see that her irascible subordinate's front teeth were resting on his lip to produce the *'ver'* syllable of *verpiss dich*. Not a good move to actually tell *Bild* to fuck off. Not with a circulation of two and a half million.

'He's on the hit list, when are you lot in Stuttgart going to act?'

As they drove off she could see Jurgen shouting, 'You'll have blood on your hands, you Saxon, Commie-loving, fag hag!'

She rolled her eyes.

Lucas said, 'It's a shame it had to be Gunther Hart, he was one of the good guys.'

Al-Ansaar al-Akhdaar.

The Green Companions.

Green from the colour of Islam, and the Companions, named after the earliest followers of Muhammad. It was rumoured they were formed from hardened ISIS terror fighters who had joined the stream of *Flüchtlinge,* the refugees from Syria that Merkel had invited in. It was rumoured the group contained German-born Muslims, rebelling against the land that had sheltered them and brought them up. It was rumoured… It was all rumours really, although the death of Gunther Hart wasn't a rumour, it was a blood-soaked reality.

She sighed irritably as the car roared off through the cobbled streets of the old town. The quiet, art deco buildings mocked the turmoil in her mind. What a bloody awful day this was turning out to be.

CHAPTER TWO

The Reverend Mike Andrews put his head round the door of the church hall. He did a quick head count: maybe thirty people. He closed the door and went back into the kitchen, doing a quick sum in his head: thirty people, half a litre each, fifteen litres of soup. The large stockpot they had on the stove held thirty and was two thirds full, plenty for everyone. Then bread. They had sliced white – brown had proved unpopular – whose sell-by date was the previous day, donated by a local supermarket. It was still perfectly fine to eat. There were twenty slices per loaf and they had five.

He thanked God; Jesus had loaves and fishes, they had loaves and leek and potato soup made by Rowenna that morning. He said a quick prayer of gratitude for the unlikely assistance of the diminutive anarchist activist, who although a self-professed atheist, was perfectly willing to help out the forlorn souls, a mixture of rough sleepers, street drinkers and a sprinkling of sad-eyed refugees who were the customers. That was more than could be said of his regular congregation, more's the pity.

He went back inside the kitchen.

'Thirty, Rowenna.'

She was standing on a stool stirring the soup, so it didn't catch and burn on the bottom of the pan, with a long-handled metal spoon.

She nodded and picked up the ladle. 'Ready to go when you are…'

The Revd Mike gave her the thumbs up. He disapproved of her politics and certainly felt alarmed by her anti C of E rhetoric, but he felt that there was more innate goodness in this multi-pierced tattooed girl in her ragged clothes than in the majority of his well-heeled sanctimonious flock.

He started pulling the screens up.

Old Harry said to Elsa, 'Oi, oi, darling, here comes lunch!'

He looked with affection at his companion. If only she'd take care of herself, he thought with concern. She was only seventy-something, a spring chicken. He was eighty-five. He didn't need to use the soup kitchen but if he stayed at home round the corner all he would see was his carer once a day and she only stayed about ten minutes. Got to keep busy, he told himself, got to keep the mind active.

Elsa certainly helped there, when she wasn't 'tired', as he thought of it.

She had been lecturing him on an artist called Frank Auerbach. Harry had never heard of him. He didn't know many painters; he'd heard of Constable and his mum had had two pictures in the parlour: *Bubbles*, a little Victorian girl blowing a bubble with a clay pipe, and *Rannoch Moor*, some Highland cows in Scotland. Elsa was saying,

'… and he returned to the same subject over and over

again, not everyone liked his thick use of paint…' She fell silent and her kindly blue eyes grew puzzled. Harry could see that she'd forgotten what she was talking about.

'What's happening, dear?' she asked him. He mentally shook his head, what a waste. She had once lectured in Art History at one of the colleges, he'd forgotten which one, but now her mind had gone. She was still attractive, or rather she would be if she had a clean-up. He was glad that after his bad fall a couple of years ago that had left him with a six month concussion, blinding headaches and confusion, he had lost all sense of smell. He suspected that Elsa might whiff a bit.

He had tried to take her home, but she had grown frightened. She had lived so long on the streets that indoors physically scared her. She was like a rare bird that you couldn't put in a house.

'… I'm hungry, Harry, oh, I do hope it's soup! I like soup.' He loved her girlish enthusiasm for things.

He looked at the queue forming and stood up. 'I'll go and fetch you some, me old Dutch.'

'That'd be nice, Harry, you're such a kind man.' She beamed at him. She had a dazzling smile.

Old Harry got slowly, awkwardly to his feet, pushing himself up with his arms, feeling the habitual fizzing pain in his left knee from arthritis, and straightened his back. He looked down at the thick white hair of Elsa, her Roman nose and beautiful large eyes. If only they had met when they were younger.

You stupid old fool, he thought to himself, like she'd have given the likes of you the time of day.

He handed her his stick to look after, he'd need both hands for the tray.

'All aboard the Skylark,' he said. He knew that she liked simple, optimistic declarations, no matter how meaningless.

Now she was beaming at him.

'What fun, Harry, what fun!'

Slowly, he went to take his place in the queue.

CHAPTER THREE

'Who the hell is Wolf Schneider and why on earth should I care about him?' asked Assistant Commissioner Corrigan. Deputy Commander Henry Gower from SO1, the specialist protection branch, smiled wearily.

'How good is your German and your knowledge of German politics?'

'Non-existent on both counts,' said AC Corrigan, firmly. 'Why are we even having this meeting? Julie, I mean Commander Hatton is your boss, not me.'

Gower inspected his fingertips. He'd been gardening at the weekend and he was concerned that bits of soil were trapped under his nails despite several showers.

'She's on holiday. This came up and she wants you to deal with it...' He resumed his inspection. A couple of them looked a bit grimy. He was fastidious about his personal appearance.

Corrigan looked suspiciously at the bald, fat figure of Henry Gower who appeared to be avoiding eye contact. He kept looking at his hands, it was beginning to get on Corrigan's nerves.

'Why me, Harry? Diplomatic protection does not fall under my remit.'

'But PR does and this is a tricky situation. It just needs a little careful thought and it will cease to be a problem. Colonel Mortimer, you know him, I believe.'

Corrigan nodded. The colonel was one of the police liaison officers who dealt with diplomatic protection. He was a man that Corrigan respected.

Gower said, 'Schneider's a politician and a controversial one, he's a right-wing zealot with a very anti-Muslim message and he's on some kind of jihadi hit list. They've already killed one prominent businessman in Germany, Gunther Hart. So, there's a very real threat to him, and he is an elected MP in Germany.' He paused and looked at Corrigan whose eyes were flickering towards his phone and screen. Gower was keenly aware of the emails building up like waters behind a flood barrier. He carried on.

'But he's not part of the government or that powerful and we don't want to be seen to be being overly friendly to right-wing parties. So, it's one of those slightly awkward problems.'

He put his hands flat on the table and looked at Corrigan.

'Basically, we don't him killed while he is over here. We want good protection but done without any fuss, no big numbers, and done as cheaply as possible.'

'Oh.' Corrigan managed to invest the syllable with a suitably ominous tone. He was beginning to see why Julie Hatton was anxious to wash her hands of Wolf Schneider. She was in charge of Special Operations but his main job was to enhance the Met's reputation. An assassination attempt would be a terrible blow to prestige; equally, the Met did not want to be seen to be favouring fascists.

Corrigan's head might roll.

'How long is he over here?' he asked.

'One week, I believe, and then he's off to the Netherlands. He's been invited to speak at some conference or other, one organized by Dutch right-wing MPs.'

Corrigan rubbed his prominent jaw with a rasping sound. Idly, Gower thought they could use Corrigan as a human shield in diplomatic protection. His enormous size would make him ideal as a kind of mobile barricade and his vast strength would come in handy for manhandling any protestors out of the way. Despite the expensive suit, Corrigan looked very much like a bouncer from a grotty nightclub in Kilburn. He wasn't the kind of man you wanted to get in the way of.

'Who's he seeing here?' Corrigan's voice was polite but sceptical. While it was true that PR was part of his remit, a straightforward babysitting job should not have to reach his desk at all.

Schneider was not really big enough to warrant diplomatic protection but he was maybe slightly too important to simply farm the job out to a divisional support team. He was kind of on the cusp.

Gower shrugged. 'He's doing the media rounds, talking to a UKIP meeting in Islington, at the Union Chapel. They don't associate themselves officially with his views on refugees but they say he's anti-EU so that's why he's there. There's a lunch at the House of Commons, he's a guest of a couple of MPs. That's London really. Then Oxford, he's been invited to speak at the Oxford Union in a debate with some left-wing speaker, who it is hasn't yet been finalized. They wanted Owen Jones originally but he couldn't make it. So it'll be someone like that, maybe a prominent Muslim if they can get one.'

'So that'll be Oxford's pigeon.'

Gower shook his head.

'No, policing the event and maintaining public order is their job, not preventing assassination.'

'Preventing assassination!' Gower thought to himself that the look on Corrigan's face was hard to pin down. Surprise mixed with incredulity mixed with exasperation were some of the contenders.

'Yes, sir. Seemingly there's credible evidence to support this. The home secretary does not want a dead German on her hands right now. Particularly at this time. Nor, I would imagine, do the Met need an international incident in London. Wolf Schneider's head of staff, Christiane Hübler, is due tomorrow to fill us in on the precise details.'

Corrigan breathed deeply. 'And what do you expect me to do?'

Gower slid a folder across the desk to Corrigan.

'This is my plan of action to protect Herr Schneider – numbers of police are noted together with relevant stations. It's only really the Islington event that's a problem.'

'How do you figure that out?' asked Corrigan.

'Well, the House of Commons has its own security. Oxford: Thames Valley will deal with that. They can always call on Firearms from Kidlington if they feel the need.'

He held up a hand to forestall any protest. 'It's fine, it's all cheap and low-key. SO1 will provide the specialist officers, just a small team. We just need a few bodies to deal with a small protest when he's at the Commons and the same for

Islington. I've got a DI who's worked out the details. We'll need a couple of cars with drivers to accompany Schneider and that's about it. I just need authorization.'

Covering your back, thought Corrigan. Just in case anything does happen to Schneider.

'And when you say "a small protest", how small is small?'

Gower scratched his head. 'Probably no more than about fifty to a hundred people, just a few from the SWP and Labour, now they've become a bit more radical. But Schneider's fairly unknown in this country, as is "New Destiny", that's his party.'

'New Destiny, it sounds like an act from *X Factor*.' Corrigan's voice was scathing.

Gower shrugged. 'Neu Schicksal, maybe it sounds better in German, but I think they like to abbreviate it to NS, you can chant it when you have a march, then it works.' He took his laptop out. 'Have a look.'

Corrigan did so. The pictures revealed a night sky, flares, police dogs, riot police, a couple of thousand skinheads in bomber jackets chanting. At their head a stocky, good-looking blond-haired man in a blue two-piece suit flanked by two women.

Behind them was a bearded giant with an equally powerful-looking dog on a leash. He guessed he was Schneider's bodyguard.

'What's that they're shouting? No to refugees?' he asked.

Gower nodded. 'Exactly. There's a big party called the AFD, Alternative for Germany, who are more mainstream, but he's snapping at their heels. And he's photogenic, and he's media savvy, and women like him.'

'I get the picture,' said Corrigan wearily. 'So, just a signature then?' he asked.

'There is something else, sir.'

I knew it, thought Corrigan.

'It's more a PR thing really.' Gower sounded almost apologetic. 'I thought it would be good for our image if we had a non-white policeman as his protection officer, particularly as we're going to be facing crowds shouting the odds that we're protecting fascist racists.'

Corrigan nodded thoughtfully. It made sense, it might even help to calm things down. Gower continued, 'The trained POs will be in the background, I want window dressing. Do you have an officer who is bright and keen, maybe who even fancies moving into Protection Command? Someone who'd like a bit of glamour maybe, for a change.'

'Possibly.' Corrigan's voice was guarded. Could guarding Schneider count as glamorous?

'He'd just have to be from some ethnic background, I'm not choosy,' said Gower. 'Black, Asian, any colour but white.'

'It smacks a bit of tokenism,' demurred Corrigan.

Gower shrugged. 'Life's not perfect, sir. We'd be out of a job if it was, but have you got anyone you could recommend, level-headed, not rash?'

'Yes,' Corrigan answered firmly.

'Calm, alert...'

'I do know what you're after, there's no need to spell it out,' said Corrigan.

Gower was taken aback by the senior policeman's helpful attitude. He'd been expecting a locked and bolted door, not to have it thrown open in welcome. He began to smell a rat.

'Great,' he beamed, covering his suspicions. 'Well, thank you very much. Have him drop by my office tomorrow about three. Ms Hübler will be there and we can all make sure we're singing from the same hymn sheet. They won't get a Glock or a Smith and Wesson but they will get to do something out of the ordinary with a chance for bigger things, if it all works out well.'

'Mm-hm.'

'Which borough's he from?' asked Gower.

'Hackney at the moment, a DI.'

'Well, I'm sure he'd appreciate seeing something other than Haringey,' said Gower. 'They'll kick up but they must have a fair few DIs.'

'I asked him that once, I think it's about fifteen, not so many.'

'Well, when the cuts bite they'll have to scale back anyway, do them good to practise.'

'I'm sure they'll agree.' Corrigan's tone was sarcastic. Now his voice turned dismissive. 'I'll speak to them, the chief super's a mate,' he said. 'Until tomorrow.'

They shook hands and Gower left the office, pleased with what he had managed to extract from the assistant commissioner.

Corrigan stood up and walked over to the window overlooking the Thames from his new office on the Victoria Embankment.

The great river rolled its muscular might far below him.

He did not want an issue with someone trying to kill a right-wing politician on his patch.

Even if he was German.

CHAPTER FOUR

Christiane Hübler looked at DI Enver Demirel with ill-concealed disgust. It was the kind of look that did not just express dislike or disapproval, but almost naked dislike.

Enver was wearing a new, dark blue suit and a white shirt and tie. He looked like he was attending a job interview which, in a sense, he was. Corrigan scratched his head with irritation.

Hübler was being astoundingly rude. She also did not seem to realize how honoured she was that he was there at all. Corrigan was not a vain man but he had a keen sense of his own importance. He had much more pressing things on his plate than to be embroiled in the political shenanigans of a foreign politician. Gower's face was inscrutable. Schneider's visit was causing trouble far beyond what it should have done.

'Wolf Schneider is currently under the threat of death from an extremist Islamic organization that we suspect has a great deal of sympathy within the Turkish community.' Hübler's English was flawless, her pointed finger accusatory. 'And you,' her icy gaze switched from Enver to Corrigan, 'want to have him guarded by a Muslim Turk.'

She shook her head saying in German, '*Das ist ein Witz*?' adding a translation as an afterthought: 'Is this some kind of joke?'

Corrigan sat silent and massive, glowering at her.

'DI Demirel…' he began. Hübler rolled her eyes as if Enver's surname was some sort of added provocation.

'DI Demirel is a British police officer, and will be treated by you with the respect and courtesy that his position entails.'

The trouble is, thought Corrigan as he made this rather pompous speech, that she's got me by the short and curlies. I'd love to just storm out and let them get on with it, let them be hacked to bits maybe, but I can't, and she knows that.

Enver stroked his thick moustache, a gesture he often made when he felt nervous. Gower looked at him with interest. He was always keen to see how officers who were potential recruits would behave under stressful conditions and this had to be very testing for DI Demirel. He had interviewed him earlier and come away with a very favourable impression.

It was as he had suspected. Demirel was bored to death with his current role in CID at Wood Green, finding himself shunted more and more into community liaison work. It was work he was uniquely qualified to do, although he very much didn't want to do it. He hated community politics. As a policeman it was the most thankless position he could think of. It was ironic that being half-Turkish had worked in his favour in North London and was now screwing up his chances with this crack at diplomatic protection.

Enver wanted very much to be taken away from his rather dull duties in Wood Green. He wanted to run around the woods firing Heckler and Koch sub-machine guns. He wanted to have his driving skills brought up to professional standards; he wanted to design protection plans and be part of a Strategy and Tactics team.

He wanted excitement.

'If I may be allowed to answer Ms Hübler's point, sir,' he said now, his voice calm and reasonable.

'Go ahead.' Corrigan glared at Christiane Hübler. She looked pretty non-Caucasian herself, come to that, he thought. She had very black, coarse hair, brown eyes, swarthy skin. She was buxom and slightly running to fat. He guessed she was in her mid-twenties. She was no advert for white Judaeo-Christianity, so it seemed hypocritical of her to be criticizing Enver.

Pot. Kettle. Black. Corrigan's thoughts.

Enver turned to look at her and Gower noted the impressive musculature of Enver's body visible even through the material of his suit.

'I'm sorry you feel that way, Ms Hübler.' Warmly polite, noted Gower, no trace of sarcasm. Diplomatic, grace under pressure, good for you. 'I am, it is true, half-Turkish but my mother was British and I was raised in a fairly liberal household with Western values. I can assure you—'

'You can assure all you like, DI Demirel,' said Christiane Hübler acidly. 'The fact remains that far from providing the reassurance of protection, you're a potential danger.'

Corrigan leaned over the table menacingly. 'I will not have my officers insulted in my presence. Perhaps it would be best for all concerned if Mr Schneider remained at home in Bavaria in some reassuringly Christian enclave.'

'Baden-Württemberg,' corrected Gower.

'Enver stays,' Corrigan said bluntly.

It had now got far beyond the original idea of placing an ethnic minority policeman in a prominent role. It was now a battle of wills.

'No, he doesn't,' countered Hübler.

Corrigan got the impression she was almost enjoying this, that she thrived on antagonism. Well, it was stalemate, he wasn't going to back down and neither was she.

There was a knock on the door and a uniform appeared and beckoned Gower out. He muttered an excuse and left the office. A difficult silence reigned in the small room.

Corrigan stared intimidatingly into space. Enver sat with his big hands, fingertips steepled, on the table in front of him as though they were potential assassin's weapons and Hübler would feel reassured if she could see what they were doing. She was the only one who seemed happy, glaring with hostility at the others.

Corrigan thought, I bet she's Schneider's Rottweiler. Many powerful figures employ a human attack dog, he'd done it himself. He thought nostalgically of Hanlon.

Still off on sick leave sanctioned by himself after the business with the Russians. Well, at least that seemed to have died a quiet death.

The door opened and Gower appeared, accompanied by a blond-haired man in his early thirties wearing an expensive leather bomber jacket and an easygoing smile. Christiane Hübler looked up, startled.

'Wolf, *was gibt?*'

It was Schneider.

CHAPTER FIVE

The two men walked down past the Ashmolean museum in the centre of Oxford, turning left into the broad thoroughfare of St Giles.

A casual observer might have taken them to be students, at first glance. They were wearing street clothes, hooded sweatshirts, one of them in camouflage combat trousers, the other in tight, skinny jeans. But if you looked closer the taller, stockier one was in his early thirties, too old to be an undergraduate, and the other's visible tattoos, LOVE on one set of knuckles, HATE on the other, were not the kind of thing that Oxford students sported, not even in an ironic sense. And their hard-eyed gaze was neither studious nor academic.

'So what's the plan exactly, Mark?' asked James Kettering, the shorter, younger one.

Mark Spencer gave a bleak smile. 'You know Marcus Hinds?'

'Georgie's bae?'

'Yeah.'

The two of them walked past the Eagle and Child where Tolkien and his fellow Inklings had famously met.

'Do you know him?' asked Spencer.

'No, well, I know what he looks like. Journalist, isn't he?'

'Seemingly.' Spencer's voice was dismissive. 'Anyway, Georgie wants him taught a lesson. He's getting dangerous, according to her.'

Kettering glanced at him. 'How much of a lesson?' he asked. Spencer put his hand in his pocket and handed him a pocket knife. Kettering glanced at it discreetly: five inch blade, more or less, spring mounted, a classic flick knife. He hefted it in his hand.

'That much of a lesson?'

'You got it, buddy.'

Spencer eyed his companion. He'd been on a few riots with JK, as he was known, and knew him to be a vicious, hard fighter. They'd also been on a couple of raids on EDF pubs, 'Fascist bashing' outings. He was pleased to see that JK seemed perfectly happy, that mix of excitement and tension that both men loved before things kicked off.

'Where's it going to go down?'

They walked past one of the colleges. Kettering eyed it incuriously, they were all the same, full of privileged arseholes.

'We'll take him on the stairs. Georgie'll buzz us in. He won't know what's hit him.'

A while later they reached their destination in Summertown, a quiet residential street.

'Hinds is a journalist,' said Spencer, 'a writer, it'll be a piece of piss.'

Kettering nodded. 'Looking forward to it,' he said.

'Eleuthera will be very grateful,' Spencer said. 'And they're very generous and Georgie controls the purse strings.'

'Thought you'd say that,' said Kettering with a grin.

There was a skip outside Hinds's communal front door and, just as they reached it, the door opened and a woman pushing a bike emerged. The two of them crossed the road to avoid being seen by her.

'Thought you said the place was deserted at this time of day?' Kettering's tone was angry.

They reached the other pavement and then they saw an old bag lady, hunkered down on a step with three carrier bags in front of her and an old blanket draping her. They looked at each other and shrugged. They waited for the Lycra-clad neighbour of Hinds to pedal off and then recrossed the road, Spencer glancing at the screen of his phone as they did so. Neither of them paid her any attention, as far as they were concerned. Nobody notices street people, nobody pays them any attention. They are a smelly, embarrassing eyesore.

But Elsa was paying them attention, and Elsa, former fine art lecturer and an authority on nineteenth-century European portrait painting, never forgot a face.

CHAPTER SIX

Wolf Schneider sat back in his chair and favoured the assembled group with a high-voltage smile of easy charm. It was an inclusive smile and he particularly focused on Enver, giving him a millisecond longer and a couple of extra watts of charisma. It was as effortless as turning up the central heating a notch. It was also equally effective, a highly calibrated instrument. It was as if he were trying to make up for Hübler's intense rudeness. He didn't look like a right-wing racist demagogue, he looked like an affable entrepreneur with the confidence that only a healthy bank balance and good looks can bring.

Corrigan guessed that he was in his forties. He had blond hair and an outdoorsy glow to his features. His background had been in construction and he still had the powerful physique of a builder mixed with an amiable can-do toughness. He could see that Schneider's appeal would be to attract people who were alienated by the political class. He wasn't an intellectual or a businessman, he was an ordinary Joe, telling it like it is, telling it straight.

'I'm sorry I'm giving you all so much trouble, particularly you, DI Demirel. I'm a great fan of the Turkish people.' He raised a hand as if to ward off any criticism. 'I know that you're British, but my message is really one of tolerance and acceptance.'

Oh, God, thought Corrigan, he's about to make a speech. Schneider had a kind of messianic look on his face; four or forty thousand, the numbers were immaterial, he was determined to get his message across.

'In an ideal world, we would have no racist problems. Sadly though, our world is very flawed. I want a multicultural Europe, a multicultural Germany, a multicultural Britain and by controlling numbers of Muslims to a certain percentage and winnowing out the extremists, we can achieve that.'

Point made, he smiled winningly. Hübler looked at him admiringly.

Corrigan sighed. I'll make a speech too, he thought. Time to cut him off. He leaned forward and coughed, looked stern. It wasn't a hard look to pull off, Corrigan was a hard man, people tended to be frightened of him. He was used to dominating meetings.

'We at the Metropolitan Police are committed to protecting the public whatever their shades of opinion, sir. However, what we are not prepared to do is have the manner of our policing dictated by those we are seeking to protect.'

'I absolutely agree,' said Schneider with shining sincerity.

Gower frowned. 'I gathered from your colleague that you had reservations—'

'Oh, not at all,' Schneider interrupted him. 'Christiane, as my head of staff, was *natürlich*, sorry, naturally, concerned that after the horrific murder of Gunther Hart, being on the same hit list I might be sensitive to the proximity of Muslims, but nothing could be further from the truth.'

'So no objections to DI Demirel being with you?' Gower stepped in swiftly, anxious to have his original plan restored.

'No, but not visibly,' said Schneider.

'I beg your pardon? Not visibly?' Corrigan was confused. Then angry again. Presumably Schneider thought that it would be bad for his image if he were seen to be accompanied by a Muslim, who instead of trying to kill him was keeping him alive.

'I would like to suggest a compromise, like we had when I was in France recently when I went to visit Marine Le Pen, and we did the same in Holland when I shared a platform with Geert Wilders.'

The name-dropping was so pointed that Corrigan nearly smiled. 'Look at me, look how important I am,' was the obvious message. He'd be getting his phone out soon, showing them his selfies: 'Here's me in front of the European Parliament, here's me at the Hague…' It could not be denied, though, that Schneider was a seriously important politician.

Corrigan had, as always, done his homework. 'So, what did the French and Dutch police provide?' he asked sceptically. Schneider was a much bigger deal on mainland Europe than he was in the UK.

Schneider smiled and fiddled with his phone and gave it to Corrigan to look at. I knew it, he thought. He scrolled across the images and passed it to Gower without comment.

Photos of Schneider and politicians; next to Schneider in France a dark-haired woman, in Holland a blonde. The uniting fact, hard faces, watchful demeanour. Corrigan and Gower could smell a cop even on the screen of an iPhone 6.

The message to Schneider's followers: a man popular with women. A tough man who did not need bouncer-style bodyguards.

Vote for me.

'I will level with you, Commissioner Corrigan.' Schneider opened his hands to demonstrate his sincerity. Corrigan could feel his charm. It was a mix of intelligence, sincerity and a kind of everyman quality that politicians usually lacked. Schneider had it. You trusted him. If he wasn't exactly the guy next door he was the kind of man you hoped that the guy next door would be.

'I very much do not wish to be beheaded like those unfortunates in Syria or Iraq, and I do not want my throat cut like Gunther. Those are worst-case scenarios.' That vote-winning smile again. 'What is much more likely is that I will be pelted with eggs or flour or jostled.' He shrugged charmingly. 'Well, I'm used to that, but I'd rather it didn't turn ugly. If I could have a woman protection officer it would defuse tension. I don't want to strut around like a tough guy, I want calm, calm is good for rational debate. A female presence soothes people, in my experience.'

And she'll look good in your attempt to woo lady voters, thought Corrigan. Fine then, politics is the art of the compromise, of the possible. Since Schneider didn't object to Enver per se, he'd keep him on the team but in a backdoor role, one where Schneider wouldn't have to face the indignity of being visibly protected by the sort of person he wanted to exclude from Europe. Honour would be satisfied on both accounts. And since he wanted a woman officer, then that was what he could have.

'Fine,' he said.

'That easy?' asked Schneider, slightly taken aback by Corrigan's ready agreement. 'You have someone in mind? Can I meet her first?'

'I don't see why not,' said Corrigan.

'Is she tough?' Schneider looked slightly worried. He wanted someone feminine enough to look attractive on his media pages but hard enough to deter aggressors. He wanted a Twitter/Facebook/Instagram decoration. Someone who appealed to his demographic support, who would attract both women and men voters. A difficult juggling act.

Corrigan smiled. 'That you can judge for yourself.'

CHAPTER SEVEN

Marcus Hinds knew he had very little time, but he was a resourceful man. He had discovered that morning his PC had been hacked. That meant beyond a shadow of a doubt his phone had too. Carrying it, with its built-in tracking device, would be tantamount to wandering around with a megaphone and a hi-vis jacket shouting, 'I'm here!'

His car was out of the question too. Eleuthera were highly organized, very computer literate. Some of its members were, unsurprisingly, part of the Anonymous hacking network. If his security had been compromised then he felt sure a tracker, costing peanuts and easily available, could well be attached somewhere to the old Renault that he drove.

Pulling his clothes on in the grotty one-bedroomed flat, he glanced down at the huddled form of Georgie Adams, Eleuthera's press and communications officer, under his duvet. Strands of her dark hair – the ends of her swept-across fringe coloured green – and the tips of her painted fingertips were visible. He heard a faint snore. That girl would sleep through anything.

Nine thirty a.m.

He and Georgie hadn't gone to bed until two, she had no college today, she'd be comatose until noon.

Georgie was typical of the Eleuthera membership: young, idealistic, committed. Attractive. That's really what had made him notice the anarchist group first, the fact that there was a hard-core of extremely desirable women, and he, as a genuine member of the proletariat, a real working-class hero, had been of equal interest to them as well.

Like many of the anarchists who belonged to Eleuthera, she chose to keep her membership a discreet secret. Although they weren't a prohibited organization, they preferred to operate under the radar. It had taken Hinds considerable ingenuity to track them down.

Well, now things were going terribly wrong. He had uncovered things he shouldn't have.

He had looked under the wrong rock.

He glanced out of the window. The street outside was quiet. Those going to work had done so and the school run was over. The street was occupied mainly by young professionals – the old and middle-aged had sold up and students couldn't afford the rents.

One more issue for Eleuthera to get fired up about.

Redistribute the property!

Occupy the colleges!

Smash the rich!

Destroy.

End the stranglehold of elitism. That would play well in Oxford.

The small block of flats he was in would be deserted

apart from himself and Georgie. All the other occupants at work. He found the silence during the day quite eerie.

The same could be said about the whole road.

There was, however, one resident impervious to economic conditions. That was the old bag lady who often slept opposite. He could see her out of the window now. Huddled in her layers of blankets, bedding that she would often roll up and push around in an old shopping trolley. She had a variety of locations. He often saw her outside St John's when he passed by in the morning, she liked to spend her days there.

Someone had told him she had a bus stop she liked to use as well, somewhere on the outskirts of town where the council wouldn't harass her for upsetting the tourists with her non-picturesque grime. But this morning she was huddled in the doorway across the street. No trolley today, just a few large, plastic bags.

He felt a twinge of pity when he saw the alcoholic homeless, coupled with an uneasy feeling that he could be looking at his own future.

There was a half-smoked joint on the desk by his open laptop. He lit it and drew the smoke deep into his lungs. He quickly copied several files to a spare memory stick and thrust it into his pocket, then he disconnected the small external hard drive and added that to it.

Can't have too much information, he thought, in a slightly fuddled way.

He looked out of the window again. No one in the street. The bag lady was searching for something in one of her plastic carriers. This morning she was sponsored by

Sainsbury's. Today he felt a stab of jealousy. Nobody was going to try and kill her, except maybe herself. She'd be alive today; he doubted he could be so sure about himself.

He laced his boots up and looked in the mirror at his handsome, stubbled face and pushed a hand through his dark, tousled hair. There were lines now starting to appear on his forehead and crow's feet around his eyes, but he was still good-looking, a Byronic East Ender living on his wits.

He bet most of Eleuthera hadn't heard of Byron. They'd think he was a burger chain. He poured himself a shot of Courvoisier from the bottle on the stained table, toasted his reflection, downed it in one and quietly let himself out of the front door.

As he did so, and the door clicked to behind him, Georgie sat up in bed and looked around the empty bedsit. Her face was hard and imperious, her naked upper body toned and tattooed with geometric designs. She recalled her instructions to her fellow anarchists. She took her phone from the bedside table, fingers moving swiftly over the screen.

He's on his way.

She put the phone down. She'd miss Marcus. Well, the sex anyway. But he lacked ideological commitment, that was for sure.

Perhaps she'd attend the funeral, she thought, as she pulled the duvet over her. She looked good in black.

CHAPTER EIGHT

Corrigan, with Wolf Schneider in tow, climbed the creaking wooden stairs to the boxing gym in Bermondsey.

Schneider had looked out of the rain-streaked window of Corrigan's car with approval at the housing estates and the red-brick railway arches of the borough where the gym was located. It was his kind of place. It's where his roots were, industrial, working class, white, unloved. Even the boxing club was familiar to him from one that he had belonged to, years ago. Again, it epitomized what he felt he represented, the true voice of his country. A sport that the intellectuals and theorists who ran Germany despised, but that the blue-collar society, their jobs undercut by cheap foreign labour or taken overseas, loved.

Bob's Gym was not for the faint of heart. It was run-down, unglamorous. It smelled of sweat, damp, effort and pain. It was old-school, it didn't offer boxercise classes or go in for white-collar boxing where businessmen could act out fantasies about being real fighters. It was a serious gym for serious athletes. Hanlon was the only woman to belong, mainly because Laidlaw, the owner, liked her and allowed her to use the place when it was closed. Sometimes he would train her or, when it was closed to all but the handful of boxers that he managed, she would spar with them at lightweight or welterweight, on occasions heavier. Any qualms they had about fighting with a woman soon disappeared once they realized that pound for pound Hanlon was exceptionally gifted.

Power in a punch doesn't come from big muscles, it's a whole body involvement. It was partly what made her so formidable. If Hanlon hit you it was from her feet upwards, it was explosive. And that force, allied to her speed, accuracy and concentration, added up to an astonishingly good boxer. If Freddie grew tired of explaining this verbally, he'd put them in with Hanlon, let them experience it physically.

'Go on, Hanlon,' patting her head-guard, 'paint me a picture. Better than a thousand words.'

Corrigan and Schneider reached the top of the narrow stairs and went through the scuffed glass-panelled door into the reception area.

Schneider looked around him with interest. He'd boxed to a reasonable level himself in Stuttgart as a kid and still had a keen interest in the sport. A lot of boxers, young kids from deprived backgrounds, were members of the NS too. They were a fertile audience for his message. Occasionally his rallies would be attacked by the militant left or the anarchists, and then the hard-nut, skinhead kids could be let off the leash.

The lobby was low maintenance, a couple of old armchairs, a dusty, glass-topped coffee table and threadbare carpeting. Old framed posters for long-gone contests featuring long-forgotten boxers decorated the walls.

Corrigan was talking to a young kid behind the desk with a beard and some serious tattoos.

'Yes, she is here.' The kid looked at them unfavourably. 'But we're closed. She's sparring with Chris Campbell.'

Corrigan leant over the desk. He showed his ID. The young boxer was tiny in comparison to his looming height, he must have been a bantam or lightweight, thought Schneider. He was intrigued by this unexpected jaunt to the seamier side of London. He looked around him appreciatively. This was more like it, no intellectuals here.

Schneider hated intellectuals even more than he hated Muslims.

Intellectuals, the great betrayers of the people. The backstabbers. People who had rejected what had made Germany great.

Not the scientists who had made Germany the intellectual powerhouse of Europe.

Not the engineers and industrialists whose legacy still lived on in the great names of cars and machinery.

Corrigan glanced at his companion. He had gone strangely quiet.

'Who's Chris Campbell?' asked Corrigan of the kid.

'He's got a shot at a southern area heavyweight title.'

'Heavyweight?' Corrigan was baffled. Against Hanlon.

The young kid behind the desk gave a bark of laughter. 'It ain't a mismatch, mate. Not with Hanlon. She's class. Freddie wants to show Chris how fast a good fighter can punch. Chris is a bit slow. He's up at the York Hall soon, he'd better buck his ideas up. He's been babied up till now.'

Corrigan nodded appreciatively. The York Hall, Bethnal Green, home of British boxing.

'So if you two gentlemen want to come back in an hour or so…' The kid indicated the door with his head, just in case there were some misunderstanding.

Corrigan, suddenly enormous and menacing, leaned over his desk.

'Didn't you read what it said on my ID?'

'Yes, Assistant Commissioner, I did.' The kid swallowed slightly nervously. Obviously he had wondered what had brought someone so high ranking here. Normally the police were a red rag to a bull for him, especially as he'd done nothing wrong. It was just a natural reaction, the way he'd been brought up.

Don't talk to coppers.

Corrigan knew that. He didn't care about his attitude. He didn't give a fuck. The kid's attitude was insignificant. Corrigan's face filled his vision. The scars and lines on his face, his large battered nose. It was a face designed by nature to intimidate and he knew it.

'Good.' Corrigan pointed at Wolf Schneider. 'Now we know who I am, this gentleman has come all the way from Germany to see Hanlon. We don't want to disappoint him, do we, sunshine?'

It wasn't only the air of quiet menace in Corrigan's voice that was so effective, it was the absolute certainty of getting his way that led the kid to say, 'Yes, Assistant Commissioner, now…'

'Don't worry,' said Corrigan dismissively. He'd had enough of the conversation. 'I know the way.' He turned to Schneider. 'Come on,' he said. 'Follow me.'

Wolf Schneider, ever the politician, nodded politely at the

receptionist, gave him a comradely wink and followed the broad back of Corrigan as he headed to a scuffed door at the rear of the threadbare reception area and opened it, revealing a narrow staircase.

The kid watched the two backs disappear up the stairs that led to the gallery that overlooked the gym. He shrugged, he wouldn't mind joining them. He always loved watching Hanlon fight. It was beautiful.

CHAPTER NINE

Marcus closed the door behind him and started down the stairs. They were broad and unadorned, zigzagging three storeys towards the front door, around a central well.

He was wishing he hadn't smoked the grass now – he felt unpleasantly stoned, disassociated from reality. It added to the nightmare, hallucinatory quality of what was happening.

There were three flats per floor, his was on the third. The heels of his boots clattered as he descended the steps. Sounds always echoed in this block. At night a firmly closed front door would sound like a gunshot. As he went down, he heard footsteps coming up the staircase towards him. He rounded a corner. A momentary impression.

Two men, their heads bowed, wearing hoodies.

If they hadn't had the hoods over their heads, things could have turned out very differently. With the hoods up it was like displaying a warning banner, screaming, WE MEAN BUSINESS.

Marcus, keyed up, expecting a fight, was already almost as high on the adrenaline pumping round his body as he was on the THC and the booze.

No one in these flats dressed like that. But nobody. There

were a couple of hipsters, a couple of Boden wearers and a Hooray Henry, upper class LAMF red trousers guy. None of them would wear a hoody and trainers, not even in a gym. They wouldn't be seen dead in them. These two didn't belong.

He recognized them immediately as trouble.

Well, that was just fine with him.

Most of Eleuthera were middle-class intellectuals, grammar school or privately educated, unused to violence. Not so Marcus Hinds. He had grown up in Bethnal Green and Hayes fighting Somali gangs. His family had form, and he had a vicious streak.

Right, you wanky, nerdy anarchist muppets, used to harassing women or filming yourselves pushing a policeman and uploading it to the net, let's show you how we do it in Bethnal Green.

Not fucking Sevenoaks.

Let's party.

His fingers clenched into fists, his eyes narrowed. Concentrate.

Rather than pass them on the stairs, his body a defence-less target open to attack from all sides, he pressed his back against the wall. Without making eye contact, heads bowed, they walked abreast up the stairs towards him and then changed to single file to get past him, Grey Hoodie leading.

As he walked up the stairs past Marcus, Grey Hoodie suddenly wheeled towards him, left arm curving round. Marcus sensed rather than saw the blade in his hand. He was ready, he'd been expecting this. Blue Hoodie was not an immediate threat, behind his companion he was blocked by his body.

It wasn't the first time in his life Marcus had experienced a knife being pulled on him. For a year he'd worked doors in nightclubs and pubs back in Bethnal Green and points further east to pay living expenses for his journalism degree at City University. He was a hard bastard and he knew it. After a year of minding on the Mile End Road and Plaistow he was a damn sight harder. Frankly, he was lucky to be alive. People he'd ejected from the premises or refused to allow in had tried to stab him, glass him, bottle him. Some nutcase had even fired two shots at him one night from a handgun. Luckily, they'd missed.

So, on sensing the knife, most people, understandably, would freeze in such a situation. Not him.

He almost welcomed the fight.

Marcus grabbed the arm with the knife. Grey Hoodie was seriously unbalanced, the lead foot carrying all his weight. Marcus, who was higher on the stairs, headbutted him, driving his forehead into Grey Hood's face, smashing into his nose and simultaneously pushing with his right hand and pulling with his left.

'You cunt!' he shouted, frenzied with blood lust. It was a Hinds family trait. They were a violent lot, even the women. He wasn't a rational human now, he was like a crazed animal, all intellectual thought gone. He just wanted to smash these two until they were bloody pulp.

Both his dad and his uncle had done time for GBH, he was carrying on the family tradition.

His assailant crashed into Blue Hood and Marcus lashed out with his foot, anchoring himself with his hand on the banister for balance. Then, like he was kicking a ball with all his strength, the tip of the toe of his boot smashed into Grey Hood's face. It connected with his chin and he fell back down the stairs.

Blue Hood had had enough. He turned to run away but Marcus from behind him put his foot on his lower back and gave an almighty shove. Blue Hood was on the edge of the step and the impetus of Marcus's leg propelled him into the void.

It wasn't a long fall, maybe a couple of metres, but it was two metres head first onto concrete. His head slammed into the corner of the wall of the landing with a deafening crack.

Marcus breathed deeply, sucking oxygen into his lungs. He felt dazed and his heart was thundering like he'd been injected with speed.

'Fuck!' he said. It was the third word that had been spoken. He looked at the scene below. Grey Hoodie, his face now revealed, blood covering his mouth, was sitting on the stairs by his fallen companion.

Mark Spencer was his name. Marcus knew him as Eleuthera's head enforcer. The guy who would lead the charge against the police horses at Stop the War or End Austerity or whatever demo they'd tagged along to.

He was the kind of person who enjoyed hurting people. One of nature's bullies. He'd kill someone one of these days. It was the kind of thing he'd enjoy. If he could have, if he'd been the right religion, he'd have joined ISIS for the lifestyle, the chance to kill and maim. Spencer liked cider and drugs too much though to have gone down well with the jihadi brigades.

The knife, a slim flick-knife, was on the floor next to Marcus.

There was absolute silence on the stair and the stairwell. He could almost hear his heart beating. Marcus was glad of the emptiness of the block of flats. He felt he couldn't have coped with a door opening, someone demanding what was going on, certainly he did not want anything to do with the police.

He picked the flick knife up and walked slowly down the stairs. Spencer glared at him aggressively as he edged past, their eyes locked on each other with mutual dislike and mistrust. Spencer wasn't kind of man you would turn your back to. Marcus was very glad he was holding the knife meant for him. The weapon in his hand a very potent deterrent to any further action.

Once he was on the next flight down he ran to the front door and then he was outside in the cool autumn air. He pulled the door closed behind him and looked down the street. Parked cars on either side of the road, a skip, nothing unusual. He dropped the knife in the skip and hurried across the road.

Old Elsa, the lady tramp, was still in her doorway. She was about seventy – it was hard to judge – toothless, a Tibetan-style hat with ear flaps on and voluminous layers of clothes. She knew him, he'd given her money before now, slipping her the odd fiver when he was feeling flush.

Sometimes they'd have a chat together. He was aware of how far she had fallen: from senior common room to park bench. Mental illness is no respecter of intelligence. He needed a messenger and right now Elsa would have to do.

He could smell her as he approached. She was awake and he crouched down beside her. She looked at him calmly.

Hardly the answer to a prayer but she was all he had. He pulled the memory stick out of his pocket, together with his wallet and a biro. He took a tenner out and an old receipt. She watched him silently. He gave her the money, the memory stick and hastily wrote a few explanatory words: *DI Huss, Summertown police station.*

'Go to Summertown nick, ask for this woman, give her this. She'll pay you, OK?'

She looked at him calmly and put the money, memory stick and credit card receipt into an inside pocket.

On an afterthought he took the external hard drive from his pocket. He knew that she never threw anything away. Even if she failed to deliver his message she'd hang on to the hard drive, of that he could be sure.

'Hang on to this for me, will you?'

He looked into her cornflower-blue eyes as he did so. They were full of intelligence this morning. Thank the Lord, he thought, she's with it. Some days he spoke to her and the shutters were down, she didn't know who he was. But not today.

She took it from him, examined it curiously, she had never seen one before, and stowed it inside her stained blouse.

Marcus stood up and without a backward glance started off down the street towards the centre of Oxford and the bus station.

London, here I come, he thought grimly.

Sanctuary.

CHAPTER TEN

Laidlaw had finished putting the wraps around Hanlon's strong, long fingers. She flexed them and then she held her bandaged hand out and he slipped on the gloves. She threw a couple of experimental punches, jab, jab, then a quick combination, jab, jab, right cross, left hook. As always, she was fast and, above all, elegant.

'Let's go.'

They walked down the short, silent corridor that led from his office to the cavernous, empty gym. Hanlon felt light and strong on her feet. She had that pleasurable sensation in the pit of her stomach that she always had before a fight, even though this was simply a sparring session.

Her opponent was waiting for her in the ring. He was huge, a head taller than she was. He said nothing as she climbed through the ropes, the point of no return. They faced each other momentarily, her hard grey eyes locked on to his brown ones. Any doubts he felt about fighting a woman disappeared at that moment. Joe Paulson, his manager, a sceptical look on his face, sounded the bell.

From the viewing gallery at the top of the large room

that was the gym, lost in the shadows and unseen by those below, Schneider and Corrigan watched.

The two boxers in the ring were completely unaware of their audience. For them the whole universe had shrunk down to the canvas and its rope borders.

The German wondered what the hell was going on. The contest looked ludicrously one-sided.

The large figure of the black boxer advanced on her, trying to close the ring down, flicking the occasional jab to find his range. Campbell would have been much more used to fighting men of his own size and height. Hanlon, as his opponent would be in his upcoming match, was much shorter, making things awkward. He had to punch down at an angle.

He was also large and lumbering, ponderous on his legs, whereas Hanlon could move with whiplash speed and balletic agility.

For now, Hanlon contented herself with avoiding his gloves as best she could. She was a slim, hard to hit target, never motionless, her head continually bobbing and weaving, her body, side on, light and flexible, and she had exquisite footwork.

Campbell frowned in frustration as his gloves aimed blows at a target that suddenly was no longer there, or she would slip low and rise under the punch, his glove finding air where he had expected her head.

Then she saw a chance, his hands were low and his face exposed, she decided to punish him, to show him what happens when you make mistakes and underestimate your opponent.

Her hand flicked out, hard, fast and accurate and she caught him on the side of his face. There was no great power behind the punch, they were just sparring, but if it had been serious it was the kind of mistake he couldn't afford to make, particularly in his approaching fight.

His challenger there would not be landing warning shots, that was for sure.

The round continued, frustration visibly growing on Campbell's face as she slipped under and around his punches, occasionally moving up close underneath his reach and hitting him with hooks to the body.

The bell sounded. Corrigan could see Laidlaw was delighted, Paulson quietly angry.

'She's amazing,' whispered Schneider, happily.

They sat in their corners. Hanlon could hear Paulson berating Campbell for not keeping his guard up. She could see him gesturing with his left – she soon found out why.

Another round went by, this one not so good for Hanlon. Campbell was getting used to his low target and several times his gloves made contact with her padded headguard. Despite the protection and despite the lack of power in his punch, there was enough there to make her head ring. But most worrying was his left hook.

She had no real answer to it. Unlike his forward punches, his jab and right hand, it could cover all of the side of her body. If he'd put power into the shots she'd have been knocked off her feet.

Back in her corner Laidlaw hissed, 'Get right up to him, right up close, and go even lower, do the unexpected.'

She took a drink of water and nodded. Her top was

soaked in sweat now, clinging to her body, but her arms and legs felt amazing. All those hours and hours of training paying off. All that cycling, all that swimming, all that running. Hanlon was super-fit even by boxing standards.

Laidlaw watched with proprietorial pride as she took the fight to the bigger man like a terrier against a mastiff. Campbell's skin a mahogany shade against the paleness of Hanlon. She advanced on him and he jabbed lazily at her and then she was through, under his guard, practically touching his body.

She unleashed a couple of left hooks of her own, her left foot swivelling inwards to add to their power, the force of the shot coming not from the arms but from the body. Her left elbow was perfectly angled, protecting her face.

He could see the bafflement on Campbell's face as he tried to deal with her but she was too close, almost as if they were dancing, to be able to get any real angle on his punches.

Hanlon suddenly upped her game. It was like watching a Ferrari race a Ford Mondeo. Class, power, speed.

She suddenly stepped back and, with lightning speed, launching herself off her back foot, delivered a flawless three punch combination to Campbell's face.

Corrigan heard Schneider say, '*Scheisse, sie ist ausgezeichnete!*' He turned to him: 'She really is good.'

'Break!' Laidlaw shouted.

Hanlon and Campbell dropped their hands and he gently tapped her gloves in a show of respect.

Hanlon walked over to Laidlaw and he undid the straps of her headguard and pulled it off. She shook her sweat-matted hair. Her top was glued to her upper body with perspiration. He could smell the leather of her gloves, her perspiration and a faint residual perfume.

'How was that, Hanlon?' he asked.

She took her mouthguard out and grinned wolfishly at him. 'Better than sex, Freddie, better than sex.'

Laidlaw smiled and pointed upwards. 'You've got admirers.'

She lifted her head. There, leaning over the balcony of the gallery, was a familiar figure.

'I think you've demonstrated that you're fit enough to come back to work now, Hanlon,' Corrigan called down to her.

'Yes, sir,' she called back.

CHAPTER ELEVEN

DI Huss was having a frustrating morning. She had been working on an analysis of burglaries in the Summertown area of Oxford, matching the MO with known offenders and trying to predict which streets might be next targeted. Then two of her team had been pulled to bolster a planning exercise to deal with the demonstration that was going to greet Wolf Schneider's debate at the Oxford Union in the heart of the city.

And now, she had just been informed that responsibility for planning the police presence outside the debate was her responsibility, her problem.

'But this is not our department,' she'd said to Templeman, her dour Scottish boss, fuming with annoyance. 'It's a public order matter, it's between uniform, the university authorities and the council.'

Templeman, despite his forbidding exterior, was a pleasant man, usually supportive, and in turn expected his officers to support his decisions, not query them.

'I dare say you're right, Melinda, however, the chief constable wants a woman's touch, and you're that woman.'

'Oh, for heaven's sake, sir. Next you'll be telling me that I'll be working out the costings for this!'

Templeman was sitting behind his desk, reading some report or other. Now he looked up with irritation.

'Yes! Yes, you can do that. Oxford CID is not here for your amusement, to furnish you with jobs you happen to find congenial.' Templeman was Glaswegian and rolled his r's when he spoke. It was something that got more pronounced the more irritable he got.

'Now, I usually find that the quicker a job is started, the quicker it's finished.'

Schneider, she gathered, was attracting headlines for his hard line on immigration as well as his more right-wing views, so Anonymous, End Austerity, the Socialist Workers, Liberty, just about every protest group in the city was primed to attend. Her heart sank. All the noisy, aggressive nutters.

Most of them didn't know who he was or what he stood for, other than he was 'a bad thing'. Stop the War were going to be there too, even though Schneider was implacably opposed, Huss gathered, to any form of intervention outside Europe.

Then again, she thought, the plus side was that it was going to be on a Tuesday night, the long-range forecast was bad – rain always helped thin the protestors' ranks – and nobody knew who Schneider was anyway.

There was a buzz of news and talk in the office that she worked from. Reports were coming in of an incident in some street near St Clare's college, just down the road. One man critically injured on a stairwell, presumed assault.

Nothing to do with her.

Back to her German problem.

Huss returned to the endless task of going through the

requirements for Schneider's safety. Would he need a personal protection officer and a driver with specialist skills?

How many uniforms? Maybe four divisional teams, nearly forty police. Would she need to contact Kidlington for a firearms team? Surely not.

She ground her teeth. Templeman, I could strangle you. This is not my job.

Council crush-barriers, road closures? What about a pre-visit to Schneider's hotel to check security and, theoretically, vet the guests? Where even was his wretched hotel?

She checked the inadequate paperwork that Templeman had given her.

Picked up the phone, call this Commander Gower's office, a London number.

Before she could key in the numbers, a voice behind her said, 'Melinda, Pete wants you at the front desk.'

She swore quietly to herself, put the phone down and made her way through the office to the front desk. Pete Gainsborough, the lugubrious desk sergeant, pointed through the glass at the mound of clothing sitting on a bench in reception that was Old Elsa.

'She wants a word with you, if that's OK. Be as quick as you can, Melinda, she whiffs a bit.'

'Why does she want to talk to me?' she asked.

Gainsborough shrugged. 'She's not all there, but she's a sweetheart really.'

Even from behind the glass, the penetrating scent of Elsa was making itself felt. Huss saw the tea that the old woman was holding and the sandwich container that had obviously come from the canteen.

'Thanks, Pete,' she said. She recalled other examples of the sergeant's good deeds, kind turns he had done people. He was one of those people who disliked it if people knew about it. She smiled warmly at him, conspiratorially, the freemasonry of the good at heart. He noticed that she had noticed and pulled a face.

'Don't tell anyone or they'll think I'm going soft. Elsa used to be a don, you know, at Somerville. Before...' He tapped his head expressively. 'Anyway, she's all yours. Oh, don't bring her back here, she'll freak out. She's quite paranoid. To be honest I can't say I blame her. I nicked a couple of students who thought it funny to piss on her a while ago. Then the council would like shot of her. Poor old thing.'

He buzzed her out and she sat by the old lady on the bench opposite the reception window.

Huss looked into her face, framed by dirty locks of grey hair that had escaped from the grubby, turban-style hat that she was wearing. Dirt had so engrained Elsa's skin it looked like she was tanned. Huss wondered what had happened to her to transform a once respected academic to this. Alchemy in reverse. But, she reflected, that's mental illness for you. It doesn't require a reason.

'You're Huss?'

'Yes, Elsa.' Huss's voice was gentle.

'Like the fish?'

'Like the fish,' agreed Huss.

Elsa nodded, apparently satisfied. Her vowels were cut-glass, old-style BBC RP English.

She looked around her conspiratorially. 'He said to give you this...' She handed Huss a memory stick and a Post-it note.

She examined it. On one side it read: *Schneider. Akhdaar. Eleuthera. Rosemount.* On the other side was her name, underneath, *xxx Marcus Hinds.*

She blinked in surprise, not a particularly welcome surprise.

Hinds – there was a name she wasn't going to forget, although she had successfully managed to suppress the memory.

Huss was twenty-eight. Four years earlier, drunk, at a friend's party in Oxford, she had met Hinds. The attraction had been incredible, one of those rare things that was just meant to be. They had spent what was left of the night having amazingly energetic sex on his sweat-soaked bed. He had been gorgeous and, she remembered, she had wanted more, more and more.

The grey light of morning had come and she had quietly pulled her clothes on and slipped away from his flat and out of his life. Huss wasn't one for regrets. A relationship with an investigative journalist would have harmed her career and Huss was ambitious.

She had fond memories of the evening. His body had been great.

More memories.

His one-roomed flat had smelt of incense and faintly of weed. A student smell. He had been twenty-one, she remembered. A boy.

She closed her eyes momentarily. She could even remember his body, hard beneath her, as she straddled him. She shivered then pulled herself together.

It had been great, but not that great. She occasionally

heard his name mentioned, and once their eyes had met at a press briefing. She had looked away. It wasn't like anything was over, there had never been anything to begin with.

Now here was Schneider's name, this time on a piece of paper, yet again pursuing her like a demon in a nightmare. God alone knows what it had to do with Hinds. Presumably Hinds had some hot information on the German politician. Maybe trying to get back into her good books.

Elsa stood up and looked at Huss. Huss opened her eyes.

'I've got to go, dear,' she said firmly, as if she had appointments to keep.

'Oh yes, of course.' Huss suddenly realized what was expected of her. She stood up and tapped on the window. 'Lend me twenty quid, Pete.' He pulled his wallet out, handed her the money and she gave it to Elsa.

'Thank you very much,' she said. She tucked the money inside her clothes in her grimy bra. Obviously that was a repository for valuables.

'If you need to find me,' Elsa informed her, 'I'm at home every evening in the bus stop near Wilson Road, Summertown.'

'I'll remember,' said Huss, solemnly.

With quiet dignity Elsa exited the police station. Huss, holding the memory stick, returned to her desk, lost in memories of the past.

She heard two of her colleagues at the next desk talking as they pulled their jackets on. She turned her attention back to her screen.

'That assault victim's just died.'

'So it's murder now?'

'It's murder now.'

'Anyone in the frame?'

The DS who was in Serious Crimes buttoned his jacket. 'Someone called Marcus Hinds.'

Fuck, thought DI Melinda Huss.

CHAPTER TWELVE

Hanlon walked out of Oxford's surprisingly ugly train station, it reminded her of a giant Portakabin, to be met by Huss.

On the journey down from Paddington she reviewed her meeting with Wolf Schneider. She was due back later to escort him from his hotel in London, the art-deco wonderland of Claridge's, to the Union Chapel in Islington where he was speaking.

Claridge's was five hundred pounds a night for a cheapish room and Schneider had a suite. He must have some seriously wealthy backers.

As she had sat on the train, the countryside rolling by, she reflected that it was tough being a German right-wing MP. Behind you there was always another, baleful example from fairly recent history. Whatever your message, no matter what denials you issued, there it was.

Someone would forever be standing at your shoulder.

The elephant in the room.

Hanlon reflected that with the police in general, and the Met in particular, embroiled in yet another scandal, the last thing that Corrigan needed was the murder of a right-wing German politician at the hands of Islamic militants.

Disastrous too for London tourism and the economy.

She thought of the growing power of the right, of their insidious appeal.

Recent ISIS atrocities in France and other European locations only increased the power of the right. She could well imagine the charismatic Schneider doing well in such a climate. In uncertain times people turn to strong men or women and he certainly fitted the bill. He was a born leader.

Well, she didn't share his politics. Hanlon didn't really like politics full stop. But she owed Corrigan and she would do her utmost to ensure Schneider stayed safe and well during his time in London and Oxford.

Huss was standing waiting for her under a cold October sky, her wavy blonde hair flattened by the dispiriting moisture. Hanlon's own coarse, springy black curls were impervious to anything the weather might throw at it.

Hanlon thought that the usually good-natured Huss looked uncharacteristically gloomy, preoccupied. That's my job, she thought. How dare she. Stealing my look.

'Hi,' said Huss, opening the door of a Golf for Hanlon. 'Nice to see you again.'

She looked at Hanlon as she climbed gracefully inside the car, admiring slightly jealously her slim, athletic body. I could never get into those skinny jeans, she thought mournfully, not in a million years. Hanlon looked stronger and fitter than ever. Mind you, thought Huss, she exercises for about two hours a day and I've seen her kitchen. She shuddered at the thought of Hanlon's sparse, rigorously balanced diet, the brown rice, the tofu, the lentils and white meat. Huss liked her food, Hanlon viewed it with dispassionate lack of emotion.

Hanlon, for her part, had been unsurprised when she heard that Templeman had put Huss in charge of Schneider. Huss combined tact, organizational flair with a huge capacity for hard work. She was impressed with Huss's abilities. Although capable of hard work, Hanlon was a poor organizer, impatient, hard to work with, occasionally slapdash. She really wasn't the kind of person that you would want to run anything, and her abrasive personality clashed with so many people.

She guessed that Corrigan had heard from Gower that Huss was involved and that was partly why Enver had been offered the protection job.

It was only a short drive to St Wulfstan's College where they had an appointment with the master.

Huss filled her in on what had happened so far, including the Hinds incident.

'And what did the memory stick contain?' asked Hanlon.

'I don't know,' said Huss. 'File names but it wouldn't open them. Systems support have it now.'

Gower had wanted them to understand the kind of organizations they might be up against. He lived and breathed his job and one reason why he was such a success at diplomatic protection was that he insisted that his teams understood the kind of specific threat that their charges were facing. He was a man who planned meticulously and when he had heard sensible questions at the end of the phone from Huss the day before he had pulled strings and organized this briefing from one of the country's authorities on terrorist organizations, in this case Al-Akhdaar, whose death list Schneider headed. He happened to be conveniently situated not far from where Huss worked, in central Oxford.

The seventeenth-century college's honey-coloured Oxford stone was muted in the late autumn gloom. Term had started and students wandered to tutorials or back to their rooms along the paths bordered by intricately cut low box hedges, or via the cloisters that ran beside the college lawns.

They followed the directions that they had been given to the senior common room where the college dons met communally. The master of St Wulfstan's, Paul Smithfield, young to be in charge of a college at forty, a noted economist and adviser to the Bank of England, was to meet them there. Smithfield was behind the invitation to Schneider to speak at the Oxford Union.

Huss knew a linguistics lecturer, Laura Thompson, who worked at the college. She had helped Huss on forensic matters a couple of times. She had called her up to find out what kind of a man the master was. Laura had said that Smithfield had a slightly sinister reputation but that he was an internationally acknowledged expert on extreme political movements and political terrorism. He often briefed COBRA and several leading think tanks.

His opponents said that there was a dark side to Smithfield. Some of his colleagues claimed he sympathized with right-wing extremism. There was another school of thought that said he was an Ayn Rand-style libertarian and allied himself spiritually with the anarchist movement, holding the opinion governments were bad, full stop. The kind of anarchism that led to the dark net, untrammelled freedom for sexual expression, bestiality, paedophilia, rape, drugs, weaponry, internet trolling.

The two women walked into the SCR. It was a beautifully

proportioned, airy oak-panelled room, overlooking the central quad with its perfect lawns and the knee-high box hedges they had noticed and admired earlier, cut over the centuries into complex geometric designs.

It was also easy to imagine it as Schneider would, a shining example of the culture that was under threat from the barbarian forces yowling outside the decadent remains of a magnificent but tottering European culture like the Goths ready to plunder the Roman Empire and inaugurate the Dark Ages of ignorance and savagery.

The furniture in the room was heavy, old-fashioned, masculine. Leather sofas and armchairs, dark wood proliferated. An elderly don was the only other person in the senior common room. A pile of manuscripts, essays waiting to be marked, sat patiently on a small table next to him as he dozed like a senior, tweed-suited, moth-eaten cat in the warmth of a nearby radiator.

The master, by contrast, was in his early forties, tall, saturnine, good-looking in an arrogant kind of way. He had the lazy confidence of a man buttressed by wealth and success. Smithfield's eyes ran appraisingly over the women in front of him. He did it in a totally obvious way, almost as if they should be flattered by his attention.

Hanlon ran her eyes over Smithfield too, in a markedly hostile fashion, as if measuring him up for where she would strike the first blow. Huss decided they had better get what they had come for quickly in case hostilities broke out.

'Thank you for taking the time to see us,' she began. 'This is DCI Hanlon of the Met, currently on secondment as a protection officer for Wolf Schneider.'

Smithfield nodded graciously.

He was compelling too, thought Hanlon, but in a different way to Schneider. The German politician believed passionately in what he was saying, he was an idealist. Smithfield exuded an air of tranquil evil. She guessed he was a man who believed in nothing but himself and this was allied to extreme intelligence.

'Basically, we're after any information or ideas that might help with protection issues regarding Mr Schneider. I gather there have been death threats against him in his own country and in Europe too.'

The master smiled and waved them into easy chairs near a fireplace. He pressed a bell on the wall, a uniformed college servant appeared and he ordered tea.

Over the Darjeeling, he filled in Schneider's rise to political power. From true blue-collar bricklayer origins, a real man of the people and a member of the Socialists, to increasing disillusion with the Left.

The master was a practised speaker, fluent, to the point.

'He's doing well in Bavaria, Hesse-Mecklenburg, Saxony and of course his own home state of Baden-Württemberg. In Heidelberg he has been taking votes from the National-demokratische Partei Deutschlands, the NPD...' Huss found herself switching off mentally as the heavy, sonorous Germanic names rolled through the warm air of the senior common room. It was the names on the list that she wanted to hear about. The list that Hinds had given her. In Huss's mind the fact that it came from a man wanted for murder added to its probable authenticity.

Hinds's list, she ran through it mentally again: Schneider, Al-Akhdaar, Eleuthera, Rosemount.

The words of a man on the run for murder, presumably he thought that these would either explain his behaviour or clear him. Time to see what Smithfield thought.

'That's fascinating,' she said, casually. 'The name Al-Akhdaar has come up, do you know anything about that?'

'Indeed I do,' he lifted a surprised eyebrow, 'and so should you.'

Hanlon glared at her. She had been enjoying Smithfield's lecture. She was one of those people who actively liked learning new things, she was even prepared to forgive the master's lecherous glances.

'Um, could you elaborate?' asked Huss.

'Al-Ansaar al-Akhdaar, the Green Companions. Green is the colour of Islam,' explained Smithfield, 'and the Ansaar were the companions of Muhammad. But, as far as we're concerned, they're a German jihadi group. No one had ever heard of them until they sent death threats to Schneider and also a socialist MP in Heidelberg, Gunther Hart. Gunther Hart was found dead a couple of weeks ago, they'd cut his throat and uploaded the footage to YouTube.' He carried on for a while, elaborating the sketchy history of the group, until Hanlon interrupted him.

'So, basically, they're the ones we should be worried about?'

'Sure,' said Smithfield, 'they're basically like IS in Germany and as German citizens they can be over here easily enough.'

'And how about Eleuthera?' Huss asked. Hanlon's eyes narrowed in thought as she looked at her colleague. She hadn't expected Huss to be remotely interested in these existential threats to Schneider. Huss's job would be prising enough uniforms out of the system to ensure Schneider got to and from the Oxford Union and enough crush-barriers so no one got injured. That was assuming anyone actually turned up to protest.

Smithfield grimaced. 'They're a very unpleasant anarchist group. Hang on.' He picked his tablet up and showed them some images, twisted, blackened metal, the remains of a car, splashes of blood in the street, an inert form huddled under a blanket.

'Athens last year, an economist from the IMF, a friend of mine as it happens, that's their work.'

'"Troika scum!" Eleuthera tweeted after that,' he added. 'Basically they are prepared to kill, they are also extremely well-financed. But nobody really knows who they are or what they really represent.'

He drank some tea. 'They appear online, they have a website on the dark net, using TOR, of course, to avoid detection. Sometimes they appear at rallies, masked with flags. Is it them really, or just wannabe anarchists? No one knows. Some think Russian money is involved, some say that they're linked to organized crime, others that it's money funnelled by the FSB, the Russian secret service, to destabilize the West. Nothing's proven. But I'd really worry if they were involved.'

Another picture, armed cops in riot gear, clouds of tear gas, Smithfield elaborated, 'Eleuthera-inspired demo in Toulouse outside a Front National meeting, twenty-seven delegates injured.'

Another image. A stretcher being loaded into an ambulance.

'Hungarian,' said Smithfield. 'Junior justice minister in Viktor Urban's government, assassinated, suspected Eleuthera.' He turned off the tablet. 'It's Greek for freedom. Are you sure they're involved too? I do hope not.' He smiled coldly, he certainly didn't look worried. 'Like I said, some people say, do they really exist? I would say, they do an awful lot of damage for a non-existent group.' He continued, 'At least we can keep Al-Akhdaar at bay if we keep an eye out for Muslims, Eleuthera are a throwback to Baader Meinhof and the Brigate Rosse, they're disaffected mainly middle-class student intellectuals. There's bound to be a couple in my college, almost certainly doing PPE, my specialist subject. Or maybe IT.'

He frowned thoughtfully. Hanlon wondered if he was taking it as almost a personal slight that Eleuthera should come from this background. Religious fanatics such as Al-Akhdaar would be practically insane in Smithfield's view; rabid, foaming nutcases stuck in the fourteenth century. Eleuthera too, addicted to a political extremism that was as dated as the sideburns and flares of the seventies where it belonged. A place, a mindset, where the government were 'the Man' and people who worked for a living 'breadheads'.

'Eleuthera,' he smiled this time, 'so idealistic, so old-fashioned, fighting last century's battles. Schneider's doing very well at collecting dangerous enemies, you two are going to have your work cut out, that's for sure.'

'I'm sure we'll rise to the challenge, Master,' said Hanlon, with offhand sarcasm. It wasn't lost on Smithfield. He frowned at her.

'I hope so, for your sake, DCI Hanlon, and I'd lose the attitude if I were you. If you don't, your politician, and maybe even you, are going to end up very dead.'

He smiled pleasantly at Hanlon and his voice was quiet but his gaze was cold. His eyes met Hanlon's. Hers grey, his blue. Like a flicker of swords.

Hanlon thought suddenly, He really dislikes me. The thought didn't bother her at all. She was supremely indifferent to the opinions of others.

'What kind of people join Eleuthera?' she asked, to mollify him.

'Generally middle-class idealists with a taste for extreme violence. The kind of people who enjoy hurting and killing people but dressing it up in ideological clothes. Just like the killers who join IS, it's an excuse to do harm. If you were religious, you might call them evil.'

Hanlon nodded. She wasn't religious, but she believed in the power of evil.

'Any other questions?' asked Smithfield.

'Rosemount?' asked Huss.

Smithfield's head jerked up in almost a pantomime of surprise. 'I beg your pardon?'

'Rosemount,' repeated Huss.

'That's the hotel near here that Schneider is staying in for a week. Only his people and I know about it, it's supposed to be a closely guarded secret.' He looked at Huss with a perplexed expression. 'And just how on earth did you hear about it, DI Huss?'

Fuck, thought Huss for the second time that day.

CHAPTER THIRTEEN

Marcus Hinds gazed out of the grimy window at Bethnal Green High Street. Clifford Hinds, his uncle, joined him, resting his powerful fingers on the window sill. Marcus looked at the heavy gothic lettering on the top joints of the fingers, CLIFF HINDS. When he'd been a child he had wanted his name on his hands like Uncle Cliff and had been annoyed when his dad had pointed out Marcus had six letters.

Marcus wondered how many people had managed to read the message on Uncle Cliff's knuckles before they had rearranged their face. The last image they would have: the script on his skin as his large fists battered them into unconsciousness.

Nowadays, Uncle Cliff, to Marcus, had become simply Cliff and his gut was massive. His longish hair was still there but he had to wear a pork pie hat at a jaunty angle to conceal his bald patch. But his eyes were as bright and full of amusement as ever and the air of latent violence that hung around him like aftershave was still as strong as ever. Sixty-five now and still as scary as when he'd been in his prime. Right now, though, his eyes were troubled.

'There's a warrant out for your arrest, old son, murder.'

'Shit.' He turned and paced Cliff's front room. It didn't take long. He had a small, neat flat above a shop opposite the Museum of Childhood. If you leaned out of the window you could see the York Hall, home of British boxing. Heavy traffic rumbled outside.

Cliff had been in touch with old friends from Oxford who had police contacts. What he had learned wasn't good.

Now he was looking at the screen of his phone. 'You didn't knife him, did you?' His tone was light, conversational, the kind of way you might ask someone if they'd remembered to buy milk.

'Do what?' Marcus was puzzled. 'No, of course not. I booted him down the stairs. It was self-defence.'

Cliff looked up from his phone at his brother's son, twenty-five now but looking lost and worried, like a small child almost. He sighed. This wasn't supposed to happen. Marcus was the golden boy of the family, beating the shit out of people was for those with limited options like himself and his brother, Paul. Paul had wanted Marcus to be the editor of the *Guardian*.

'The Old Bill say he died of being stabbed in the leg, femoral artery, he bled out.'

Marcus raised his eyes heavenwards and shook his head wordlessly.

'You got a drink in here?'

'In the kitchen.'

Cliff heard a pop as Marcus uncorked the Bell's and he came back into the room with a tumbler full of Scotch. He sat down heavily on the sofa.

'Do you want a drink, Cliff?'

The older man shook his head. 'Nah, mate, I'm fine. I'm on tablets for me heart, have to look after the old ticker.'

Marcus nodded silently. 'I'm being fitted up.'

'By that anarchist mob?' Cliff rubbed his chin thoughtfully.

Marcus nodded. 'By Eleuthera, yeah.'

'They'd top one of their own just to fit you up?' Cliff cocked his head questioningly.

'Yeah, it's the sort of thing they do, they're idealists.'

Cliff gave a bark of laughter. 'Funny old ideals.'

'Yep.' Marcus took another drink of Scotch. 'Probably Georgie's idea.'

'That bird you were shagging?'

'Mm-hm.' Marcus nodded and drank some more.

'Well, Marky, you can certainly pick them. Mind you, lovely tits.' Cliff had met Georgie when he'd come up to Oxford to visit Marcus. The boy had thought that the anarchist girl would be blown away by Cliff's anti-authoritarian record, that and his disadvantaged, proletarian background. They had hated each other on sight.

'She's no anarchist,' said Cliff, 'she's a fucking intellectual snob.'

'That's true,' said Marcus, with feeling.

'Why would they want to do that anyway?' Cliff asked. 'Fit you up?'

'Because they found out I was a journalist and going to write about them. They're in bed with a Muslim terrorist group, like IS, Al-Akhdaar. They want to kill a German politician who's over here.'

'Oh,' said Cliff. He shook his head. They had all been so proud of Marcus, still were, the first Hinds to go to university and one of the few members of the family not to be on the wrong side of the law. Who could possibly have imagined it could end up as dangerous as this?

Dangerous and stupid.

Not the way to get to run the *Guardian*.

'Why are the anarchists involved?' asked Cliff.

Marcus continued, 'Al-Akhdaar don't have any operatives in Britain, so they've contracted the job out to Eleuthera. Al-Akhdaar are bankrolled by IS, they've got loads of money and, obviously, loads of weaponry. Eleuthera need both, it's their chance for glory.'

Cliff shrugged. It was all a bit beyond him.

'Well, old son, they're taking fucking liberties, muppets.' He shook his head. In his youth he'd have got a few trust-worthy mates, people like Beard and Malcolm Anderson, and given the anarchists a lesson they would never forget. But he was too old now, like a declawed mangy lion.

'So, what do you think I should do?' asked Marcus.

Cliff rubbed his bald patch, he did that these days as a sign he was thinking. 'Turn yourself in,' he said simply.

Marcus looked at him in surprise. It was the last thing he thought he'd hear. 'Do you really think so?'

Cliff laughed loudly. 'Course I fucking don't.' He shook his head at the absurdity of the idea. 'No, you're going to go and stay with a bloke I know, I was a mate of his dad's, cos the Old Bill will be round here soonish looking for you, and I'll get a message to that woman copper you think you can trust and arrange a meet. You can put your side of the story. That'll help to a limited extent. I'll arrange a place to meet that the Old Bill won't dare raid to get their hands on you.'

Marcus looked at his uncle and felt a surge of affection tinged with relief. It was a huge weight off his shoulders to have someone else deciding what he should and shouldn't do.

Hopefully the files on the memory stick would make it abundantly clear to Melinda Huss the kind of people that Eleuthera were. The information there would prevent the Schneider assassination and with luck all charges against him would be quietly dropped.

His head throbbed but he took another mouthful of Scotch. It was easily the worst day of his life. He was beginning to get some kind of insight into the stresses that Uncle Cliff had faced throughout his life: extreme violence, someone out to get you, and the very real danger of a lengthy prison sentence.

Another day at the office for Uncle Cliff, but not for him.

There was a ring on the doorbell. Marcus looked up in alarm. Cliff made a placatory gesture.

'It's Mick the Beard, he's your driver. I'll wait here for PC Plod. They'll go to your mum's first, then here.'

He went into the hall and Marcus heard voices, then a burly figure in leathers and holding two motorbike helmets followed Cliff into the room. He had a shaved head and a long, curly brown beard streaked with grey. He looked tough and evil in equal measure. Like Cliff he'd been around the block.

'Mick, this is Marcus.'

They shook hands.

'Better head off now, Beard,' Cliff said, 'before we get company.'

The old biker nodded. 'Put this on,' he ordered Marcus.

Marcus took the helmet. 'Where are we going?'

'Up north.'

'North?' queried Marcus. Manchester? Scotland?

'Edmonton.' That was about three miles away. 'The Three Compasses.'

Marcus's heart sank. 'Is that...?'

'Yep,' said Cliff, grinning. 'Today's your day for meeting gangsters.'

Reluctantly Marcus pulled the helmet on and followed the broad back out of the flat and down the stairs.

Just when he thought his day couldn't get any worse.

The Three Compasses. Home of Dave Anderson, head of one of north London's leading crime families.

CHAPTER FOURTEEN

The demonstration outside the Union Hall in Islington was smaller than Hanlon was expecting but much more unpleasant. She had done her share of demo policing but they had been for big events, attracting thousands of protestors. This was very low-key. The fact that Schneider was unknown, the leader of a small, albeit controversial party, from a state few people could find on a map, certainly helped.

There were maybe twenty or so protesters with slogans such as *Smash Fascism*, *Schneider = Hitler*, *Racism*, *Nein Danke*. They stood pushed up on the pavement under a watery autumn sun inconveniencing passers-by.

'There he is!' A cry went up as Schneider and his people climbed out the black Range Rover that had been loaned to them. The chants and abuse increased in volume.

Gower had said that he had two armed protection officers ready and waiting, should the need arise. Hanlon found this slightly pointless, what was she supposed to do if someone just, for example, shot Schneider? Stand and wait for them to do something?

But, as always, the immediacy of action drove any worries or doubts from her mind. Gower had told her they'd be photographing faces to compare them against the database of known violent political activists. Again, she thought this would probably come in useful only after the event. It wouldn't help right now.

An egg hurled by a screaming girl demonstrator brushed past Hanlon's head and exploded over the bodywork of the car.

Hübler and Schneider followed Hanlon, Schneider with a hard, tight smile fixed on to his face as they marched toward the doors of the venue.

There were about half a dozen police in hi-vis jackets controlling the protesters, more than adequate to stop any direct attack, but there was obviously nothing they could do about the abuse.

'Fascists!'

'Nazi bitch, I hope you get raped!'

'Fascist whore!' This one directed at Hanlon by a pretty dark-haired girl with a pierced nose and green streaks in her hair.

Most of the abuse was directed at Christiane Hübler and Hanlon and most of it was graphic threats of rape, a lot of it from women. They seemed to hate them more than Schneider.

Hanlon was used to being abused by mobs from her early days as a uniform in riot control or football duties, but this was different. There was a visceral hatred that twisted the faces of the protestors into snarling animal masks of aggression.

As they neared the steps to the venue a girl and a man broke through past the police and ran at Hanlon and Schneider.

Two of the uniforms grabbed the man, who was shouting and kicking, trying to shake off the burly officers hanging on to him, one on each arm, as he shouted at Schneider.

'Fascist scum!'

He was white, with dirty brown matted dreadlocks, blue and green tribal tattoos visible on his neck.

The girl was the one that she had noticed earlier, the one with the streaks of colour in her very dark, short hair. Hanlon noticed that she was startlingly attractive. She blocked Hanlon's path and drew her head back. Momentarily Hanlon thought she was going to headbutt her but then she darted her head forward and spat in Hanlon's face.

Hanlon twisted her body, dropping her left shoulder down, and the spittle struck her right shoulder. With the two police wrestling with the girl's accomplice and the general confusion of the situation, Hanlon retaliated. Before she really knew what she was doing, she had straightened up and driven her balled left fist in a very short vicious hook into the solar plexus of the girl. The spittle landing on her jacket had enraged her. It disgusted her.

The girl doubled up in pain then looked at Hanlon with an expression of almost feral rage.

'She assaulted me,' she screamed, pointing at Hanlon. 'Arrest her!'

Hanlon looked at her more closely now. Her eyes had an almost almond shape to them and her accent was genteel Scottish, she guessed Edinburgh. She was expensively dressed in a cashmere jacket and scarf, her skirt was very short and she had excellent legs. Her boots were high quality suede.

Fortunately for Hanlon there was no press and the

attention of the protestors and their ubiquitous camera phones was mainly on the bald guy and the police.

'Pig scum!'

'Smash the fascists!'

'Come on.' Christiane Hübler pulled her arm, her voice urgent. 'Inside.'

She practically dragged Hanlon into the building and the doors closed behind them as another couple of eggs smashed on the glass followed by a dull thud as a bag of flour landed.

Schneider calmly wiped some spit off his cheek with a tissue and binned it. He smiled and waved at the protestors through the doors.

He turned to Hanlon. 'I saw what you did' – he wagged a finger – 'naughty, naughty. Don't get me wrong, I'm delighted, but we have to be seen to behave. Now, if this were Saxony or Hamburg, well, things would be different, but please,' he smiled to show he wasn't really cross, 'no attacking anyone. Well, not unless I ask you to.'

A fresh wave of inaudible abuse burst from the protestors outside. He looked at the mess on the door.

'If you added sugar, you could make a cake,' he said, pleasantly.

A couple of security men from the Union Hall took up positions by the door as three men wearing suits appeared in the lobby to greet them.

'Hi, I'm Paul Samuels,' said one of the suits, shaking Schneider's hand. 'Let me take you inside, get you freshened up. We kick off in about an hour, hopefully that lot will go away now you're inside...'

He took Schneider by the arm and they drifted away, leaving Hanlon and Hübler in the lobby.

Hanlon looked at Hübler who was staring at her in irritation.

'If you attack the demonstrators you play their game. You of all people should know that.' She shook her head. 'It was very unprofessional of you.'

'It was self-defence,' countered Hanlon. 'She could have had a weapon.'

Hübler smiled bitterly. 'Well, I suppose so. But welcome to our world, DCI Hanlon, you'll have to get used to a lot of abuse, I'm afraid.'

Hanlon thought, actually just now was almost certainly the high point of the difficulties that she'd foreseen. The House of Commons lunch would be a breeze and then he'd be off to Oxford and out of everyone's hair.

'Don't worry,' said Hanlon, 'I'm used to people not liking me.'

'I'm sure that's the case,' said Hübler acidly, 'but at least Wolf and I have the consolation that history is on our side, as is the side of right.'

Hanlon's chilly, grey-eyed gaze met hers.

'Me too,' she said.

CHAPTER FIFTEEN

Marcus Hinds was dropped off outside the Three Compasses in Edmonton in the north of the capital.

The pub had an evil reputation. It belonged to the Andersons, who were one of the big London crime families. The building itself looked innocuous. It was a small white-washed building standing on the corner of a cul-de-sac. The terraced houses nearby had a forlorn look about them. Paint was peeling off the windows, the small gardens were choked with weeds. They were never going to be gentrified as long as the Andersons had the Three Compasses. Two shaven-headed men in Crombies stood outside the door.

Marcus Hinds was not unaware of the irony of his situation. As a freelance writer, he was standing outside tabloid gold. He could earn a year's salary with the story:

Inside the belly of the beast, an exposé of the headquarters of organized crime. It was, however, a story that would never get written. He would never dare. He knew of a journalist who had offended Dave Anderson. Hard to type with all your fingers broken.

Marcus Hinds approached the men on the door, they looked at him suspiciously.

'Sorry, mate, we're closed.'

Their faces and expressions were those of hardened street-fighters, their stubbled heads reflected the chilly late morning sun.

'I'm expected,' said Hinds.

'What's the name?' A hard, mistrustful look.

'Marcus Hinds.'

One of the doormen disappeared inside whilst the other, arms folded, regarded Hinds with wary watchfulness. Hinds slightly puzzled him. The bouncer was like a dog who is faced with a breed he has never encountered before. Hinds was educated, by the sounds of his voice, yet he had a street quality that the other man recognized. You could see at a glance that he could handle himself. He was neither fish nor fowl.

His companion reappeared.

'Follow me, mate.'

All affability now. Now that Hinds had been vouched for.

Hinds did so. The front bar was deserted. He walked behind the narrow, powerful shoulders of the doorman through to the back bar.

'Marcus Hinds,' announced his escort, like some odd toastmaster at a wedding.

Inside the room were two men at a table, both seated. Hinds needed no introductions. His journalist's eye ran over the place, noting its salient features for the well-paid exclusive story that he would never write.

The drawn chintz curtains, the pool table in the corner, the green baize suspiciously stained, three, no, four small circular tables with heavy wood and ornate metal frames.

The wall-mounted lights were shaped to look like candles with old lampshades that had yellowed with time. A swirly, busy carpet, an ice bucket on the bar advertising Gordon's and a lamp next to it designed to look like a pineapple.

It was the kind of pub only old men would drink in, a pub unchanged essentially since the early seventies.

Now he transferred his attention to the couple at the table. One man, tall, thin, grey-haired, in a beautifully cut dark grey two-piece suit, a narrow downturned gash of a mouth like a shark's. Morris Jones, Dave Anderson's minder. His eyes were half closed. Marcus had heard he had quite a big heroin habit. The rumour was true but the drugs had neither slowed him down nor improved his character.

The other, Dave 'Jesus' Anderson. Shorter but also thin, in his late twenties or early thirties (who was going to dare ask?) dressed in a T-shirt and tracksuit, the kind of knock-offs you can get from a street market for a tenner although he was worth a conservative seven million pounds. Rumours and legends had accumulated around him too. His sanity was open to question, Marcus had heard. But not his business ability, efficiency, intelligence or propensity to violence. Rat-tailed hair and those extraordinary eyes, almost burning.

The eyes of a prophet.

'Have a seat,' said Morris Jones, conversationally.

Marcus did so, feeling absurdly as if he were there for a job interview. As their eyes rested on him he felt a scrotum-tightening chill of fear descend over his body. No, not a job interview, more the professional evaluation of a couple of undertakers interested to see if he would fit the coffin.

Dave Anderson leaned forward. 'Heard you was in a bit of bother. Cliff's asked me to look after you for a bit until we come to some sort of decision.'

It was highly uncomfortable sitting there under the gaze of someone who had crucified a man to a door, someone used to issuing orders for punishment beatings and occasionally worse. And although he wasn't too concerned about his own safety, he knew he would be forever beholden to Anderson, and that was not a good feeling.

Anderson's voice was harsh, brutal, the words slapped down like cards in a winning hand on a table.

'So, Marcus.' Morris Jones smiled at him, or rather the corners of his mouth turned up in the parody of one. 'Tell us what happened.'

Marcus took a deep breath, and did so.

CHAPTER SIXTEEN

'I'm sorry, DI Huss, there's nothing usable on this memory stick.'

Evan Collins from Systems Support ruefully handed Huss the bagged memory stick. There had been three files on it and when Huss had clicked on them to open them nothing had happened other than an error message.

So she'd gone in search of help.

Evan's presence at the police station was somewhat mysterious. It certainly wasn't to do with lack of ability. Far from it. He had a degree in IT from Warwick, nobody could fathom why he had elected to work for Thames Valley CID instead of in the City. He seemed overqualified to be doing what he was doing. He was still on his first three months but already people were frightened in case he decided to leave. They could all remember his irritatingly incompetent predecessor. Huss personally put his presence there down to laziness and maybe a heavy weed intake. Some people like doing a job they can do blindfold, no stress, regular pay, pleasant working conditions. Nobody breathing down their necks anxious to supplant them. Certainly Evan looked a little zonked out some mornings, but then again, so did many of the police, although that was mainly alcohol rather than drug related.

'Nothing at all?' She was puzzled. Marcus Hinds had gone to considerable trouble to get this to her.

'No, there was something, there were files there, but they've been corrupted.'

'Accidentally or deliberately?' asked Huss looking at Evan's serious face. He looked exactly as one would imagine a systems support guy to look, nerdy, indoorsy, intelligent, habitually dressed in T-shirt and jeans. Today he had a retro Led Zeppelin sweatshirt on.

'Oh, deliberately, I would say. Without a doubt. But you can take it from me they're unusable.'

'Oh, well, thanks, Evan.' Huss took the useless memory stick. She might as well chuck it in the bin. She went back upstairs and sat behind her desk, staring into space. She would have to do a run-through on security with the Rosemount, she decided. She added it to her mental to-do list. At least she'd get to see one of England's most exclusive hotels, that wouldn't have happened otherwise.

She walked along to DCI Templeman's office and knocked on the door.

'Do you have a moment?'

Twenty minutes later she returned to her desk even more full of gloom. The case against Hinds's was looking increasingly black.

Templeman had happily shared his preliminary notes with her. Georgie Adams, his girlfriend and a PhD student at St Anne's College doing her doctorate in Eastern European Political Thought, had stated that Hinds's behaviour had been increasingly erratic lately, maybe due to heavy drug and alcohol abuse. He had been smoking worrying amounts of high strength skunk and she thought it was leading to cannabis psychosis. He had been violent and verbally abusive and had accused her and her friends several times of being in league with Islamic extremists.

'He's got a bee in his bonnet about them,' she said.

Huss frowned. She could believe Adams about the drugs, but she found it hard to imagine Hinds as violent towards women.

Adams went on to say that he was unhinged.

'I'm pro free speech and pro rights for the individual,' she had said, 'but in his mind to be a Muslim was to be a jihadi. I kept saying there are millions of British Muslims and just a few IS sympathizers. He was having none of it.'

That morning, he had started drinking early and smoking skunk (Templeman said a plastic container of weed had been found in his flat. As well as that there was an ashtray with a half-smoked joint in and roach ends were in the bin in the kitchen). She'd been frightened by his behaviour, 'muttering to himself, paranoid,' and had texted a friend to come round.

'He doesn't like me going to Russia either. I say to him, look, I'm doing a doctorate in Post Communist Political Thought, where else would I go, Surrey? Chechens, he says, Tajiks, Muslim fanatics.'

Two of her friends had come to give her moral and, if necessary, physical support and it was these two, Mark Spencer and James Kettering, the man who had subsequently died, that Hinds had attacked on the stairwell.

The knife was being analysed for prints. Door-to-door enquiries had established only that two of the flats in the block had heard noises but nobody had actually seen anything. There hadn't been that many people to interview. At that time of day the block had been virtually empty.

A warrant had been issued for Hinds's arrest on suspicion of murder and Serious Crimes alerted in the Met. It was assumed that Hinds, a Londoner, would hide out there with friends and family.

'There's still no sign of Hinds,' said Templeman, 'he's still on the loose. Hardly the actions of an innocent man.'

Or maybe, thought Huss, the actions of a very frightened man. A man on the run from a violent criminal organization.

'Why the interest, Melinda?' asked Templeman. Huss had decided that her previous relationship with Hinds, brief as it was, was of no concern to the police. She hadn't mentioned the reason for Elsa's visit or the memory stick to anyone.

'I suppose that I'm just keyed up over this Schneider visit, sir. I had heard some rumour that this Georgie Adams was a member of an anarchist group called Eleuthera. They can cause quite a lot of trouble, I believe.'

Templeman looked baffled. 'Who told you that?'

'The master of St Wulfstan's.' Huss decided not to mention it was her own belief that Adams was a member of Eleuthera. Eleuthera were not actively banned in the UK but Huss guessed that their activities would be of interest to the security services. Adams had merely said that she was 'left-wing, libertarian'.

Huss continued, 'He's organizing Schneider's visit. He

arranged for the debate at the Oxford Union.' Just to underline Smithfield's importance, she added, 'He knows the chief constable.'

Templeman said, in a tone that cut down any chance of debate, 'Georgina Adams seems a very respectable young lady and she has no criminal record. Her political views are her own concern, not ours. Marcus Hinds, on the other hand, has a conviction for drug possession and I gather his family appear to be well known to the police in London. His dad did time, as did his brother. His uncle's a nutter, seemingly. And, from the injuries inflicted upon the deceased, even if we discard the fatal final knife wound, Hinds has inherited his propensity for extreme violence.'

'Well, I can probably discount that rumour then, sir.' Huss hid her disappointment. Templeman was not going to allow her to see Adams. It rather looked as if he had decided that Hinds was guilty.

Then Templeman asked, 'How are the arrangements for Schneider's trip going?'

'Fine, sir.' She sketched out the arrangements she'd put in place for security for his speech at the Oxford Union. Templeman seemed happy.

'And this assassination threat? I don't want him dead here in Oxford. Not in this current hysterical Middle East atmosphere. That's all we need.'

'I've been liaising with Protection Command, sir,' said Huss. 'They are taking it very seriously indeed. I'd like to go up to London just to run through some protocol with them, check out their arrangements with the Rosemount, since it's on our patch.'

'The Rosemount, very nice. Schneider must have a lot of money. By all means, Melinda, go up to London, and, oh, if you could, I'd like you to meet Georgina Adams.'

Huss looked startled. The DCI went on, 'She needs to go back to Hinds's flat, pick up some of her stuff. Obviously with him on the loose she needs someone with her to babysit her. Can you do that? I'd also like your opinion of her. If you're not too busy?'

Yesss! thought Huss.

'That'd be fine, sir. If you give me her number I could do that this lunchtime.'

'Sure.' He took his notebook out and jotted down a number and gave it to her.

Huss went back to her desk and called the number. She spoke to the well-bred, educated voice on the other end of the phone with its genteel, modulated Edinburgh vowels and they agreed to meet at Georgie's college.

'I'll pick you up at twelve,' said Huss.

She put her phone back in her pocket.

She thought of Marcus Hinds. Was he the innocent boy she remembered coming to her for help, or had he really gone off the deep end as Georgie Adams claimed? She guessed that both were possible. Look at Elsa, brilliant don and bag lady/street drinker co-existing in one body, co-existing in one mind.

She was looking forward to seeing Adams. She smiled grimly to herself, I could always introduce myself as his ex.

CHAPTER SEVENTEEN

Hanlon met up with Schneider, Hübler and a member of his German team that she hadn't met before, Frank Muller, his head of security, at Claridge's for breakfast. Despite the fact that Muller was wearing a suit, a bearskin and a club would have suited him better.

Huge, with an unkempt black beard and shaggy hair, he reminded her of Rasputin or the seventies British wrestler, Giant Haystacks. He must have been a good twenty stone. He was squeezed into an ill-fitting electric blue suit that was slightly too small for him. His arms bulged through its cheap fabric. The waiters looked at him with fascinated contempt.

'This is Frank,' Schneider introduced him. His eyes as they met Hanlon's sparkled playfully and he raised his eyebrows in mock apology. There was a side of Schneider that Hanlon found very attractive, a kind of playfulness that was unusual in those that she had met who had, or aspired to, high public office.

'*Guten Morgen, Frau Hanlon. Leider, kann ich nicht Englisch sprechen,*' grunted Frank, his voice deep and slightly hoarse. His eyes regarded her with lack of interest.

Having spoken, Frank returned to demolishing his full English breakfast. Not a pretty sight. His eating lacked finesse.

Hübler leaned forward. 'He says unfortunately he can't speak English,' she said, 'but he says he's delighted to make your acquaintance.'

Hanlon doubted that. She couldn't imagine Frank was remotely pleased to meet any representative of the police. She was certainly pleased not to have to talk to Frank. She doubted he'd be an Oscar Wilde, his conversations a flow of entertaining witticisms.

His looming presence was out of place with the well-heeled clientele in the dining room. Frank created a kind of force field of aggressive silence at whose epicentre he floated serenely. She wondered if Schneider had brought him in to beef up security after the Islington incident.

She suppressed a yawn and drank some of Claridge's excellent coffee. She had been up at five for an hour's run eastwards along the Thames, down through the City to East Ham and back. As she'd run, her hair bouncing in rhythm with her stride, the sweat running down her spine, her mind had floated free. The huge river, shrouded in darkness when she started, was gradually revealed as another cold dawn illuminated the great city. Hanlon's two loves, Mark Whiteside and London, the eternal city. Sod Rome, she thought. Give me London.

She had reflected as her feet pounded the narrow streets that these were the sorts of districts that, in Germany, would form the bedrock support of Schneider's party, the dispossessed white working class.

They were equally mutinous over here, shafted from all sides, feeling that their jobs were under threat. If the country were flooded with migrant lawyers, judges, journalists and TV presenters undercutting the law and the media and taking their jobs, they argued, coverage would be very different indeed.

Well, here she was with the heroic defenders of the faith.

Frank, as if divining her thoughts, scowled at her across the tablecloth. Like I care, thought Hanlon. Her cold grey eyes locked on to his. She felt utterly indestructible. She could feel the energy of her super-fit body coursing through her veins.

Their gaze was mutually challenging. I can take you, she thought scornfully. You might be big, but you're slow, and stupid, and you might have big muscles but how quickly can you move and how long before you're puffing, out of breath?

Schneider, aware of the tension, leant across the table and spoke to Frank who nodded and stood up, leaving the room.

Immediately it became a brighter place.

Schneider leaned forward over the table, the immaculate heavy white linen cloth under his elbows. He seemed very at home in the grandly intimidating room. Hanlon cared little what people thought of her but she was aware from the occasional disapproving glance, from staff and guests alike, that she somehow didn't belong. Not to the same extent as Frank, it was true, but hotel staff are extremely good at placing people and Hanlon was definitely not a Claridge's person.

Schneider, however, had the successful politician's ability to transcend barriers. You got the impression that he would be just as welcome at the boardroom of Mercedes as in some down-at-heel *kneipe* in the backstreets of Munich. The staff looked at him with devoted affection.

'I'm here for three more days, but there are no public engagements. During the day I won't need you, but I have three dinner appointments and I'd be glad of your company just in case.'

Hübler added by way of clarification, 'Herr Schneider has had problems in Germany with being recognized and it only takes a few phone calls to get a few anarchists or lefties to start throwing their muscle around.'

Hanlon nodded. 'What's Frank going to be doing, sight-seeing?'

Schneider smiled. 'Frank's like having a bull mastiff around. You heard about what happened to that unfortunate man in Heidelberg,' he grimaced, 'my old friend Gunther.'

Hanlon saw Hübler glance sharply at him. An odd look. Schneider ignored it.

'I'm happy to take risks of being shot or blown up, but something about throat-slitting or beheading makes my flesh creep. I know it sounds stupid, but I sleep much better with Frank dozing on my sofa, even if he snores and ... *was ist "furzt" in Englisch?'*

'Farts,' supplied the ever reliable Hübler.

'Speaking of mastiffs,' Schneider said, 'Frank's brought over Wotan, my dog. Claridge's won't have it in the place, but the Rosemount will.'

'It's a Presa Canario,' said Hübler.

The name of the breed meant nothing to Hanlon whose knowledge of dogs ran purely to shepherds and spaniels. She looked at her watch.

'Well, I'm going to check on the arrangements for Oxford, is that the name of the hotel that you'll be staying in?'

'The Rosemount.' Hübler smiled. 'They have offered Wolf the use of their Garden Lodge, we'll be there for a week.'

'A week?' Wasn't a week a long time in politics? Hanlon thought to herself.

As if reading her mind Schneider said, 'I am meeting like-minded politicians from the USA, Scandinavia and several extremely wealthy individuals, entrepreneurs and indus-trialists who are interested in funding us. You saw those *Abschaum den Menschheit.*'

'Scum of the earth!' supplied Hübler, beaming happily, enjoying her translation role.

'These enlightened gentlemen I shall be meeting feel there's not much point in making money if people like that are going to take it from you,' said Schneider, 'or kill you! We're their bulwark against the red hordes.'

Although Hanlon personally detested the anarchist movement, she thought describing them as a 'horde' might well be a slight exaggeration. Dangerous, possibly. Numer-ous, certainly not.

'Naturally there is a price to pay,' said Schneider. 'A pol-itical party is only as strong as its funding.'

'Well,' she said, 'I'll let you get on with your day, Herr Schneider.'

I'll go and see Huss, she thought, see how things are in Oxford.

'See you this evening, DCI Hanlon.' He drained his coffee and stood up, leaned forward and shook her hand.

Accompanied by the faithful Hübler she watched his broad back as he walked across he thickly carpeted room. Once again she was struck by the power of the presence of Schneider. She had looked him up on a YouTube clip, addressing the faithful at a rally. It had been like a rock concert, dramatic lighting, choreographed movements, cunning use of multimedia anytime the audience's attention looked like flagging.

He carried this star quality with him even now. Several women in the room followed him with their eyes even though she doubted they would have a clue who he was.

Schneider had charisma.

He had it in spades.

CHAPTER EIGHTEEN

Elsa was having lunch with Old Harry; today it was butternut squash soup. Rowenna would go down the weekly market in Summertown and badger the veg stall holders into giving her the unsaleable stuff for free. Today she'd come away with a dozen squash, a sack of potatoes, carrots and celery.

Elsa was unsure about it. 'It's very orange, Harry.'

'It's supposed to be that way, Elsa. How've you been keeping anyway? I haven't seen you for a couple of days.'

She ate some of her soup thoughtfully. It was lovely and warm.

'I've been out of town, Harry,' she said grandly. He nodded. He knew that she had a place in the woods on the outskirts near the ring road where she slept. It was quieter out there and she had a tarpaulin and a couple of sleeping bags that she kept hidden under a spreading holly bush, so she could wrap up warmly and not get hassled by passers-by.

'I'm looking after something, it's from a computer, I think, that the nice young man who lives in Pretoria Road in Summertown gave me.'

Harry frowned. 'That street was on the news, someone got killed there.'

'That's right,' said Elsa. 'In fact in, oh, my Lord, what's his name…' Harry watched with amusement as she banged her head angrily with her fist, he often had the same problem. Names refusing, obstinately, to come.

'Marcus, that's it, Marcus Hinds.'

'Shouldn't you speak to the police about it?' asked Harry.

'Maybe I will, or maybe I won't,' said Elsa mysteriously.

'Have you finished, Elsa?' asked Rowenna. She was going round the tables clearing the bowls and plates away. She had learnt that it was best to get them back as quickly as possible in case of breakage or spillage.

'Yes, thank you, dear, anyway.' She turned her back on Rowenna who was stacking the bowls and plates on a trolley and looked at Harry. 'Marcus Hinds said he'd be back for it at some stage, so I'll speak to him then. He'll probably want it back. Those computer drive things are probably important.'

'Are you finished too, Harry?'

He nodded and Rowenna moved their bowls on to her trolley.

She pushed it back to the kitchen. So, she thought, Elsa knows Marcus. What a small world.

CHAPTER NINETEEN

Huss picked up Georgie Adams outside St Anne's College. It wasn't far away from Summertown, near the part of Oxford known as Jericho.

Huss had found her image on Marcus Hinds's Facebook page but the small photo had done little justice to how attractive she was.

Both she and Huss were the same height, but there things diverged. Huss had thick, springy, wavy blonde hair and a sturdy, no-nonsense frame. She was powerfully built, the kind of woman who could swing a half hundredweight bag of feed effortlessly over her shoulders. Georgie was much slimmer but Huss could see that she was toned. She also had a watchful air about her and a hardness to her face that was quite daunting. She was exceptionally good-looking but there was a disturbing air about her. Her dark hair with its green highlights should have looked playful, quirky, but seemed oddly sinister. Her slim body was expensively accentuated by the leather jacket, the kind of leather that is soft as butter.

Ironic, thought Huss, trying to control an irrational and visceral dislike of Georgie. She supports class war and she's from the background of the 'oppressors', unaware that she's part of what the workers hate: unthinking privilege.

'Hello, you must be DI Huss.' She smiled coldly. Her smile was as expensive as her clothes. Templeman had told her that her father was a prominent Edinburgh lawyer. Huss felt a further stab of irritation. She was a farm girl, had left school at sixteen and, she felt, knew the value of peasant-style labour. Georgie, expensive private schooling, still being elitist-educated at one of the country's top universities, determined to try to smash a system that had showered her with every gift known to man.

She championed the proletariat but, thought Huss, had probably never done a day's manual labour in her life.

Or was it simply revolution as a fashion accessory? Something to go with that handbag, which Huss guessed to cost about five hundred pounds.

She felt patronized by Georgie. Not just patronized but treated with contempt. 'Fascist bitch'. 'Pig whore'. Words like that would be hurled by Georgie at her if Huss chose to attend the police line at the Schneider talk, plus volleys of gob. Now, she seemed happy to see Huss to protect her from her nut-job boyfriend.

And, annoyingly, she was better-looking than her.

But Huss was a fair-minded person and determined not to let her own prejudices stand in the way. Even though she would have cheerfully consigned her companion to compulsory 're-education' Mao-style in the countryside.

I've had to literally shovel enough shit in my lifetime, she thought. Let's see how you'd like it. Put those expensively manicured hands to some use.

She put the car in gear and they drove round to Hinds's flat.

All traces of the police investigation were gone. Huss had read the notes, and as they walked up the concrete stairs, their footsteps echoing in the stairwell, the faint smell of disinfectant in her nostrils, she could imagine the scenario, the curled-up body in the corner, the blood pooling underneath him. His friend's attempts to staunch the flow of blood as it seeped inexorably out. The medical officer had said it would only have taken a couple of minutes for him to have bled to death.

A stab wound to the leg.

The knife had been found next to the body.

Why did you do it, Marcus? she wondered.

As if reading her mind, Adams said, 'I don't suppose for one instant Marcus thought he was going to kill him. I think he just wanted to incapacitate him.'

'Had you ever seen him with that knife before?'

She was watching Georgie Adams's face closely and there was a moment of flickering indecision.

'Yes, yes I had.' I don't believe you, thought Huss. Liar. 'But I still like to think Marcus just stuck it in his leg thinking in his mixed-up way that would stop him following him.'

They reached the top of the stairs and Georgie opened the door to the flat.

'I'll go in first,' said Huss, 'just in case.'

Marcus's flat was an attic conversion and it didn't take long to look around. There was one main room with kitchen facilities and a bathroom. There was an odd, almost chemical smell that Huss recognized as that of old skunk smoke. The bed was screened off from the room by a storage unit. Light came in from large, velux windows. He was not a houseproud man; the flat was dusty, clothes lay strewn about the floor.

'OK,' said Huss. Georgie came in. She barely glanced around and went straight to the bathroom, emerging seconds later with a washbag.

'My stuff,' she explained.

'Is that everything?' asked Huss.

'I wouldn't leave clothes in here, can you not smell that weed?' Georgie shook her head. 'I blame that for what he's become.'

'And what's that?' Huss was looking at the table under the window. It was obviously the place that Marcus sat down to work. There was an anglepoise lamp, a coaster, an ashtray.

'A nutcase.' She sat down on the old sofa and looked up at Huss. 'I've got some friends in Occupy the City, the libertarian group, and I'm a member of the SWP. It's not exactly like I'm some sort of terrorist, but at times he became convinced that we were committed to heavy duty armed struggle. He thought I was mixed up with crazy anarchists.'

She gave a harsh bark of laughter at the idea.

'What, like the Red Brigades?' Huss asked.

'Exactly,' Georgie nodded, 'he was really paranoid sometimes. I don't mean that in a joking way, I really do think he has a serious medical problem. And now James is dead because of it. Weed isn't like it used to be, it's a seriously fucked-up drug these days, and then if you add a bottle of vodka on to that...' She shook her head sadly.

Huss had to admit that she sounded authentically worried. It was a plausible enough story.

'Or Eleuthera?' Huss tossed the name out lightly but Georgie blinked, startled.

'Who?' It was such a transparent lie.

'Oh, just some anarchist mob.' Huss's voice was dismissive. Her eyes were on the table, in the centre of which was a rectangle that was free of dust. Given that the rest of the flat had a fine film of it everywhere, it was conspicuous. A rectangle about the size of a laptop.

'Did Marcus have a laptop?' she asked.

'Yes.' Georgie nodded, looking relieved that the conversation had shifted from anarchist groups. 'He must have taken it with him.'

Huss looked out of the window at the street below and the terraced houses opposite. It was lined on both sides by cars. Directly opposite, one of the houses was boarded up and on the steps leading up to the door was old Elsa, the bag lady.

'I see you've got a resident tramp.'

Georgie nodded. 'Her, yes. She stinks to high heaven. I spoke to her once, offered her help to get into a hostel. She more or less told me to eff off. I wish she would.'

Georgie's tone made it clear that there would be no place for people like Elsa in her bright new dawn.

'Is she here often?'

Georgie shrugged. 'Often enough. She told me she had another residence. That's how she put it: "residence".'

There was no attempt to lecture Huss on Oxford council's railroading of rough sleepers out of sight of the tourists, out of the city, or an attack on government policy to the homeless. Huss guessed they weren't glamorous enough for Georgie.

The bus stop, thought Huss. The other residence. Suddenly Huss wanted very much to speak to Elsa, alone. She wished she didn't have Georgie with her.

Marcus must have run out of the front door of the flats and given Elsa the memory stick. He must also have taken time – how long, a minute? – to jot down the words for Huss to read. It didn't seem like the actions of a man fleeing a stabbing, but fleeing he obviously had been.

Eleuthera?

'Shall we go?' she said.

Georgie shook her head. 'No, not just yet. I know this sounds silly but I want to be alone here to think.'

'Oh well, if you're sure.' Thank you God, she thought.

'I'm sure. I can't imagine Marcus turning up here, can you? Not now, not after all of this.'

Huss let herself out of the flat and walked back down the echoing stairs. The heavy door of the house banged to behind her and she walked round the side of the skip that took up two precious bays for the residents-only street parking and crossed the road.

Elsa huddled in her layers of clothing, topped off by a once fawn-coloured man's Burberry raincoat, now rain-soaked and torn, but still quite stylish. Huss thought, if you gave her a makeover she would look quite presentable. There was a faded beauty still discernible in Elsa's features.

Huss took her purse out of her bag and extracted a five pound note.

Elsa's shrewd blue eyes regarded her inscrutably.

'Hello, it's me, remember me?' Huss asked.

'Of course I remember you, dear.'

'Did you see anything that happened? With the man who gave you the note to give to me?'

'Yes.' Just that, just the one word. Elsa took the note.

'Can you tell me any more?'

Elsa raised her head and looked across the road, up at roof level.

'I will. I saw lots. Meet me at my other address. I'm not talking here.' She looked upwards. 'Walls have ears.'

'Wilson Road.' Huss remembered the name from earlier. Elsa nodded.

'Ten p.m.,' she said. 'I'll have finished all my chores by then.' She smiled at Huss. 'He gave me something to look after.'

'What's that?' Please God let it be the laptop, prayed Huss.

'It's called a "superdrive", dear. Ten p.m.! Don't be late.'

'I won't,' said Huss with feeling. So, not the laptop but an external hard drive. Just as good.

Elsa rose to her feet and gathered up her bags. Huss watched her slowly hobble off down the street in the direction of the main road.

She turned to go herself in the direction where she had left her car. As she did she noticed movement at the window high above the street. A curtain twitched.

Georgie Adams had been watching.

CHAPTER TWENTY

Hanlon met Huss in the cafeteria of the Natural History Museum of Oxford. She'd spent twenty minutes in the attached Pitt Rivers ethnography museum looking at the shrunken heads. Severed heads had always fascinated people and now, she reflected, it was the Islamic terrorists' turn to benefit from the hold they had on popular imagination.

Gunther Hart's head hadn't been severed but his throat had been spectacularly slit. The act itself hadn't been filmed but the attackers had been filmed, balaclavaed, posing with his corpse. The usual depressing performance.

She'd been researching Al-Akhdaar – it was slim pickings. They had only really come to prominence in terms of their threats to Schneider and the murder of Hart. The concierge of Hart's townhouse had disappeared, was rumoured to be in Syria. So the group, although possibly minuscule, couldn't be discounted. They had followed through on one major promise. She couldn't blame Schneider for wanting to sleep with an attack dog, human or canine, at the foot of his bed.

Huss had just finished telling her of the meeting with Georgie.

'So what do you think?' asked Hanlon.

'I think that Marcus Hinds was running for his life. The dead man, James Kettering, has one conviction for affray from a Stop the City march, and has been linked to anarchist groups like The Wombles and Class War. These are fairly tame organizations,' said Huss, 'and much as they might like to, they haven't beheaded any capitalists yet. Eleuthera are anything but tame. They've got a rock solid history of violence, bombs, beatings, murder. That's on the continent, of course. And they're well-funded. I'm assuming that they have linked up with Al-Akhdaar to commit a high-profile assassination of Schneider, like they did with Hart.'

'And Hinds knows about it?'

'I would think so.' Huss drank some of her coffee. 'He is a journalist. I spoke to a couple of his mates. He'd been bragging about it to anyone who would listen. He was going to do a big exposé of Eleuthera – names, photos, everything – and was going to sell it to one of the Sundays. He had a deal lined up. Big money, it would have been front page. Normally he does in-depth crime, either profiles of well-known criminals or exposés of types of crime. Face it, he's got the connections.'

'I was there once when his uncle was nicked,' Hanlon suddenly recalled. 'It must have been twenty years ago, under Detective Superintendent Tremayne.'

'What was he like?'

'Quite a laugh, larger than life, an old-school villain, had an eye for the ladies. He was very good-looking, actually. Cliff, that was his name.'

She drank some coffee then asked Huss, 'So, you think that Hinds has been framed to make him disappear or to discredit any claims he may make regarding Eleuthera?'

'Well, it's working,' Huss pointed out. 'Hinds is on the run and his girlfriend's claims that he's mentally impaired through drugs and booze are quite cleverly laid out. Sow doubt as to his credibility, make it look like Hinds's report is the ramblings of a drunk, paranoid stoner.'

I'll reserve judgement on that, thought Hanlon.

'What does she look like?' she asked Huss.

'Slim, dark hair, beautiful.' Huss thought. 'Hang on, here's her Facebook photo.' She took her tablet out of her bag and showed Hanlon.

'We've met,' Hanlon said sourly. Huss looked at her in amazement and Hanlon told her about the incident of the previous night. Huss shook her head.

'You assaulted a protestor!' Her voice was scandalized but really she thought, Good.

'Yes, well, it was self-defence.' Hanlon was unapologetic. 'I seem to have got away with it, no one's made a complaint. Anyway, she was there. Probably sizing Schneider up for his coffin.'

'I'm amazed you haven't been sacked, DCI Hanlon,' said Huss.

'So am I, but I'm a bit past caring, to be honest.'

Huss stayed diplomatically silent. Hanlon was forever pushing at the boundaries, but she had a very powerful protector in the sizeable form of Corrigan and she had brought in some spectacular results. Corrigan had a tendency to block or shut down anti-Hanlon investigations. Sometimes he had to have 'a word' and officers' memories tended to become confused. He could play the system like a virtuoso could a violin. Crime reporters might be gently bribed, 'distracted' with a juicier story. He headed internal investigations. People knew better than to cross Corrigan, a capricious friend but a monomaniac as an enemy.

The assistant commissioner, raised a hellfire Catholic, now staunch atheist, had as much forgiveness in him as the Old Testament Jehovah.

One of these days, thought Huss, Hanlon would really overstep the mark, but she knew that Hanlon probably wouldn't care.

'So what are your plans regarding Schneider?' asked Huss.

'I thought I'd go and have a look at the Rosemount, introduce myself to the management and have a look at where they're planning to put Schneider. Evaluate it from a security point of view. We've only got to keep him alive for a few days, after that it's not our problem. I can do that much for Corrigan. I do owe him several favours.'

Huss shook her head. 'Until the next time. Eleuthera won't go away.'

'So what?' Hanlon was unimpressed. 'They're tiny, they're insignificant.' She put her head on one side and looked at Huss. 'It's hard to underestimate how insignificant they are.'

'They're violent,' said Huss, protesting. 'They might decide, oh I don't know . . .' she cast around in her mind for an example, 'to bomb the Dragon School here in Oxford because it's fee-paying and kill a load of seven-year-olds because they're capitalist scum. Or some college because they're a bastion of the elite. Or chop *your* head off,' she pointed at Hanlon, 'because you're a violent tool of tyranny. I think they killed James Kettering on that stairway to frame Hinds and they'll probably kill again.'

'Fine,' Hanlon raised her hands placatingly, 'just so long as you're sure that they exist outside of Hinds's imagination. It's all well and good, they *might* do this, they *might* do that, let's wait until they actually do something. You realize Hinds might just be crazy like Adams says he is? She's not necessarily lying. I told you I met his uncle Cliff, and he was handsome and a charmer. He was also a nutter. It's coming back to me now. He used to debt-collect for the Andersons. Dave Anderson's dad. He bashed someone's head in with a claw hammer, they were late with their payments, that's what we nicked him for. His brief got it reduced to self-defence, eight years or something, I seem to remember he got.'

'You really think that?' Huss was incredulous.

'Why not? Neither of us knows Hinds, he's a not very successful writer with a heavy drug and alcohol problem and a criminal family background. The only "evidence" you appear to be working on is a scribbled note and a memory stick that's full of gibberish.'

Huss eyed Hanlon with irritation. 'Well, I've got a witness who says she knows what happened and tomorrow I'll call you and hopefully I will be able to give you some evidence.'

Hanlon stood. 'Well, good for you.' She zipped her jacket up. 'Happy times! In the meantime I'll go and check out that hotel. Make sure that Schneider's safe from the Phantom Menace.'

Huss watched Hanlon's lithe figure with her arrogant, confident strut walk away through the café to the street outside.

Bitch, she thought. Well, come ten o'clock I'll have Marcus's hard drive and then we'll see.

CHAPTER TWENTY-ONE

'Hello, Rowenna,' said Mark Spencer. Rowenna turned around in the small kitchen of the church hall as he quietly closed the door behind him.

Rowenna looked at Mark uneasily. She had been attracted to the anarchists because of a libertarian streak in her and a visceral hatred of politicians. She had started the soup kitchen by herself because she had wanted to do something for the rough sleepers of Oxford whom she saw as being shamefully betrayed by the local authorities. But her romantic view of the anarchists was challenged by people like Mark Spencer, who she thought was a dangerous thug, and also Georgie Adams, who she thought was uncommitted to their ideology. In fact, she had a feeling that Adams was using them for her own ends.

'Hello, Mark,' she replied.

'Busy?' He went over and peered into the enormous stockpot the size of a dustbin on the stove. It had a metal handle on each side, riveted on. He went to hold one of the handles.

'Be careful,' warned Rowenna, 'the handles get very hot.'

He gingerly touched one and winced.

'I see what you mean,' he said. He turned and looked at her. 'You know old Elsa, don't you?'

She nodded.

'You know that she sometimes sleeps in Pretoria Road, near Marcus Hinds's gaff?'

'I didn't know that, no.'

He took a step towards her. There was something menacing about the gesture and she instinctively backed away so that she was trapped between him and the stove. His shaved head gleamed under the kitchen lights, contrasting with his stubbled chin. He looked very intimidating. Disturbing memories of rumours she'd heard of his behaviour troubled her mind. She had put these down to right-wing propaganda, wanting to discredit their cause. Suddenly she wasn't so sure.

'Has she been saying anything about Marcus?' he asked.

'No . . .' She shook her head and then gasped as he grabbed her forearm. She struggled but he was much stronger than she was and he pushed her wrist against the very hot metal handle of the stockpot.

She gasped at the pain. Her legs turned to jelly and she felt a sickening knot in the base of her stomach. He pushed his face close to hers and his eyes were hard.

'I don't believe you,' he said.

'OK, I'll tell you.' It was excruciating. He let go of her arm and she could see the ugly red weal on the pale, delicate skin where she had been burned.

'He gave her something, something computer related, maybe a hard drive or a memory stick, I really don't know.'

He nodded, digesting the information.

'And where can I find Elsa? She's not in any of her usual places.'

'I honestly don't know.'

This time he grabbed her by the hair and forced her face over the pan. They both looked at the lentils bubbling away, a couple of large onions and some carrots bobbing around in the boiling liquid.

Spencer pulled his jacket sleeve over his fingers and gave the stockpot a sharp tug. The soup sloshed around alarmingly, nearly spilling over the sides.

'It'd be terrible if this pan fell off the stove and over you,' said Spencer. 'You'd be so badly burned, now, please help me?'

Rowenna thought of the effect of pouring boiling water over tomatoes, the way their skin blistered and slid off. She imagined it happening to her.

'Please...' she begged. He kicked her ankles away from beneath her and she thudded down on to the tiled floor of the kitchen. He pulled the enormous pan so a third of it hung over the edge of the stove directly above her. Its dented, blackened bottom loomed huge and menacing.

She stared up at it in horrified fascination.

'Old Harry knows where she lives,' Rowenna said, hurriedly, hating herself for what she was doing.

'And what's his address?' asked Mark Spencer.

Five minutes later he left the kitchen, nodding to himself with self-satisfaction.

Inside, Rowenna carefully turned the heat off under the soup.

'I'm sorry, Harry,' she whispered.

CHAPTER TWENTY-TWO

'So, DCI Hanlon, what was the Rosemount like?' He paused and smiled his thanks as the attentive waiter poured Schneider a generous glass of white wine from the bottle.

'Luxurious.' She looked around the Michelin-starred restaurant they were sitting in. 'You'll like it.'

Vacherin, the restaurant, with its predominately French menu, would have sat quite comfortably in the Rosemount as far as food went, but not décor. You have to work awfully hard to be young and relevant but classic is classic. The modish room they were sitting in now, essentially minimalist in its styling, just off Bond Street, would have clashed horribly with the Rosemount's pseudo-Gothic style. It was modern, with composite moulded plastic tables, expensively done, the kind of faux-marble effect that one might get in an expensive fitted kitchen. There was quite a lot of Miró-style art on the walls, interspersed with pieces of interesting abstract sculpture. Everything was beautifully, expensively lit.

The lights didn't just light, they enhanced. Even Hanlon was impressed.

'You live very well, for a man of the people,' she said.

Schneider looked at her, amused. 'I came from a really shit

background, Hanlon, a classic slum. I can keep it real, but I'm never going back.' He shook his head. '*Niemals*. I'd rather die.'

She believed him.

She looked at the menu and her eyebrows rose fractionally. No wonder they could afford the lights.

That which was artfully illuminated included Schneider, who tonight looked like a Hollywood actor playing a minor Germanic god, relaxed, powerful, strongly handsome. Hanlon noticed that Hübler, sitting next to him on the banquette that ran the length of the wall, was almost pressing her body against him and she also noticed that Schneider was looking slightly embarrassed by this. She wondered if maybe they'd had some kind of one-night stand at some time and he had found himself embarrassingly stuck with her. She plainly adored him, and he was now regretting it.

Hanlon mentally filed this information and thought back to her visit to the Rosemount earlier that day.

Like Claridge's, the Rosemount Hotel was classical luxury rather than the contemporary chic that Vacherin embodied. It had been built as a home for a Victorian industrialist, a large imposing baroque pile, swirly stone decorations everywhere, a huge clock tower, a massive Italianate fountain with nymphs, dolphins and gods frolicking around, manicured grounds, gates like those of a London park. It was a stone-built hymn to money. There was a red carpet, secured with brass runners, going down the steps and, once inside, the luxury baronial theme continued. A minstrels' gallery, suits of armour, enormous gloomy paintings. Everything was on a massive scale. Walls were wood-panelled, ceilings incredibly high and rococo-plastered. There was a dining room that hadn't just been copied from a Loire chateau, it had been ripped from a Loire chateau and transported, piece by piece, back to Oxfordshire and reassembled.

It was two fingers up to the boutique hotel, with its transitory fads and its egalitarian atmosphere. This was a place where everybody knew their place and the main concessions to modernity lay in plumbing, bathrooms and Wi-Fi.

There was a helipad for guests and prices were to match. Strangely, thought Hanlon, from what Huss had told her, Georgie Adams would have been very much at home here. She was the interloper at the Rosemount, not the upper-class anarchist.

The hotel was built on an escarpment, giving its dining room a majestic view of the flat, dull Oxfordshire countryside. The duty manager, Irek Czerwinski, pointed to a building visible from the terrace at the rear of the hotel.

'That down there is the Presidential aka the Garden Lodge. It's where Herr Schneider and his party will be staying, come and see.'

He looked at the woman by his side as they walked down the balustrade stone steps and along the path to the lodge. The wind blew her dark corkscrew curls and he noticed the way her cold, grey eyes evaluated her surroundings. He had met her before, at a different hotel, and he doubted she would remember him, but she had caused a great deal of trouble then and indirectly nearly got him fired. Like all good hotel managers, he had an almost psychic ability to read people's characters.

Hanlon was trouble.

He had no doubt whatsoever of her ability to create trouble again at the slightest provocation. He knew he would be heartily glad to see the back of her. He carried on with his tour.

'The lodge was built to accommodate the prince regent and his party in 1889 when they stayed here over Christmas for the shooting.' Czerwinski had automatically fallen into his hotel spiel. 'Discretion was the order of the day, and so a hawthorn hedge was planted around the lodge to screen the prince's shenanigans. Nothing ever changes, there's only the one entrance.'

Hanlon evaluated the three-metre-high hedge, beautifully trimmed but with vicious thorns, that surrounded the property. It was impenetrable.

All the better to protect the prince from prying eyes as he got on with his womanizing. A function it was still serving well over a century later. She looked back at the hotel above, dominating the landscape, its grey stone staircases and manicured lawns.

'We won't go in.' There were barred gates the height of the hedge controlled by a keypad.

'So what is it now?' asked Hanlon.

'A four-bedroomed self-contained cottage, gym and spa room in the basement. Staff will come down from the hotel as arranged.' The manager indicted the hedge. 'Nobody could get through that hawthorn, or cut through it, and your friend Mr Schneider can let his dog run free, it won't be able to get out and bite anyone.'

He looked at the hedge. 'Have you seen his dog?'

'No,' said Hanlon.

'It's fucking horrible,' Czerwinski shuddered, 'and I like dogs!'

They had finished walking around the hedge. It was close to the perimeter of the grounds and a wood ran up to where the hawthorn started to grow. Czerwinski pointed at it.

'There are jogging trails in the woods that guests can use, and an outdoor gym. There is also one thing that I should show you. It's not something I would usually mention, but you are responsible for Mr Schneider's security, so, come and look at this.'

He led her to where the trees met the hedge and walked with her into the wood. He pointed to a section of the hedge. 'Look down there.'

Hanlon did so. There were concrete steps leading down to a rusty steel door. Brambles overgrew it. If it hadn't been pointed out to her she'd never have seen it. She looked at Czerwinski questioningly.

'During the war, the main house,' he pointed back up at the hotel, 'was used by military intelligence; it was linked up with Bletchley. The officers had the cellars of the house as bomb shelters but the plebs, the junior staff and the ATCs, et cetera, who were billeted in the grounds had this.' He pointed at the steps. 'It's a kind of Anderson shelter, cut-and-cover; the other end comes out in the lodge grounds, behind a shed.'

Hanlon walked down the steps to the heavy steel door and tested it. The hinges were rusted but you could open it. She looked up at the manager.

'What about the other end?'

'It's like this, but there's a window, well, a kind of hole really. The whole thing runs under the hedge. I think they built it like that in case the gate got blocked – it would serve not just as a bomb shelter but also an emergency exit. You can understand they'd be worried about incendiaries turning the inside into a sea of fire and everyone trapped.'

Hanlon looked at it closely. 'Well, I can't see it being a problem. Schneider's got that dog of whatever sort it is.'

Czerwinski led her back towards the hotel, noting absent-mindedly her athletic fluidity as she walked along, her eyes perpetually busy.

Hanlon asked him, 'Is the lodge popular? I mean, do you book it a lot?'

They had reached the grassy terrace now and they were looking down on the roof of the lodge. He nodded.

'Pretty much fully booked. People are happy to pay a high premium for security. Sometimes I guess it's justified, we have Hollywood stars who've had problems with stalkers or the paparazzi, or Russian businessmen anxious to avoid "business" rivals, and then you get legitimate business people who I think would probably be perfectly safe anywhere but they like to feel that they're so important they need this level of security, an ego thing. They sometimes hire bulletproof limos – they like that touch. Nobody gets gunned down in Oxfordshire, for heaven's sake. It's not Moscow or Mexico.'

He paused and looked at her inscrutable face as she surveyed the bleak Oxfordshire countryside. A red kite wheeled high overhead.

Hanlon watched it, her eyes as grey as the skies above,

as the great bird wheeled effortlessly overhead, borne on its giant wings.

'So Herr Schneider will have his dog,' she said again.

He nodded. 'And an alarm that goes directly through to Kidlington police station. There'd be an armed response team here in minutes, or so they say.' He shrugged, theatrically sceptical. 'And I've got two of the Specialist Protection boys in the hotel, they must think Christmas has come early. They're armed. And there's our security, they're ex-marines so, to be honest, I'd back them over your lot in a fight. I can't imagine there'll be any problems at all.'

Hanlon nodded dubiously. 'We'll see,' she said.

A magpie flew down on to the grass in search of food.

One for sorrow, thought Hanlon.

Back in the dining room at Vacherin, she looked at Schneider and Hübler. They looked like a successful married couple, like the world, the future, belonged to them. She wondered where the minder, Muller, was. Eating raw meat somewhere with the mastiff. A meeting of minds.

Christiane Hübler's eyes rested on Schneider with proprietorial love. Once again Hanlon wondered at their relationship. Someone is always in charge but such was the mixed messages that the two of them were sending out, it was difficult to say who had the whip-hand, or was Schneider one of those powerful men who like to be dominated?

'You'll like it,' said Hanlon. 'So will the dog. It's very you.'

CHAPTER TWENTY-THREE

Huss returned to the station at Summertown feeling slightly irritated. She rubbed the small of her back. She'd pulled a muscle there helping her father on the farm and it was really starting to bother her. The first sign of ageing, she thought gloomily. She ran through her emails, checking allocations of the team that worked for her, following up on the arrangements for the Oxford Union debate.

No we do _not_ require street closures, she angrily wrote to Oxford Council, underlining as she went. This was emphatically not CID work and she felt a surge of resentment towards Templeman for having landed her with it. The problem was, nobody was really all that sure as to what to do with Schneider. They were trying to forestall a crime rather than clear one up.

Yet again, she went over the Hinds's conundrum in her mind. Had he murdered a man, as seemed the case, or was it something connected to the anarchist group Eleuthera and/ or Al-Akhdaar, as Hinds's scribbled note to her suggested? Was Georgie Adams connected with Eleuthera or was she just an innocent political protestor? Eleuthera were not a banned organization in the UK, so did it matter anyway?

Presumably Hinds's hard drive would contain proof of a criminal Eleuthera connection to a plot to kill Schneider.

There was a slight cough and she looked up.

'Hi, I was thinking about that memory stick. Could I have another look at it?' Evan was wearing a tie-dye Grateful Dead T-shirt today and an apologetic expression.

'Sure, Evan,' said Huss, cheering up at the sight of him. 'Do you think you might be in with a chance?'

It was typical of life, she thought, that now she would very soon have access to gigabytes of Marcus's data, in the form of his hard drive, it seemed likely that Evan might be able to restore the content of the memory stick to a readable format.

'Yeah, well, I was kind of rushed off my feet yesterday and there are a couple of things I could try. No promises, mind you.' He looked suitably apologetic.

'No pressure, someone's giving me Hinds's external hard drive tonight anyway, but if you wouldn't mind having another go.'

'That'd be fine, Melinda, just bring it down to me whenever.' He stood there fiddling with the evil eye bracelet that he wore on his wrist. The stylized white eye on the blue glass bead stared at her glassily.

'I've been feeling kind of guilty about giving you the brush-off on that, sorry.'

She smiled and watched him as he wandered off. She had a bit of a soft spot for Evan, as did one or two other women at the station. He was quite good-looking in a slightly effeminate way.

*

It was about nine o'clock that Huss got the news. She was in the canteen when DI Ed Worth, one of her favourite colleagues, came up to her looking worried.

'Thank God, you're still here, Melinda. There's been an almighty fuck-up. I can't find the duty officer and there's been a serious incident called in, I've got two cars responding. Fire and ambulance are on the scene but could you get down there and hold the fort until Harry deigns to put in an appearance?' Worth was temperamentally a bit of an old woman, thought Huss. Right now he looked so nervous he might throw up.

'Templeman will do his nut,' he added, miserably.

'Sure,' said Huss, on her feet and moving to go and get her coat. 'I'm on my way.'

Worth visibly brightened up now Huss had taken charge. Not only was he secretly in love with her, a condition he'd managed to conceal for about three years, he had a great deal of respect for her judgement. He was not a man born for leadership and, to his credit, he knew it.

They strode through the practically deserted station, just the skeleton evening shift on duty.

'What's it all about?' she asked as they pounded along the blue carpet that ran throughout the place.

'There's a body on fire,' said Worth. 'A jogger called it in. Thought at first it was something to do with Hallowe'en. Up by the university parks near Jericho, off Wilson Road.'

A horrible sense of dread started to rise within Huss.

'Wilson Road?'

They had reached the big glass door to the car park. Ed Worth hit the button and the door swung slowly open. They walked towards Huss's Polo. It was a cold night and their breath steamed in the air under the brilliant floodlights of the car park. The razor wire on top of the walls glinted menacingly.

'One of the uniforms said it was that old tramp woman you see around there quite often. Really nasty, someone seems to have doused her with petrol and—'

Huss yanked open her car door, her face furious. 'Tell them I'm on my way.'

Worth watched her drive away. In the five years he had known her, he had never seen her look so upset.

He wondered what was going on.

CHAPTER TWENTY-FOUR

Hanlon found Huss easily enough. It certainly wasn't hard. There were three police cars with lights flashing, a parked up fire engine and half a dozen uniforms sealing a perimeter off with tape. There was still a smell of burning, of charred meat, in the air.

Traffic lights had been installed so the lane that ran past the bus stop was sealed off, and within the traffic cones Huss was talking to a man in a suit. Huss shook hands with the detective and walked over to where she could see Hanlon waiting.

Huss said to her, 'That's Brian McKenzie, he's the SIO on this. What a mess.'

Hanlon looked at the activity – she could see the inner and outer search perimeters indicated with fluttering tape, the entrance and exit walkways to the crime scene. At first light there'd be God knows how many police on their hands and knees crawling around, doing a fingertip search.

'What happened?'

'You see that bus shelter there.' Huss pointed to the clear Perspex structure, now also cordoned off. 'Elsa Worthington lived just behind it, there's a couple of trees and a clearing on the ground. The woman who found her told me she'd been there at least five years. She hated hostels, said they were smelly and full of nutcases.'

'They must be grim if people prefer sleeping out here.' Hanlon shivered. It was a cold, starry night. She'd driven straight here as soon as Huss had texted her. North London is not far from Oxford.

'We're quite tough on the homeless here in Oxford,' Huss explained. 'You can be done under the 1824 Vagrancy Act. We'll bus you off to Coventry to get rid of you so you don't upset the tourists. Nobody goes to Coventry. Well, not unless they have to. That's why she had this, her "country retreat", I'm guessing, hiding away from the council.'

Her attractive face was hard as she contemplated Elsa's sad life. Commuting from her bus shelter to the centre of town, to the colleges where she used to lecture.

'At nine thirty, Marian Keys, that's the jogger, ran along the road – she jogs here most evenings, there's not much traffic and the pavement's wide – saw flames and went to investigate.'

'So that's when she was found.'

'She'd had petrol tipped over her and was set alight. Burnt alive.' Huss's voice was grim. She was thinking of the gentle eyes of the former don. What a way to have your life taken from you.

'Why?' asked Hanlon.

Huss said, 'When they examine her and cut what's left of her clothes off, there'll be what's left of an external hard drive in there. Under the rags.' She looked at Hanlon. 'That's why. Killed for something she didn't know the reason for.

Let's go back to the station, I need to do the paperwork on what I've been up to tonight for McKenzie so he can make a start on his incident log.'

'I'll follow you back. Is that your Golf I'm parked behind?'

'Yeah, that's mine.'

The two women walked back to their respective cars.

'So, you think Eleuthera did this?' asked Hanlon as they passed the shelter.

'Yes,' said Huss, testily. 'Who else? Clean Up Oxford?'

Hanlon shrugged. 'Could be an attack on the homeless.'

'Yeah, right.' Huss's voice was scathing. 'In Oxford the students sometimes piss on them, or give them a good kicking, but not this.'

They had reached their cars.

'So how did Eleuthera know you were due to meet Elsa tonight?'

'That,' said Huss grimly, 'is what I'm going to find out.'

CHAPTER TWENTY-FIVE

Hanlon decided not to accompany Huss back to the station. She had her own plan of action.

Georgie Adams, she thought, as she drove through the quiet Oxford streets. You came to my meeting, time to return the favour.

CLASS STRUGGLE
Do we still need the WORKING CLASS?
Are the true Proletariat the UNWAGED & STUDENTS?
Summertown Church Hall Sat 7-10.00
Bring bottle, open mind and revolutionary fervour!

The venue wasn't far from St Wulfstan's where she'd been with Huss the other day.

She parked her Audi a couple of streets away where its sleek lines wouldn't attract unwanted, revolutionary attention. That being said, the anti-capitalists seemed strangely drawn to consumerist goods. The ones at the protests she'd seen were walking billboards for major tax-evading companies. The anarchists didn't do irony.

She reached down into the passenger well and took out the two two-litre bottles of cider that she had brought with her, the price of her admission. Merrydown cider. Drink of revolutionaries.

There were a couple of anarchists on the door: one white with dreadlocks, the other a traveller type, burly in second-hand military cast-offs and steel-toed workboots.

Hanlon strode up to them with her customary arrogance as they politely blocked her entrance.

'Lambeth Feminist Collective,' said Hanlon, curtly.

They nodded and opened the door.

It gave way onto a small entrance hall. There was a kitchen on the left, toilets on the right and in front were the double doors leading to the hall. I should have got here earlier and picketed them, thought Hanlon, gobbed at them as they walked past and shouted rape threats. See how they like it.

There was a goth girl with a nose piercing and multiple ear-studs bustling around the kitchen, laying out food, opening wine. Hanlon handed her the cider. She recognized the girl from the demonstration as the one who had spat at Hübler and called her a 'German bitch'. She looked blankly at Hanlon – she was quite stoned and there was no glint of recognition.

'You shouldn't be reinforcing gender stereotypes,' said Hanlon nastily, handing her the bottles, then turned on her heel and went inside.

There was a good turnout for the meeting, the hall was full, all the seats taken. On stage the speaker was just coming to an end.

He was a good-looking man in his thirties with a leather

jacket. The number of vegans on the revolutionary left and right must be infinitesimal, she thought. In many ways, the speaker was not too dissimilar to Schneider in his appearance. And they both favoured leather. But a cut-price Schneider. The real deal would have had them on their feet, ready to burn the colleges, bastions of privilege and knowledge, to the ground. Here there was quiet approbation, nothing more.

The audience applauded and Georgie Adams, who had been sitting onstage with another couple of organisers, walked forward. The hall was in darkness, there were just a couple of spotlights on her.

Their first meeting had been fraught and brief. She hadn't had a chance to look at the girl properly. Under the spotlights, now she did. Hanlon thought, she's breathtakingly beautiful. You couldn't blame Marcus Hinds for flirting with the devil when the devil took such a form. Her very dark hair with the green highlights haloed her fine features, her slim body in figure-hugging jeans and a simple white tailored blouse had surprisingly generous curves. The blouse was unbuttoned slightly to show the swell of her breasts and the mysterious geometric tattoos that she favoured. Most of the men in the audience would be salivating.

Had it been her who had doused Elsa in petrol? No, she thought, she was the type who would have ordered someone else to do it and watched. Watched appreciatively. There was a hint of cruelty to Georgie's beautiful face that Hanlon could imagine would drive men wild.

'Thank you to Paul Mattocks from Camden Active for that thought-provoking talk. In a moment we'll have refreshments.' It was the kind of cut-glass middle class Scottish accent that might introduce a fete in genteel Morningside: 'And now, in the pavilion, the major will be judging the vegetable produce…'

'While that's happening we'll be collecting for the Calais migrant camp for Smash the Borders. So, I'd like to ask again for another big hand for Paul and an even larger one for yourselves, thank YOU for coming!'

The audience applauded, whistled and stamped. Georgie certainly knew how to work a crowd, thought Hanlon.

She thought of the burned remains of the old bag-lady.

She thought of the hate-filled faces of Georgie's fellow anarchists.

'FASCIST WHORE!'

Hanlon moved to stand close to the door. Any moment now. A moment of dispassion, seeing herself from outside, tough, grim, flexing her fingers.

You shouldn't be doing this!

The same pleasurable feeling of anticipation filling her body as when she had climbed into the ring with Phil Campbell earlier that week. The adrenaline building. Heartbeat rising. Pupils dilating.

ARE YOU READY TO RUMBLE!!!

Someone switched the lights on and the audience started talking, stretching, coughing, all the pent-up noise of a group of people forced to sit silently and now released. Chairs squeaked on the polished parquet floor of the hall as people stood up.

Georgie raised her eyes from the lectern where she had been standing and caught sight of Hanlon. She did an almost theatrical double-take.

That's shattered your poise, thought Hanlon.

Hanlon was leaning by the door, her arms folded in an aggressively challenging posture. For a moment Georgie had struggled to place her. The last time she had been wearing a short skirt, jacket, blouse and boots. Now it was a bomber jacket, combat trousers and high-sided DMs, but there was no doubting the tough, good-looking face, the hard eyes. Her hand involuntarily went to her stomach where Hanlon had hit her.

It was like a slap in the face, a gauntlet thrown down, a challenge.

Georgie turned to one of the men on the stage, a man with a shaved head and more tattoos that she guessed had been at the demo, and pointed at Hanlon and said something. His face turned to one of ugly rage and he hurriedly made his way towards her.

Hanlon slipped out through the door, through the lobby and the small crowd, the anarchists keen to get to their sausage rolls and cider, and into the night.

The two men who had been on the door were no longer there, probably inside getting a drink, she thought.

There was a small car park in front of the hall and Hanlon hung around momentarily until she saw the doors burst open and shaved head accompanied by the traveller appear.

She walked swiftly and purposefully away from them. She had no need to look back, she knew that they would follow. She continued into New Inn Hall Street. St Wulfstan's, like all the major colleges, was located in the centre of Oxford. The buildings were brilliantly lit and she moved with her customary grace through the heart of the town.

The two men were in pursuit but they didn't want to start anything, not here, not in the centre of town.

Although it was a Saturday night, this part of Oxford was practically deserted and it felt like walking through an empty film or stage set. Most of the students would be drinking in the college bars and the historic centre was not overburdened with pubs and nightclubs. The graceful stone buildings rose up around her, a tableau of living history.

As she walked along St Giles, the very broad road that ran past St John's College, she put her hands in her pockets and slipped on a pair of gloves, thick, black leather, to ensure her knuckles wouldn't break.

The clock in St John's College was striking ten; the two men following Hanlon lengthened their stride.

Action time. Shaved head was keen to vent his wrath on the tool of capitalist oppression. Or maybe he was just keen to beat up the woman who had hit his girlfriend. Hanlon had caught the look that he had given her on the stage.

As she walked her mind raced. She doubted they would attack her in a brightly lit street like the one she was on, so she turned down one of the small side streets off St Giles. She knew this area well. It was near where the brothel had been, that Arkady Belanov had owned and run.

It was October. The men were wearing bulky coats that would protect their stomachs from a punch, or at least muffle the blow, but their faces would be exposed. Hanlon intended hitting them very hard.

The thought made her feel strong, made her feel confident. She'd fought Arkady Belanov and won.

She smiled a cold, sinister smile. She wasn't going to lose

to these idiots. Anarchist pricks. I'm not a helpless old lady you can set on fire. I'm not someone you can gob at who'll just stand there and smile and wipe it off.

She felt anger well up in her heart. I don't do defeat, she thought, grimly. Her strong fingers tightened and she tossed her hair provocatively as she walked, the men a few steps behind.

In her mind she remembered Freddie Laidlaw's comment to her:

'You're the best I've got, Hanlon, the fastest and the brightest and you're hard to hit.'

The streetlights here were dim and the houses in darkness.

She tensed, ready for action.

I love you, Freddie, I won't let you down.

She heard the footsteps quicken behind her and sensed rather than saw the blow about to fall. The iron bar that shaved head had been carrying arced through the air. He had no intention of messing around. This woman was destined for intensive care or the morgue. The centre of Hanlon's unruly corkscrew hair its target. As the bar came down, Hanlon exploded into movement.

She sprang backwards into the body of her attacker. The bald man. In boxing, most of the power in a punch comes from springing forward off the back foot, here she used the same principle in reverse. She also knew that by getting so close to him, any strike with his arms would go over her head and body. And that is exactly what happened.

The steel bar, about a foot in length, overshot her head but the man's arm crashed down on her shoulder. As it did so, still moving back into him with the momentum of her body, she drove her elbow back hard into his stomach. Even his heavy coat couldn't cushion the blow as the tip of the bone slammed into his solar plexus with explosive power.

It drove the breath out of him.

He gasped and swore and she spun round and slammed her fist into the side of his head in a vicious left hook, twisting her body into the punch, driving it home with all the terrific power in her hips and thighs. Then, as his head snapped to the side, she brought her other fist forward in a powerful right cross into the front of his face.

There was a snapping sound as her leather glove smashed home. His head flew back and he gave a moan and toppled over. As he went down she snatched the iron bar from his hand and swung it at the shorter one, the traveller.

The sheer speed of Hanlon's attack had left him frozen to the spot. That hadn't been in the script.

Not at all.

He put an arm up to defend himself and cried out as the metal thwacked into the bone on his forearm above his wrist. His head would have made a perfect target but Hanlon had other plans.

The bald man that she had knocked to the ground was starting to haul himself upright. She glimpsed tattoos on the side of his neck. Hanlon kicked him as hard as she could between the legs and he gave a choking gasp and curled up into a foetal position, fighting the incredible agony that was engulfing his body from his badly hurt testicles. There was no fight left in him now. Hanlon's two punches had left him barely conscious and now there was this sea of gut-sickening pain. Even if he'd been capable of movement he had no intention of getting anywhere near her.

The shorter man was clutching his injured arm. Hanlon shot her hand out and grabbed a clump of the matted hair on his head, yanking him forward viciously. He had thick curls, almost dreads, ideal to hold fast. He cried out but didn't struggle. She knew he was hers for the taking. It was like when a dog shows submission to another dog by rolling over. His hands hung down by his sides. Whoever this man was, she could feel by the lack of resistance that he wasn't going to put up any more of a fight.

Still holding his hair so his head was forced to look down at the pavement, she reached inside his jacket, thick quilted army style, with her free hand. Then her fingers found what they were looking for in his inside pocket.

She drew the man's head close to her mouth. 'Tell your anarchist friends that the fascist whore wants to leave a message, you got that?'

He muttered something and she tightened her fingers in his hair and twisted.

'I'm sorry, I didn't hear you,' she hissed, her voice taut with anger.

'Yes,' he moaned with pain. Any more strain on his hair, she thought, and it'd probably come out in a bloody clump.

'Here's the message,' she said.

Hanlon slammed her left fist into the side of his head, just above the ear, and he fell down to his knees. The pain from his eardrum made him retch into the gutter and he nearly blacked out.

Still carrying the iron bar like a relay runner, she broke

into a jog and the two would-be assailants, one on all fours, the other still with knees drawn up to chest on the pavement, watched her back disappear down the street.

Hanlon was back inside her car five minutes later. She smiled to herself. For the first time in a long while she felt truly happy. She even hummed the opening of the 'Internationale' as she glanced at the Samsung she'd taken from its owner. She pressed it and the keypad appeared for the code. She smiled again and took her own phone out, scrolled down, found the name she was looking for.

'It's me. I'll be round at your gaff in about forty minutes. Don't go to bed. I need you to open a phone.'

She smiled at the squawking protest, spoke again.

'Stop moaning, you old fruit. Dear God, Albert, you've got three-quarters of an hour, even a man of your age ought to be able to finish having a fuck in that time.' She started the engine, still talking to the enraged Albert. 'Well, tell him to get a move on. If he is a porn star he should be used to coming on command! It's a Samsung, by the way. That's right, the new model, just like the man in your life.'

She swung the Audi TT around and pointed it in the direction of London. She looked triumphantly at the phone beside her. A major link in the chain that would take her to Schneider's would-be assassins. For the first time in a week she felt she was making progress.

It was a huge step forward.

She wondered if Huss had found out who had tipped Eleuthera off about old Elsa.

You can run, she thought, but you can't hide.

CHAPTER TWENTY-SIX

Back at the station, Huss wrote up her actions that she had performed at the crime scene of Elsa's death prior to McKenzie's arrival. While the phrases flowed into her report

> *As Acting Crime Scene Manager I created a common approach path... (see appended)... Inner and outer cordons were established... DI McKenzie to supply further details of personnel and actions undertaken together with Forensic Team...*

memories of Elsa's fate riffled through her mind. The loud, thrumming noise of the generator brought in to power the lights, the charred bulk of her body. The blackness and fragmentary state of her clothing had made her remains look like a gigantic dead crow. The child's rhyme 'four and twenty blackbirds baked in a pie' had run through her head. The terrible smell of burning lingering in her nostrils.

Overlaid on these memories, how had Eleuthera found out about her proposed visit to Elsa?

Other memories resurfaced.

Bending over her in the street outside Hinds's flat, the

sight of Georgie Adams at the window. Her beautiful face, pale through the glass above.

Who else had known about the visit?

Hanlon.

Hanlon had known she was going to visit Elsa, but Huss, although she didn't like her, would trust her with her life. And Hanlon was famously close-mouthed.

Darker thoughts.

Evan Collins. He had known. Evan Collins, their over-qualified stoner slacker. The one that people said, 'What is he doing here?'

The one that people said, 'Oh, he's so cute.'

Well, Evan Collins wasn't the only computer expert in the building. He also wasn't the only man who fancied her either.

Ed Worth was in the other office. He looked up when Huss entered and smiled. He found Melinda Huss incredibly attractive. Tonight she was wearing thick tights, an above-the-knee skirt and a low-cut sweater. Her stocky, buxom form managed somehow to combine chunky sexiness with assertive practicality.

I bet she goes like a train, he thought.

Huss came straight to the point. 'Can I get access to Evan Collins's personnel records?'

'No,' said Worth. He didn't ask why she wanted to know, quite frankly he couldn't care less. His mind whirred, seeking for a way to ingratiate himself with Huss. 'But I can get his CV for you and that includes his social media data. That lies in a part of personnel that I happen to have the passcode for, rather than the main data.' He reflected that, although they had changed the system now, it used to be that job applicants' details were held in a kind of pending file and they never really got moved.

'That's brilliant, Ed.' She smiled at him. I love your chin, he thought, dreamily, his long, strong fingers resting on the keyboard in front of him, feeling the raised indentation on the F key in front of him. Her fingernails were painted blood red.

He shook his head free of his Huss-inspired fantasies and applied himself to the keyboard.

'Shall I send them to you?' he asked.

Huss shook her head.

'I'd rather have a hard copy – I don't want anything showing up on the system.'

Worth nodded. He could see the outline of her bra under the wool of her sweater. If only … he thought … If only. He applied himself to the keyboard in front of him and a minute or so later the printer in the corner whirred into action.

Huss went over and retrieved the half-dozen pieces of paper, said her goodbyes to Worth and went back to her desk.

Worth closed his eyes. If he concentrated he could just make out a faint memory of her scent lingering on the air of the office. I love you, Melinda Huss, he thought.

A while later she had her answer.

A selection of social media images and posts that someone had idly downloaded when his application to join Thames Valley had been made. Pictures that had then seemed innocuous but now had a very different connotation.

A photo of Collins with James Kettering, the dead man on the stairs.

Another image: Evan Collins and Georgie Adams toasting the camera with cans of cider in Whitehall, Lutyen's Cenotaph visible in the background.

Say NO to War, Fight Fascism, said their placards.

Evan Collins, another placard, this one ironic given his current job. A cartoon pig, red in the face, huffing in outrage as a superimposed cut-out photo of Karl Marx in a crude collage-style stood in close proximity to its backside: *FUCK THE PIGS!*

Collins was a member of Eleuthera.

CHAPTER TWENTY-SEVEN

Enver Demirel, dressed casually in chinos and a pea jacket, parked his old Volvo in the car park of the Rosemount Hotel. The estate car was sandwiched between a top-of-the-range Mercedes – Enver was hazy on car makes – and a Maserati.

So far, his involvement in protecting Schneider had been minimal. He had attended a couple of diplomatic protection briefings on protocol and on the law, been given a sheaf of literature to read and signed up for a firearms course at the police training school outside Reading that would take place long after the German politician had left the country. Then an order to visit Gower at New Scotland Yard in the replacement headquarters at Curtis Green House on the Embankment.

Gower's desk was untidy, piled high with briefing documents and buff envelopes. He didn't warrant a river view, it seemed.

'There's been a significant development in the Schneider affair,' he told Enver. He filled him in on the death of Elsa, which was being regarded as possibly linked to Eleuthera. Enver had heard about this from Huss but feigned ignorance.

'As you can imagine, DI Demirel, this has considerably ramped up the danger level that Eleuthera posed. This is obviously not the work of Islamic extremists. The death of that anarchist on those stairs in Oxford that we attributed to Hinds in a random act of violence has to be reconsidered too. Some of us, myself included, tended to regard them, the anarchist movement, as a bit, how shall I put it, insignificant. Well, that's changed.'

He paused, shuffled some papers.

'DI Huss, from Thames Valley, who I gather you know, has discovered that Marcus Hinds's girlfriend, a Georgie Adams, has possible links with Eleuthera, and there is also credible evidence that some form of attack on Schneider may be launched while he's staying at the Rosemount Hotel.'

'Yes, sir,' said Enver.

'The manager of the hotel, some Polish guy,' he checked his notes, 'Czerwinski, has been very helpful and given me the staff employment records. In my experience, Enver, in an attack on a big, rambling building like a hotel, there's usually someone on the inside. Hotels employ so many low-grade temporary staff – cleaners, gardeners, chambermaids, kitchen porters – and they usually have a high turnover, so in general it's easy to get someone in there.

'Anyway, I digress.' He tapped his notes, settled his glasses on his nose. 'A couple of things are blindingly obvious from looking at them.'

He leant back in his chair and straightened his tie. Gower's suit was very rumpled, like he'd slept in it.

'There are some seventy people working at that hotel,

probably a third are household, cleaners, chambermaids, et cetera. They're virtually all women and predominantly all European, with a couple of Thais and Chinese. They don't fit the Al-Akhdaar demographic and they don't fit that of Eleuthera. Anarchists tend to be university educated. They don't seem overly keen on soiling their hands with manual labour.' He paused, drank some water. 'Then we have the front of house and management, a more fertile ground, and I've got two officers stationed in the hotel, just in case. Now, there are twenty-seven staff in the kitchen,' he consulted his notes again, 'of these fourteen are Muslim, including four East Europeans, a Chechen, one from Dagestan and a Turkish chef de partie, whatever that may be, do you know?'

'Head of a section, sir. Like pastry or sauces,' explained Enver.

'Impressive knowledge, DI Demirel.' Gower paused, as if Enver had passed some sort of test. 'Now guess what I want you to do?'

Work in the kitchen, thought Enver. Damn, I walked into that one.

'I don't know, sir.' I'm certainly not going to suggest it, he thought.

Gower beamed at him. 'Assistant Commissioner Corrigan tells me that you have had kitchen experience in your time. Czerwinski has had a request for a temporary chef de partie slash junior sous chef from the kitchen for a while – you're that new chef. What better place to monitor the kitchen than the kitchen itself!'

'Thank you, sir,' said Enver through gritted teeth. His colleagues would get to check out Schneider's well-being from a luxury junior suite with bar facilities, use of the pool and gym, and he'd get to work eighteen-hour, ball-breaking days and nights with the pots and pans in the kitchen.

Well, now here he was. He stepped out of his car and looked around him. It seemed very peaceful. His feet scrunched on the thick gravel of the car park.

Perhaps, he thought, perhaps a Michelin-starred kitchen might be a quieter and less manic place to work than other kitchens he had been in.

Just then an out of breath teenager in dirty chef's whites and Crocs ran up to him. 'Hi, are you the agency guy?' he panted. To Enver's eyes he seemed about twelve. He was thin, gaunt, white, dark bruises under his eyes, he looked exhausted.

'Yes, I'm Enver.'

'Oh, I'm Pete, Peter Marshall.'

'Nice to meet you,' said Enver. They politely shook hands. Peter Marshall looked even more twitchy.

'Great, Chef says could you get your whites on and your arse in gear and get into the kitchen like ten minutes ago, it's all going tits up.'

Enver sighed and took his sports bag with his whites and canvas knife-roll from out of the boot.

Or perhaps not.

CHAPTER TWENTY-EIGHT

Hanlon lay on her stomach at the top of the escarpment, looking down on the scene in the valley below.

She was about a mile and a half away from the Rosemount Hotel, the other side of the woods that abutted on to the lodge where Schneider was due to stay. A main road ran nearby the entrance to the valley and there was a little single-track road that wound its way up the opposite hill to a hamlet. Near this was a farm track that threaded its way along the bottom of the valley and in this was the encampment that she had been watching for the past half-hour.

The slopes of the valley were fields, now brown and grey and stubbly. The tops of the valleys on both sides were covered in trees, dark and mournful in the cold, autumn breeze.

There were three caravans and their attendant vehicles in the small anarchist encampment. They were two old Land Rovers and an ancient Audi A6. There were also two vans, one a former ambulance, that had been converted into mobile homes. They were parked in a circle like a wagon train in a Western.

Hanlon's friend, Albert Slater, had hacked into the

Samsung, a task that had taken maybe three minutes, and blocked the phone's tracker app. Hanlon had then been free to browse the anarchist's life as revealed on his phone.

His name was Deke Pirie. From his phone she also learnt that he was a keen game player, he was very sexually active but that he had a partner, Lizzie, (the girl with the pierced nose that Hanlon had met in the kitchen at the anarchist meeting); he was a gun enthusiast and he had a dog, a Dobermann called Jet.

She also learnt from his messages that he'd sent a text to Georgie Adams on the day that Kettering had died in the stairwell.

Mark's on his way with JK.

Time and date. Well, it corroborated one part of Hinds's story. Adams had called in the heavies.

Like Hanlon, he was a keen cyclist, there were photos of his bike, and, like Hanlon, he had an app that recorded his routes, superimposed on an Ordnance Survey map, dates and times. It was this that had led her here. The app gave detailed maps of the area showing where he began and finished his cycle rides (together with their timings, effort levels and other dashboard information), virtually all centred around the valley below. Finding it had been child's play. Was this the sort of mistake in security that Georgie Adams would make? Hanlon doubted it.

And I wonder why you chose this area to settle in? thought Hanlon. Could it possibly be its prettiness or is it due to the proximity of the Rosemount Hotel?

The slope of the field down to the caravans was covered in a light brown stubble of some harvested cereal crop, probably barley, thought Hanlon. Behind her was a strip, a thin line really, of maize, and behind that there were several blue barrels between the maize and the wood that lay between the valley and the hotel grounds, about a mile and a half distant. The feed barrels were raised above ground level on a tripod arrangement.

Huss would have known immediately what this meant. The local landowner or farmer was raising pheasant for a shoot, that's what the feed was for, to keep the pheasants in the immediate vicinity, and the strip of maize was where they would shelter.

Hanlon knew none of this.

She was lying just in front of the green strip of maize when, through her binoculars, she saw Mark Spencer appear from one of the caravans together with Lizzie, Deke's girlfriend. He was obviously part of the anarchist encampment here.

He was wearing a black T-shirt with the arms cut off, showing off his powerful biceps, and the white anarchist logo, a ragged spray-gunned capital letter A in a circle, emblazoned on the front.

He lit a joint and a cloud of smoke briefly haloed his brutally shaved head. His left eye was practically swollen shut and Hanlon could see the vivid blue and purple bruise from where she had hit him the night before. Lizzie was wearing a ragged short skirt and jumper. She had excellent legs. He passed her the joint and then Jet, the Dobermann, joined them from inside the caravan.

Hanlon moved her foot behind her and by sheer ill-luck a pheasant, disturbed by the motion, flew directly upwards, making its distinctive and very loud call of alarm. The metallic clacking noise rose over the valley and the dog barked. Hanlon looked round in irritation and discovered another of the birds practically sitting on her right calf.

The couple below her looked up sharply. Spencer reached an arm into the caravan and through her binoculars Hanlon watched as his arm reappeared holding a .22 rifle. He raised it to his shoulder and she could see the movement of his fingers as he clicked off the safety and pulled the bolt back.

The end of the muzzle moved up and down then settled in her direction. There was a telescopic sight on the gun. Hanlon guessed that if she could see him, he could see her. Her head could well be filling that sight, her face in its cross-hairs.

She froze momentarily. Then started cursing herself. Once Deke had dusted himself down after their fight the night before and discovered his phone missing, he would have informed Spencer. Spencer was no fool. Of course he could have guessed that she'd be down here. That's why there was no one around but him and the girl – they were expecting some kind of raid. Spencer had obviously moved the other anarchists out. That's why the only signs of life that she had seen had been them. The decks had been cleared for action.

Also that explained why he had a rifle handy, just in case she was stupid enough to come on her own.

The only question there had to be in his mind was did she work for Schneider or the police or security forces? He had obviously recognized her from the demo in Islington. Her unorthodox approach must have meant that he'd plumped for the former. In Spencer's mind she was obviously some kind of hired right-wing thug, probably ex-army or mixed martial arts, certainly not connected to the Old Bill. So she could expect... She rolled over immediately.

There was a sharp crack as Spencer pulled the trigger, and a fine spray of dirt and rock fragments as the bullet struck a flint embedded in the soil where her head had been a second earlier.

Well, she thought, he's certainly not messing around.

She took a look down into the valley. Spencer reloaded the rifle and started up the hill towards her at a fast jog, Jet trotting at his side. Hanlon sprang to her feet and disappeared into the strip of maize bordering the field.

If she'd expected to be hidden she was in for a disappointment.

Almost immediately a whole flock of pheasants, maybe twenty or thirty, zoomed up into the air, squawking, their wings beating loudly. Hanlon groaned to herself. If she had tried to communicate where she was going she could hardly do a better job. Spencer could have been half-blind and partially deaf and still tracked her progress. She heard the dog bark joyfully at the exciting new game they were playing.

She took another step, more bloody birds! They whirred around her, making that weird metallic-sounding alarm that echoed around the valley.

She heard the rifle crack again. God knows where the bullet went. Hanlon decided to put her faith in her fitness.

She crashed through the maize, higher than her head, leaving a trail an idiot could have followed of trampled plants, and then she was in the woods, head down and running in what she hoped was the direction of the hotel.

CHAPTER TWENTY-NINE

Enver Demirel felt he had never left a kitchen after about five minutes, which was really just as well.

The Rosemount was frantically busy. There were only thirty or so people booked in to the restaurant but there was a business conference which had to be catered for and then the preparation for the evening service as well.

Enver's job was compounded by the fact that he had no idea what any of the dishes were or where in the variety of fridges things might be found.

The sous chef was a cheery Londoner called Harry Jones.

'Will you be OK working the grill section, Enver?'

'Sure,' said Enver. He had been brought up in the family's restaurants, two kebab shops and what had eventually become an up-market Turkish restaurant. He had been grilling meat since he was old enough to peer over the chargrill.

And this was where he was standing now, as he:

- Grilled beef fillets on the chargrill (medium-rare) for beef with a red wine and shallot reduction sauce
- Roasted guinea fowl to go with a light tomato jus

- Chargrilled venison fillets, to go with a venison faggot, girolle mushrooms and a juniper and tawny port jus
- Seared duck breasts with a morello cherry and kirsch foam and piroski

And then there were things to pan fry that were the responsibility of this section: sea bass, liver.

The pressure was relentless and two or three times he cocked up and had to be reprimanded by Jones.

He had almost forgotten the superhuman memory that a chef requires. At one point he looked down and realized that he had about twenty pieces of meat, bird, fish all cooking, all needing different times and temperatures and all for a variety of different orders, while the sweat poured off him and the kitchen rang to shouts, pleas and swearing, commands and counter-commands in a variety of accents and languages.

The dishes looked superb. Enver had eaten in a couple of Michelin-starred places but he hadn't enjoyed himself, even though he was the customer. He felt he might somehow disgrace himself, eat with the wrong cutlery, commit some solecism or clumsily knock something over. A sense of unspecified dread, of impending doom, had hung over both occasions.

Now, busy in the kitchen, he was far too occupied to worry about anything. He only had a vague idea of what he was doing, he could only see his part of the picture.

There was one chef for the sauces, one for vegetables, he was doing most of the meat and fish, concentrating on the order sequence and the timings that each item needed so it would be ready when needed.

Enver thought the sous was exemplary. Jones controlled the whole operation like a conductor with a small ensemble, his nimble fingers plating up the dishes with speed, dexterity and elan. As well as that, he had to make time to ensure that the food for the function room was of a good enough quality for the hotel's exacting standards. He was a perfect example of grace under pressure.

About quarter to two, they sent their last main course and Jones took him outside. The door from the kitchen to the yard by the bins was open and a long, metal-chain fly screen hung down to protect the kitchen from insects. There was a plastic touchpad on the wall outside about shoulder height that controlled the lock to the back door. Opposite them the long low concrete staff accommodation block stood, like Soviet Union style social housing.

Jones had two bottles of Corona. He opened them with his cigarette lighter and lit a Marlboro. He offered Enver a cigarette and Enver shook his head.

'I don't smoke.'

Jones handed Enver a beer and they both drank, sitting companionably on two plastic beer crates.

'Well, you were great,' he said to Enver. 'Where was the last place you worked?'

'Çiçek,' said Enver, giving his aunt's restaurant's name, 'and some other places.' He didn't want to be put through a series of questions on the London catering scene. 'What are the brigade like here?' he asked Jones to close down this line of enquiry.

He paid close attention as Jones ran through the merits and demerits of the other chefs. Enver asked questions about the Muslim chefs, the ones on Gower's agenda. Privately, he was convinced that this was all a bit of a wild goose chase – in his experience chefs were profoundly uninterested in politics or extremist Islam.

'Anyway,' said Jones, 'you'll be in the main kitchen tomorrow and then you'll be at the lodge for the next few days after that, sorry.'

'The lodge?' Enver finished his beer and put the bottle down. It had been delicious. The kitchen had been like a sauna. His thick hair was plastered to his head with sweat. His chef's whites were sodden.

'Yeah, it's like a four bedroom house in the grounds with a big fuck-off hedge around it. It's got its own gym, massage room, and kitchen. And the kitchen has its own chef – that's you, sunshine. From six a.m. to about midnight.'

'An eighteen-hour day, then?' Enver's voice was resigned.

'Yep. But you are getting hourly paid, none of that lot would be,' pointed out Jones, indicating the kitchen. 'You speak to the client, see what he wants, then let me know cos it's a separate costing and we might need to order special stuff in, but they'll pay for it so whatever he wants he can have. I'll give you some ideas menus, or, of course, they can eat up here. But they've paid for privacy so they normally don't leave the lodge.'

'Oh, well.' Enver pointed at the plastic touchpad on the wall. 'What's that?'

'It's thumbprint sensitive, controls the lock on the door. I'll log you on to the system tomorrow.' He yawned and rubbed his eyes. 'I'm knackered. Been here since seven. I'm on a split but I'll just work straight through. I've got a hundred panna cotta to make. Fuck-nuts in there, Colin, pastry CDP, I gave him the recipe, told him to get on with it, disaster.'

'Hard to mess up panna cotta,' said Enver. 'What did he do?' He was genuinely interested.

Jones shook his head. 'I asked him just now, how did they turn out? Oh fine, he says, I added another five sheets of gelatine in case they didn't set. I said you fucking what! I took one, bit into it, you could have played squash with it, like india rubber. Unbelievable stupidity. That lot can't go out... well, not unless absolutely necessary. He was about to chuck 'em and I said don't do that yet, we might just need them if mine haven't set. They should be OK by tonight but...'

'There's always a "but",' agreed Enver.

Jones nodded. 'I've made him clean out the freezer on his break as punishment. He can reflect on the importance of following instructions while he freezes his arse off.' He put his cigarette out. 'So I'm making panna cottas now instead of sleeping. *C'est la vie*. I'll get one of the kids to show you to your room in the staff block.'

'Thanks,' said Enver.

'Oh, one last thing,' Jones said. 'Is that your old Volvo out there, the burgundy one with the dents in?'

'Yes.' Enver felt slightly defensive about his car.

'You'll want to move it round there, to staff parking. It's a bit plebby for the public car park.'

They stood up and stretched and went back inside the kitchen, the fly chains jingling pleasantly as they walked back in.

Enver, with a junior pastry chef in tow to guide him, went in search of his car so the battered old Volvo wouldn't upset the guests.

CHAPTER THIRTY

Hanlon's feet pounded through the fallen leaves on the floor of the wood. Somewhere behind her would be Mark Spencer with his .22 and a burning desire to do her harm. Hanlon's breathing was easy, her hair bouncing as she ran, her long, strong legs effortlessly eating up the distance.

Ordinarily she wouldn't have a problem. She'd seen Spencer's cycling times on Deke's Strava app and knew hers would have been much better. She knew she was fitter and she guessed he was no distance runner. If he had been he wouldn't be the shape that he was. No, what worried her was the dog. She heard it bark, closer now.

She reflected as she ran through the beech and oak trees of the woodland, the occasional clump of rhododendron, their lithe twisted trunks sinuous under their evergreen foliage, that only the fact that the dog seemed unsure of its role in the chase had allowed her to get this far. If it sank its teeth into her leg, it'd all be over. They'd be tumbling around on the floor together, the dog wouldn't give up easily. Would Spencer really shoot her? She doubted it, but she didn't want to put it to the test. He might just want to give her a good kicking, or use the rifle butt on her. She had, after all, hurt him a fair bit the other day.

Not to mention humiliated him.

He would want revenge.

Now she could see the trees starting to thin and the dark green of the hawthorn hedge that surrounded the lodge.

She heard a bark near at hand, low and aggressive: Jet. She had a terrible urge to look behind her but worried that she might fall over something or run into a tree. Then a low growl. She glanced down and the dog was running parallel to her, its lips drawn back from its very white, very sharp-looking teeth.

A quick look ahead – there were the steps that led down to the bunker and its comforting iron door.

The dog jumped up at her, snarling, and as it did so Hanlon balled her fist and slammed it into the dog's head. She felt a burst of pain from her knuckles as they made contact with the animal's iron skull. It was like hitting a metal bollard.

The Dobermann took the blow in mid-air and it knocked it sideways. It landed and shook its head then walked after Hanlon who had leapt down the steps to the bunker and was now facing the animal, her back to the door, as it stood on the ground above looking down at her.

Hanlon reached behind her with her fingers. She didn't want to turn her back on the dog. The door had been designed to open outwards. Her fingers found the handle and the edge of the door and she pulled hard. Nothing. No movement.

Jet growled, his brown eyes locked on Hanlon's grey ones.

She heaved forward desperately. A slight give in the heavy

metal door, then it moved open. She pulled harder, still facing the animal that was hunkering down, gathering itself to spring. The dog shuffled its rear, transferring its weight to its hind legs. It bared its teeth. Hanlon's blow had hurt it, not a great deal, but enough to make it wary.

The door was now open about twenty centimetres, it was enough. Hanlon suddenly slipped inside as quickly as she could as the animal sprang forward. She grabbed the handle and pulled it shut, throwing her weight into the motion.

She heard snarling from the other side and pulled again. There was a snap as the handle came off in her hand, the seventy-year-old metal, partially rusted away, had finally perished.

The door was virtually closed but she could see the dog's nose and teeth and an angry paw as it tried to squeeze through after her. She looked around. There was daylight at the other end of the bunker, shining through a rectangular hole about head height.

Hanlon ran down the length of the bunker, some twenty-odd metres. There was nothing to impede her, the room was mostly empty as far as she could see. She reached the window hole just as the Dobermann managed to wriggle its way inside. It saw her and barked, streaking towards her. Hanlon reached above her, put her hands on the window sill and heaved herself up. The aperture was wide enough to take her body and she dropped down on to the grass of the lodge's garden within the circle of the hawthorn hedge.

She looked around. From behind her she heard angry, frustrated snarling. The dog equivalent, she guessed, of swearing.

There, on her right, was the shed that Czerwinski had

mentioned. There were no steps to the bunker this side of the hedge, but the ground sloped downwards to it, so it lay in a kind of a dip.

Around the shed three rhododendrons had been planted, to screen both it and what little you could see of the bunker. Standing on the top of the dip, looking down, framed against the skyline, doubtless attracted by the barking, was Schneider's dog.

Hanlon stared at it in utter disbelief.

It was huge, and massively muscled. It emanated a sinister, vast strength. It looked like a dog that pumped iron and ate steroids. The Dobermann was big enough, but compared to the Presa, Jet was like a small, thin puppy.

Ridges of muscle lay under its short grey and brown fur, its ears, that had pricked up, looked tiny on its wrinkled head. Its paws were enormous. It was a dog from hell.

She guessed it would weigh as much as she did, if not more, and she calculated her chances of survival, if it attacked, would be virtually nil. She had never seen such vicious malice as that animal had in its eyes.

The Presa growled. Or rather it rumbled terrifyingly, an incredibly deep gargling kind of snarl, and took a step towards her. She looked back at the window, calculating her chances of getting back inside with the Dobermann.

Virtually nil.

Hanlon felt utterly powerless, it was a dreadful sensation. For once in her life, she had literally no idea what to do. There was nothing to do. The Presa took another step towards her and made a kind of limbering-up motion with its shoulders.

156

Then, there was a burst of blurred movement in the periphery of her vision and a thud as the Dobermann landed on the grass near her. In her eagerness to attack Hanlon, Jet had managed to clear the window, taking an almighty leap to bring him from inside the bunker to outside into the garden.

The Dobermann looked at Hanlon and drew its jowls back in a snarl. Compared to the other animal Jet was laughably insignificant. Go on, do your worst, thought Hanlon, see if I care. Then the dog noticed the Presa.

There was no questioning the Dobermann's bravery, although its judgement was seriously awry. It immediately forgot about Hanlon.

Without flinching the Dobermann pulled its gaze away from her and headed up the slope to the other dog.

They circled each other, the Dobermann's hackles virtually vertical, its teeth bared, growling aggressively. The Presa was ominously silent. Hanlon backed up against the door of the bunker and tried the handle, it didn't move. She took a glance at the dogs, they were engrossed in each other. She thanked God for that.

The Presa regarded the Dobermann with no trace of emotion whatsoever, no growls, no hackle-raising, then, with ferocious speed for a dog its size, it sprang forward and sank its teeth into the shoulder of the Dobermann and, as though it was as light as a toy, tossed the animal into the air with a single shake of its massive head and neck. It was an awesome display of strength. As the smaller dog landed on its back, its belly and throat exposed, the Presa lunged forward with shocking speed.

Hanlon leapt upwards, caught the window and hauled herself back inside. She heard the Dobermann howl once in anguish and agony and then a terrible silence. Her heart thudding, she ran the length of the bunker and out through the other door.

She slammed it shut and ran up the steps. She guessed that Spencer had been relying on the Dobermann catching her and incapacitating her to find her. He'd have been listening out for frenzied barking and shouts. Without those to guide him, he'd have little chance of finding her.

Quite frankly, she didn't care.

After what she'd seen, Spencer with a .22 was infinitely preferable.

From behind the hedge she heard a noise, a single loud bark of ferocious triumph.

Hanlon sank down on to her knees under the beech trees and threw up.

CHAPTER THIRTY-ONE

Huss was at the meeting of the Serious Crimes investigation into Elsa's death. There had been, according to the pathology report, severe head injuries so although she was alive when she was set on fire, it was doubtful that she was aware of what was happening to her.

'Which is some crumb of comfort,' said Templeman, wrinkling his nose in distaste at the details of the damage to her skull. 'At least the poor woman didn't suffer too much.' I hope, anyway, he thought.

'There is that,' agreed McKenzie.

Templeman was still angry with him at his late arrival at the crime scene. He went on: nothing usable from forensics, no witnesses, the fingertip search had revealed nothing, the area fairly trampled by the boots of the emergency services, the only real hope was footage from a CCTV camera that monitored a nearby junction that was an accident blackspot: a rat run that connected with the road just round from a blind bend. That was being examined now.

'OK.' Templeman sounded weary. 'Any idea of the perpetrators? DI Huss, you have a theory, I believe.'

'Yes, sir.' She cleared her throat. 'As a result of measures taken to ensure the safety of Wolf Schneider…'

Templeman audibly groaned and put his hands over his eyes in pantomime protest. Him again.

'I wish he'd stayed in Bavaria.'

'Baden-Württemberg, sir. Don't we all. Anyway, sir, while he's here for his political promotional tour, we looked into the threat posed by an anarchist group called Eleuthera. The group has a known history of violence and is said to be active here in Oxford. A freelance journalist called Marcus Hinds who is a suspect in the Kettering murder investigation passed information on the group in the form of a computer hard drive that was in the possession of Elsa Worthington.'

'And was the hard drive found?' asked Templeman.

'A hard drive was found,' confirmed McKenzie. 'It's at the lab, but the chances of anything usable being found are pretty much zero.' He gestured. 'The fire…'

McKenzie leaned forward. 'Do you think they were involved in the fire? Eleuthera?'

Templeman looked at her sharply. Huss knew she had to tread warily. Her boss would be implacably opposed to bringing in shadowy organizations as potential suspects. He prided himself on being a simple man. 'Murders are usually simple and most murderers are cretins,' he'd told her once.

'I don't know,' she said carefully, 'but we'd be remiss if we didn't have a look.'

'But why kill Elsa? Why not just take the hard drive?' asked Templeman.

'Because Elsa was a witness to what went on that day at

Pretoria Road when Kettering was killed,' said Huss. 'There was nothing wrong with Elsa's eyesight, or her memory when she wasn't zoned out.'

'Is there any evidence other than supposition that Eleuthera had a hand in her death?' Templeman, eager to shut down this line of enquiry.

'Hinds will be able to shed more light on their activities when he's caught,' said Huss. 'It's believed that he was fleeing from Eleuthera when the stabbing took place.'

Templeman shook his head in irritation. 'It's all fascinating, DI Huss, but it's just a theory.' He put his hands flat on the table. 'If Elsa was a witness to the killing and Hinds had done it, as all the evidence suggests, then he could well have killed her. In fact, I find that wholly credible.'

There was silence in the room. Huss had to admit that he had made a very valid point, and how would Eleuthera have known where to find Elsa? Hinds would have, he knew her well, but Georgie Adams?

There was a knock on the door.

'Come,' said Templeman. The door opened and DI Ed Worth stood there with an A4 envelope in his hand.

'Sorry to interrupt, sir. The council highways department have just got back to us. They've been through the CCTV footage for the six hours prior to Elsa Worthington's death. The camera in question is set to take pictures every ten minutes to measure traffic flow, part of a scheme to evaluate the need for traffic lights...' Get on with it, Ed, thought Huss. Worth was inclined to go on and on. Get to the point.

'These are the three images that I thought would interest you.'

He opened his envelope and laid out the photos.

Six thirty p.m. A black and white image of Elsa, burdened with several bags on each arm, shuffling along the pavement to her lair behind the bus stop.

Eight forty-five p.m. A black and white image of a man, a small backpack slung over his shoulder. His head was bowed, his face obscured.

Eight fifty-five p.m. The same man, this time his face was turned to the camera, a clear and unequivocal shot.

It was Marcus Hinds.

CHAPTER THIRTY-TWO

Hanlon sat opposite Schneider and Hübler in the suite they were staying in at Claridge's. A several thousand pounds a night suite. Hanlon reflected that he wasn't exactly leading a man of the people kind of life. She was disappointed; she rather liked Schneider. Opposing immigration was paying handsomely. Part of her was saddened by this hypocrisy. If you're going to be a man of the people then you should act like one, she thought.

Schneider was wearing a white silk shirt and dark chinos, no socks and loafers. He looked like an ageing rock star, an MOR rock star. Hübler sat next to him on the sofa, exuding a certain coarse sexiness, a groupie made good. Her clothes: tight sweater emphasizing her large breasts; leggings emphasizing her large thighs.

Their relationship continued to puzzle Hanlon. She was really out of her league with Schneider. A lot of it was to do with the disparity in looks. She was nowhere nearly as classy-looking as he was. It was as simple as that.

There was a disparity between the two that she couldn't fathom. She wondered if the woman had some kind of leverage over Schneider. She had heard they had been together for a long time, maybe Hübler knew Schneider's secrets and he daren't get rid of her.

Hübler said, 'So you met Wotan, Wolf's dog.'

'Yes.' Hanlon saw no need to elaborate.

'He's quite an animal,' said Schneider, a hint of pride in his voice. 'He is so loyal, a true friend, loyalty over everything, DCI Hanlon. More valuable than anything. I mean, look at this place.' He waved his arm to indicate the Claridge's suite. 'It would turn many men's heads, but not a dog's. I'm the most important thing in his life, not money or the trappings of wealth.'

The trappings of wealth indeed, thought Hanlon. Her eyes ran over the sitting room. The bedrooms opened on to it. The Germans were drinking champagne, the room was effortlessly luxurious, art deco in its inspiration, as if Hanlon had fallen through time and ended up in the thirties.

She would have fitted in. Medium height, slender, she would have looked fantastic in a strappy thirties flapper-style cocktail dress. Hübler would have struck a jarring note. Despite her obvious intelligence, despite her incredible English, despite her organizational abilities, she was not sophisticated. Or slim.

She could almost hear the voice of Soho Iris, a madam she knew in a brothel about a mile away, saying in her ear, 'Oooh, plebby, is it? 'Oo's the snob now, DCI Hanlon? Who's got sharp claws?'

Hanlon took a sip of water. The opulent wealth of the room, its cream and gold furnishings, its deep, luxurious carpet, was of no interest to her. If anything it slightly irritated her. She was indifferent to 'the trappings of wealth' as

Schneider had just put it. It was just the way it was. Strangely, it was a trait she shared with Dave 'Jesus' Anderson.

Maybe, she thought, maybe I like power. You have that in the police, you have that in boxing, the power not just to beat someone in a game or a contest, which she got from triathlon, but the power to hurt them. And she did like that. Momentarily she thought of Conquest, the Judge, Michaels. People she had done more than hurt. Oh well, she wasn't going to waste any sleep worrying about stuff like that.

What's done is done.

Let the dead bury their dead.

A thought, she reflected, that probably occurred to Anderson every morning when he saw the tall chimney of the Edmonton industrial incinerator just up the road from where he lived. His own personal crematorium.

'Loyalty,' said Schneider again. He looked at Hübler, the expression on his face enigmatic, inscrutable, and stood up. He turned to Hanlon. 'I have someone to meet at the bar.' She started to get up to follow him, he motioned to her to sit.

'Gower has arranged for someone from Diplomatic Protection to be with me in the bar.' He smiled at her. 'I fear if you were to sit at a table by yourself there would be a series of unwelcome suggestions from the gentlemen staying in this fine hotel.'

He slipped a jacket on. 'No, please stay here and look after Christiane. That way I won't need to worry when I'm away.'

He smiled and left the room. The door clicked to behind him softly. Hübler looked at Hanlon. 'Loyalty,' she said. There was an almost bitter tone in her voice.

She poured herself some more champagne.

'Want some?' she asked Hanlon.

Hanlon shook her head.

Hübler propped herself up on one elbow. 'Are you a loyal person, Hanlon?' Her voice was slurred, she squinted at her, trying to focus her eyes, and Hanlon realized that she was very drunk.

Hübler carried on talking in a slightly dreamy way. 'I'm loyal, well, my heart is, but he has other women and... well, I won't say, so if I fuck around a bit, who's to say that's wrong...'

Hanlon had her own loyalty. His name was Mark Whiteside and he was in a hospital bed, brain-damaged. Eleven thousand people a year in the UK suffer severe brain injury, of these, four and a half thousand will need full-time care for the rest of their days. That's an awful lot of people. But only one of them was her fault, her responsibility.

The woman on the sofa opposite poured and drank some more champagne.

'People say I'm racist but I'm not... I mean, it's true, I don't want blacks and Arabs and Turks in Germany, but I don't mind them in their own countries and I've got no objection, if they're attractive, to wrapping my legs round one... In fact, I love it.'

She looked at Hanlon, trying to focus.

'I don't think that makes me a hypocrite. The leader, though, is worried *Bild* might get hold of it. Keep your pants up, Christiane.' She mimicked Schneider's accent. 'Don't embarrass me...' She fixed Hanlon with a furious stare. She was at that stage of drunkenness where gushing affection alternates with sudden anger.

'*Embarrass me, embarrass me*... He's a bloody hypocrite, Wolf Schneider is... How dare he lecture me... how dare he... If the public knew who he'd been fucking, he'd be well fucked, and not just up the arse but...' She tailed off into a string of German that Hanlon didn't understand a word of.

She pulled herself together and looked across at Hanlon. 'And if he pisses me off I'll go to *Bild*. In fact, you know what, I bloody well will... You're very quiet, why don't you tell me about the men in your life?'

Hanlon could see that she was at that point of drunkenness where friendliness alternated with aggression. She wanted to hear less about Hübler and more about Schneider.

So she found herself telling her about Mark Whiteside, her injured former colleague. The hospitalization, the brain damage. He had paid the price for a crusade of her own making. This was the guilt that she carried. It was there every morning when she opened her eyes. For a wonderful second she was free as the day started anew, then she thought immediately of him. *Mark Whiteside*.

She told Christiane about the operation that he would soon be facing that she had arranged. An operation that, even if successful in bringing him out of his coma, could leave him like a babbling infant. It was almost unbearable. He was the last thing she thought of at night, and during the day her guilt walked alongside her like a shadowy, conjoined twin.

And the reason he was still alive, in the teeth of opposition from his parents and from the overstretched budget of the NHS, was her perseverance.

'*Schade…*' murmured Christiane gently. She downed her drink in one, her eyes glassy, and poured another. Quite a bit spilled on the floor.

'So, in answer to your question, Christiane, yes, I do care about loyalty, I care about it a lot.'

Both of them fell silent and Hübler closed her eyes. Her breathing deepened. Hanlon guessed she had fallen asleep.

She watched her sleep, an unlikely guardian angel. She turned over what she had learned in her mind: that Hübler was by day trying to deport non-white Germans and by night trying to get laid by them. That Schneider was finding her a source of potential major embarrassment – such a revelation would be very damaging to his NS party. Then there was the tantalizing hint that Schneider himself was involved in some form of sexual impropriety. It had certainly been an evening of revelations.

Would she reveal all to the press as she threatened?

God knows, she thought, and I, for one, do not care.

Some time later, there was the sound of the card key being swiped and the door opened, as did Hübler's eyes. She must have a head like a rock, thought Hanlon. She sat up and pushed her hair into a semblance of order and winked conspiratorially at Hanlon. Schneider came in, he was beaming.

'*Ach so*, I trust you ladies had a pleasant time. And now, DCI Hanlon, you can leave us. If you would like to meet us at breakfast again, we can all travel down to Oxford together. We can see if the Rosemount is as nice as Hanlon says it is. *Bis bald*, Hanlon.'

'*Tschuss*,' said Hübler warmly.

Hanlon stood up and left the room. Outside was one of the plain-clothes officers she had met at the talk at Islington a couple of nights previously. He nodded at her affably and settled himself down for a long and dull vigil outside Schneider's door.

She walked out of the expensive hotel into the cold evening air. She looked at her watch, eleven p.m. She walked slowly along the empty pavements outside the unbelievably expensive flats and houses in this part of town.

Mayfair at this time of night was practically empty. There was a tall, middle-aged man walking behind her on the pavement, a trilby pulled low on his head. He lit a cigarette and the faint breeze from behind him carried the smell of smoke to her nostrils.

Hanlon shrugged her shoulders. Let him try something if he dared, he'd soon regret it, she thought. No one is going to try and tackle me.

Two men walked out of a side street ahead and lurched toward her. She could smell the alcohol on them. If Hanlon had been a dog the hackles on her neck would have risen. She could sense trouble in the way they moved towards her, far from sober, slightly aggressive. They had obviously been to an upmarket formal dinner, they were wearing black tie. Middle-aged, out on the razz, hoping a wallet full of cash would make up for the jowls, the gut, the bald patch, the desperation.

'Hello, darling,' slurred one of them at her. 'Come with us and have a drink.' He leered at her hopefully.

Hanlon thought, I'm the oppressed middle. This morning it was the proletariat that were after me, now it's the high earners. The crusties and the Hooray Henries. I'm between a rock and a hard place.

She didn't really see them as a threat, then, suddenly, to her surprise, one of them grabbed her arm as she walked past, spinning her round.

'Come on, darling, smile.' He leaned forward, trying to plant a clumsy kiss on her cheek.

Before she had a chance to react there was a dull thud, and an explosive gasp of pain, and the man in the DJ sank to his knees. The tall man with the hat she had seen earlier was standing behind him, cigarette still burning in his mouth. He had slammed his fist into the dinner-jacketed guy's kidney so hard that his legs had given way beneath him from the flaring pain.

The attacker put his foot between the man's shoulder blades and shoved. He sprawled forward on the pavement. The other Hooray, red-faced, balding, looking utterly terrified, backed away from the tall man with a look of frightened alarm on his face. Hanlon bet that nothing remotely like this had ever happened to him in forty years. He obviously hadn't got a clue what to do.

The tall man took his cigarette out of his mouth and leaned towards him, his tone threatening. 'Now fuck off, you Footsie One Hundred muppet and take your mate with you.' His voice was heavy with mingled contempt and dislike.

'Come on, Benj,' said the one who hadn't been hit, helping his companion up. They limped off shakily, fearfully, westwards down Brook Street.

'Good evening, Morris,' said Hanlon, civilly.

Morris Jones looked at her expressionlessly. His eyes gleaming pinpricks under the brim of his hat.

'Dave Anderson wants a word.'

'I would never have guessed,' said Hanlon.

A waiting Mercedes with tinted rear windows pulled up and the rear passenger door opened. Hanlon, followed by Morris Jones, climbed inside.

'Hello, Hanlon,' said Dave 'Jesus' Anderson.

The car pulled away silently into the expensive Mayfair night.

CHAPTER THIRTY-THREE

It was two o'clock the following afternoon that Huss caught up with Enver. He was on his break on the split shift that he was working and he met Huss in the Oriental Garden, which was one of the many sections of the hotel's vast grounds.

There was a replica Chinese pagoda (you could, of course, hire it for picnics and parties in the summer at exorbitant expense), maple and cherry trees, bamboo groves, a Zen garden put together by an internationally famous consultant in feng shui, and a curved Japanese-style bridge that spanned a pond full of lilies and koi carp. There had been a pond with carp there as long as the house had been existence and many of the fish were rumoured to be a century old, or older.

Enver and Huss were on this bridge now, feeding them bread that Enver had brought from the kitchen. There were so many carp the waters seemed to be boiling as the huge, glistening fish fought over the scraps.

'Some of them might be as old as the house itself,' said Enver. 'Carp can live an amazingly long time.'

Huss wasn't interested in fish.

'So, any leads from the kitchen, any sign of Al-Akhdaar or Eleuthera activists?'

Enver shook his head.

'Nobody's remotely interested in politics or religion. Sex, yes, drugs, yes, booze, yes. It's a kitchen, for God's sake. Mind you, if I worked there much longer I'd probably join the anarchists. You get paid more and treated better at my auntie Demet's restaurant and she's not exactly overflowing with the milk of human kindness.'

Huss had met Enver's Aunt Demet and thought conditions must be bad in the Rosemount.

Enver shook his head gloomily. 'I think it's the contrast really that sticks in the throat. The staff here are all on minimum wage, much less really when you factor in the unpaid overtime, and the clientele can afford a lunch that costs more than they earn in a week. I'm surprised we don't all rise up and burn the place to the ground.'

'Well, don't start giving them ideas, Enver Demirel,' said Huss severely.

The grey, Gothic pile of the hotel was visible through the trees. Huss thought of the kitchen staff back in their accommodation in their two-hour kitchen break, fucking like rabbits, taking drugs, having a couple of snatched beers, sleeping in exhausted heaps in odd places, under tables, in linen cupboards, until the evening service began and they could all work like crazy until midnight.

She hoped that Enver might come across something to cast doubt on Hinds's guilt. If only he hadn't run away. And what the hell was he doing on that video? None of her colleagues believed that Hinds was anything other than guilty of two murders now. Any theories that Eleuthera were behind Kettering's death or that of Elsa were void. Even Huss was beginning to doubt herself.

As for Evan:

'We all do daft things at university,' Templeman had said. 'Quite frankly it would have been weirder if he'd been a member of the Young Conservatives. What sort of political organization would you expect to find a Comp Sci student in other than the anarchists? It's absolutely meaningless. Get a grip, Melinda.'

No one was interested in the anarchists now. Including Enver.

'I can't see any likely candidates for killing Schneider,' said Enver. 'Nobody can spell "anarchist" in that kitchen, much less want to be one.'

'Apart from you.' Huss threw another piece of bread to the fish. Enver's face wore its typical doleful expression. He was still wearing his chef's jacket under his heavy coat. It was partially unbuttoned and Huss could see the swell of his pectoral muscles. His hands lay on the granite balustrade, he had exceptionally powerful fingers. There was a painful-looking crescent-shaped burn on one thick wrist and his left forefinger had a blue plaster wrapped around it. Huss found this damage oddly compelling. The cold breeze ruffled his thick black hair and his drooping moustache bristled.

'Apart from me,' agreed Enver. 'And my fellow Muslims aren't going to be joining the Wahhabis anytime soon. One of the Chechens, Arzu, is even on suspension for "inappropriate behaviour" with lady guests.'

'Is "inappropriate behaviour" jihadi extremism?' asked Huss teasingly.

Enver failed to see the joke. 'No, it's shagging the guests.

Arzu's sex on a stick, seemingly. Mind you, some women just like fucking chefs.'

Huss moved closer to Enver and slid her arms around his body. She was shorter than he was and she rested her forehead on his chin. Her thick blonde hair tickled his nose, he could smell the shampoo she used.

Huss's hands slipped under his coat and chef's jacket. She pulled him closer to her, her palms stroking the rock-hard muscles of his lats and lower back. Her own back gave a warning yelp of pain. She ignored it. I'll go to the doctor next week, she thought. She lifted her head up and looked into his sad, brown eyes.

'I want to fuck a chef, Enver,' she breathed.

'I don't know if I've got time, Melinda,' said Enver despairingly. 'I've got to make seventy-two bridge rolls and debone thirty chicken thighs...'

Huss's hand slid lower down the front of his body, found what she was looking for.

'...for a ballotine...'

'I'm sure you'll make time,' whispered Huss. 'Now let's go back to your room.'

'But I've got to poach the chicken mousse...'

'Sod the mousse, Enver... Service, Enver, that's what you say, isn't it?'

'Yes,' he said hoarsely.

'Service, Enver, now, please.'

He nodded. The ballotine could wait.

It would have to.

Arm in arm they headed back to the Rosemount.

CHAPTER THIRTY-FOUR

Enver woke with a start about one in the morning. The staff accommodation was an ugly-looking block like a prison wing or student accommodation built out of sight behind the hotel.

The room Enver was in, which contained a washbasin, a bed and little else, had a window that overlooked the back of the kitchen and the bins. He was glad it wasn't the summer. He guessed that the noxious smell from the ten gigantic wheely bins underneath the windows would rise straight upwards into the staff's bedrooms. It would stink.

He got out of his narrow single bed, wondering what had woken him up, went to the window and looked out. The yard just at the back of the kitchens was in partial darkness, mitigated by the moon overhead and the light that the hotel itself created from the odd window here and there. Nothing was moving in the yard. He could see the bins and the upturned plastic beer crates where the chefs and waiters sat when they had a cigarette break.

He turned his attention to the kitchen door. He could see a blue glow from inside. He guessed that was from where the gigantic stockpot, the size of a dustbin, would be sitting on top of the stove, the gas turned to its lowest setting, whilst twenty kilos of roasted beef bones and dozens of litres of water would slowly reduce and gather flavour overnight to produce a highly flavoured jus.

He noticed that the kitchen door was ajar and he frowned in irritation – that shouldn't be the case. He'd been the last out, he'd made sure that it was locked.

Although there was no alcohol or money to steal in the kitchen, there were other desirable things worth having. There was ultra-high quality meat in those fridges, beef fillets, venison fillets and fish, tranches of turbot, and then the smoked fish and the oysters that were worth a small fortune. He wasn't so much worried about the truffles, five hundred pounds sterling for a hundred grams in weight. Harry Jones kept those under lock and key in a safe in his office. They were weighed out for usage on little scales like drug dealers use.

He couldn't go back to bed knowing that the kitchen was open. If I found out which moron did this, they'll be wearing their nads for earrings, he thought. He rolled his eyes. So it had come to this, he was back to thinking like a chef. *Nads for earrings* indeed. A few more days at the Rosemount and he would find himself transformed into one of those teeth-baring culinary psychos he'd become used to working alongside in his youth.

Sod it, he thought, pulling a dressing gown on. I'd better go and see what's going on. He walked into the darkness of the corridor, headed for the stairs and, as he turned the corner, nearly fell over two bodies on the landing.

Peter Marshall, one of the junior chefs de partie, was lying on his back while the ample, naked form of Kelly

Reeves, a pastry chef, her huge breasts swinging back and forth, a half-litre can of lager in her left hand, bucked energetically up and down on top of him.

She froze momentarily, her head tilted back. Can to lips. He could see, strangely, that, despite where she was, what she was doing and what she was drinking, she had her little finger crooked genteelly over the can in her hand as if she were having afternoon tea.

'Who's that?' she demanded. Her voice was quite aggressive, she was a terrifying girl in many ways.

'It's Enver, the junior sous.' He felt incredibly embarrassed by the unexpected encounter. Not so Kelly.

'Evening, Chef,' she called out cheerily, obviously reassured, resuming her motions. 'Oh, I finished those venison pithiviers by the way,'

'Oh, God,' moaned Marchant from beneath her, his eyes firmly closed, blotting out Enver from his vision. 'Oh, Christ yes...'

'They're in the walk-in, third shelf down.'

'Good,' said Enver weakly as he squeezed past them. Kelly bent over the kid pinioned beneath her and upped the pace.

'Oh, Christ, yes, Kell, yes.'

'I remembered to date and label them this time, Chef,' she called out over her shoulder. Her mighty breasts shook, her hair obscured her face and she crushed the now empty lager can in her hand and tossed it over her shoulder. Enver had given her a hard time over lax labelling earlier, heavy on the sarcasm. He'd been worried in case he'd overdone it, but all in all she seemed to have forgiven him.

He shook his head. The place was a madhouse, he thought.

He crept down the stairs, worried in case he fell over any more of his kitchen brigade. The staff block reeked of grass, cigarette smoke, sex and booze. Lights flickered from under doors as his fellow chefs got high, masturbated, listened to music, fucked, watched porn, or films, played Xbox. Some of them just cried.

It was quite a hard life really, thought Enver. The fifteen-hour days and six-day weeks, the lack of daylight, the lack of normality, really screwed the staff up, both mentally and physically. Nobody ate properly, nobody had enough sleep, nobody exercised, people shouted at them or hit them or gave them sadistic punishments, everyone drank to excess and seemed addled on drugs. Their only topic of conversation was sex and food, occasionally football. Any idea of normality had long since left the building. Many of them didn't really know where the hotel was, would be unable to find it on a map. Hardly anyone knew the name of the prime minister. Certainly nobody knew who Schneider was. Nobody would be able to find Germany on a map.

The kitchen brigade in the cold light of day looked dreadful, more dead than alive.

On balance, he preferred the police force. It was slightly saner.

He opened the door to the yard and went outside, shivering as the temperature plummeted. His breath steamed.

He rounded the bins and saw a figure standing just inside the kitchen doorway, silhouetted against the ghostly blue light in the kitchen from the gas ring and the electric fly and insect killers on the walls.

'Hello?' he called, no answer. The silent figure swayed in a slightly disturbing way, almost as if it were weightless.

Enver felt a shiver of supernatural dread and took another step forward.

The links of the steel fly chains glinted like silver in the moonlight. Standing in the chains was the figure of a woman, head bent over, long dark hair hanging over her face. Her toes in her stockinged feet were a couple of centimetres above the ground. Two of the chains had been wrapped and tied tightly around her neck, supporting her dead weight.

He sighed and looked more closely, careful not to touch or disturb anything. Her sightless eyes bulged, her mouth was open, she was evidently beyond any form of assistance.

It was Christiane Hübler.

CHAPTER THIRTY-FIVE

Hanlon met up with Huss the following day at eleven in the morning at the police station in Summertown in Oxford.

'The chief suspect is a young chef called Arzu Mansur,' said Huss. 'There's a text on Hübler's phone from him agreeing to meet up in the kitchen at twelve thirty. It's fairly sexually explicit.'

'So they were having an affair? That was speedy work on her part.' Despite what she knew about the dead woman, it seemed very quick off the mark.

Huss nodded. 'She had met him before, seemingly. She'd been down twice before now to check the lodge out and Czerwinski, the manager, said that Mansur had given her a little tour of the lodge's catering facilities. Mansur had a reputation as a ladies' man.' She paused and looked hard at Hanlon. 'You knew Hübler – did she seem the sort to put it about?'

Hanlon said, 'Absolutely. She struck me as a very direct woman.'

'What about Schneider?' asked Huss.

'I have to say,' Hanlon picked her words carefully, she wasn't sure of the answer, 'I'm not even sure what her relationship with Schneider really was, come to think of it. I thought they were having an affair, more than that, that they were an item, then I wasn't so sure and then last night, there was this weird atmosphere.'

She filled Huss in on her evening with Hübler, the strained atmosphere, the stress on the word, the concept, of 'loyalty'.

'There was definitely something going on,' she concluded.

'Is it likely she would have an affair with a non-European?' said Huss. 'Given her race views?'

'If anything, she seemed to prefer it,' said Hanlon. 'She didn't want Muslims in Europe, but that didn't mean she didn't necessarily want them in her bed; or it could have been transgressive sex, forbidden fruit? Who knows, sex is sex, it doesn't have rules.' She told Huss about her conversation with Hübler in Claridge's.

'Why would they meet up in a kitchen to have sex?' asked Hanlon. 'Hübler and Arzu, I mean. Why not in Arzu's room?'

'Arzu shared his room with another kid, it's quite common for sexual activity to take place in other places because of this. Enver nearly fell over two other chefs at it like rabbits when he was on his way down to the kitchen,' Huss explained.

Hanlon hid a grin – she could imagine how mortified the prudish Enver would have been.

Huss added, 'And from what you say about Schneider being worried that she'd embarrass him politically with her non-white lovers, she could hardly invite him to her room at the lodge. She'd want to keep it secret. No, the kitchen makes perfect sense. It's a hotbed of vice. Enver found one of the sauce chefs with his hand up the skirt of one of the waitresses in the walk-in fridge. The chefs seem to like screwing in the kitchen or by the bins, I really don't know why, but they do.'

She shrugged and looked at Hanlon and continued, 'So this "loyalty" thing that Schneider was obsessing about, could it be that he knew she was having an affair with Arzu? There was no sign of sex, by the way, on the body, nothing at all. She was strangled with that chain, pure and simple.'

'Schneider didn't do it?' asked Hanlon, half joking. 'You did check his alibi? Hübler did imply that she had some pretty impressive dirt on Schneider that would ruin his political career.'

'I did check his alibi, he couldn't have killed her.' Huss shook her head. 'He was doing a conference call with Germany on Skype and he alibied Frank Muller too, for what it's worth. The murder had to have taken place between eleven forty-five and one a.m. I find it impossible to imagine he arranged a hitman to kill Hübler in such a public place and in such a short space of time and in a foreign country.'

'And Arzu's missing,' said Hanlon.

'He's missing,' confirmed Huss, 'and it was he who opened that door at eleven forty-five, his thumbprint is logged on the system. It's a touch-sensitive keypad that controls that door.'

She took her laptop and swivelled it round so Hanlon could see the screen. She pointed at the thumbprint image and time. 'That's his, can't be anyone else.'

Hanlon nodded.

'And now there's this.'

Two figures, dressed in military fatigues, their features covered with ski masks and Arab headscarves, sat cross-legged beneath a banner with Arab writing.

'Al-Akhdaar,' said Huss. 'Uploaded to YouTube early this morning.' One of the two men had a laptop and it displayed the image of Christiane Hübler's face, a death mask, so to speak, hanging in the chains. He pressed a button, and Arabic letters appeared, overwriting her dead face.

'*Al-Mawt lil sharmouta maseehiyya*,' said Huss, reading from her notebook. '"Death to the Christian whore" is what it means.'

'Is there no audio?' asked Hanlon. Huss shook her head. 'Just the images.'

Hanlon nodded. 'Oh well, so it looks like Schneider wasn't the target.'

'Maybe he was,' said Huss. 'Maybe they didn't fancy their chances with that dog of his. Or Muller, come to that. It amounts to the same thing: an attack on democracy and Western values. There's no way either we could trace the source of that clip, it was sent via TOR.'

'Have you been up to the scene of crime?' asked Hanlon. 'This morning. The Rosemount is a real mess at the moment. Czerwinski is going crazy. News crews everywhere, guests majorly pissed off, functions cancelled, the kitchen's a crime scene, it could hardly be worse.'

'How long is the kitchen going to be shut?' asked Hanlon.

'Not long,' said Huss. 'DI Robbins, who's the SIO, reckons his team should be finished by about ten tonight, call it midnight. It's a fairly dream location, really, not like that sodding bus stop. The kitchen was cleaned down before the murder so any evidence will be easy to gather, couldn't be better for fingerprints or indeed anything, and we know who the suspect is. Ports, airports, Eurotunnel all alerted.'

'So is Schneider out of your hair now?' asked Hanlon. 'Presumably he's going back to Germany.'

'Is he buggery!' Huss's voice was angry. 'He's still doing that stupid debate at the Oxford Union: "I will not let this act of barbarism silence free speech, it is my tribute to Christiane." It's his great moment. Now even people in Britain have heard of him. He's on the front cover of *Bild*, *der Spiegel* are doing a feature. It could hardly be better for the man. You don't get this sort of publicity often.'

'So not Eleuthera.' Hanlon looked questioningly at Huss.

'Seemingly not,' said Huss regretfully. 'It looks like I was barking up the wrong tree.'

'Well, off the record...' Hanlon told Huss about her encounter with the anarchists. She could hardly have revealed how she had discovered their presence. Huss shook her head at Hanlon's actions.

'They're gone now,' said Hanlon. 'I checked on my way here, all the vehicles have moved out.'

'Well,' Huss bit her tongue, 'it hardly matters. It doesn't look like they were involved. There's another two protection officers coming, that makes four plus Enver, plus the hotel guys and that humongous hound.'

'Mastiff,' said Hanlon.

'Whatever. Schneider's very well protected.'

'I thought that they didn't want to provide too much protection in case it looked like we were condoning Schneider's views?' asked Hanlon.

'The chief constable does not want him dead in Oxford, that's the bottom line. We'd rather be accused of condoning the right,' said Huss. 'Face it, we've got, what, a couple of hundred protection officers in the Thames Valley, what with Chequers and Dorneywood. I'm sure it hasn't hurt to divert a couple of them to babysit Schneider.'

'But where does this leave you with Hinds?' Huss looked at her questioningly. Hanlon had spoken in a kind of offhand way but Huss could feel a kind of tension behind the innocuous query.

'He's facing two charges of murder.' Her voice was formal, almost stiff.

'Which you don't think he did.'

Huss said, her voice softer, 'No, I don't. Hinds is not the kind of man to do something like that. I just wish I could talk to him, hear what he's got to say.'

'Do you really mean that?' asked Hanlon, with an infuriating half-smile.

'Yes, I do,' said Huss. She looked suspiciously at Hanlon. She was obviously up to something.

'Well, then,' Hanlon stood up and stretched, 'I'll arrange it.'

She took her phone out, Huss watched her fingers swiftly text, then read a reply. She clicked the phone off and looked at Huss.

'This evening.'

'Where?'

Hanlon smiled. 'The home of British Boxing, Melinda. The York Hall, Bethnal Green.'

CHAPTER THIRTY-SIX

The York Hall, although richly evocative for the boxing community in the same way as La Scala is for the opera lover or Wembley for the football fan, was, for DI Huss, a bit of a disappointment. It's an unlovely building and inside, the boxing ring standing proud of serried ranks of plastic chairs on a scuffed wood-block floor, it is not unlike being in a school gym.

Hanlon had been before, but not Huss. Before they went Hanlon had said to her, 'You can drop any ideas you might have about nicking him, that's for sure. There's going to be about two thousand people in there tonight, a good proportion of them have been on the wrong side of the law, and a lot of them know how to fight.'

Huss nodded, she could imagine. She didn't know who the superintendent of Bethnal Green police was, but she could well believe that a request to effect an arrest there would go down very badly.

Hanlon went on, 'Anderson said Hinds will talk to you there, he wants to give you his side of the story. He says he can give you information that will prove that he's innocent.'

'That sounds fair enough.'

'And let me remind you once again, Melinda, don't try and arrest him. We're going to be in Bethnal Green, that's not a good place to use any heavy-handed police tactics, it's not Oxford. You'd have some sort of almighty riot kicking off.'

Huss looked around her. It was late afternoon, half five, and the fights went on until the last one finished about ten-thirty. The bouts were anything from three to ten rounds. This was real boxing, gritty, no-frills, low-key. The fighters weren't slick, it was where it all begins. It is a world away from the glitz of the MGM Grand Las Vegas, the O2 arena or Madison Square Garden. It's where everything slowly starts for the fighters as they make their painful way up in the fight game. The crossover point from the amateur to the professional world.

She and Hanlon leaned by the back wall, waiting.

There were quite a few other women present, mainly young, dressed up in tight revealing dresses and vertiginous heels. Lots of cleavage, make-up and perfume. All of them with either families or boyfriends. The men were muscular, short-haired or shaven-headed, probably eighty per cent white, twenty per cent black, a sprinkling of Asians. The dress code was tough.

Fleetingly Hanlon wondered what they'd make of someone like Albert Slater who, the last time she'd seen him, had been wearing pink brothel creepers, torn skinny jeans, a leopard-print silk shirt and a beret. Seventy years old and still rocking.

Hanlon was wearing a long, tailored knee-length blue wool coat, very tight dark blue jeans and high-heeled brown suede boots that reached her lower calves. She had a white V-necked cashmere sweater on underneath. She looked incredible, thought Huss, feeling awkward and burly next to her in a two-piece trouser suit. Hanlon was turning a lot of heads.

There was a fenced-off VIP section in front of the ring. Same functional plastic chairs as everyone else, maybe a tiny bit more legroom.

A gallery upstairs ran around three sides of the interior. Banners, home-made, brought by friends and relations of the boxers, hung down, cheering on fighters due later in the evening.

The hall was maybe only half-full at this time. It was early days. Then, with little warning, the MC took to the ring with his microphone. The acoustics were appalling, Huss could make out only the odd word, '... blue corner... red trunks... from Hornsea, London...'

Then the fighters came in, one after another, to their chosen music. They took their corners and two girls, shoehorned into basques that displayed a huge amount of pushed-up cleavage and which disappeared up between their buttocks, wearing fishnets and very high heels, paraded around the ring with cards saying 'Round One' on one side and 'Spearmint Rhino' on the other.

Hanlon smiled to herself. Quite by chance, at a similar place in Luton, years ago, she had seen a nineteen-year-old Enver Demirel, fleeing the tyranny of the family restaurant business, emerge to fight some black guy. A much slimmer Enver. Enver 'Iron Hand' Demirel. His surname meant, quite literally, Iron Hand, in Turkish.

Enver's entry music to the ring had been Black Sabbath's 'Iron Man', chosen by his Brummie manager. He had found it embarrassing but, typically, Enver hadn't liked to say anything.

Enver 'Let's not make a fuss' Demirel.

The girls finished walking around the ring and slipped out between the ropes. The bell rang, the fight started.

It was two lightweights. Huss paid no attention, then she felt Hanlon stiffen and followed her gaze.

Walking into the VIP area was a small group of men. One tall and distinguished-looking in a dark suit and a red tie. Next to him a shorter man dressed in a blue tracksuit and trainers. He had snakelike unruly locks of dark hair, not wholly dissimilar from Hanlon's, that fell around his face. The other two men wore Crombies and had shaved heads, like a kind of uniform, which, in a sense, it was.

Huss noticed people staring, but in a kind of surreptitious way, and the crowd of people gathered in the walkways between the chairs and the walls magically parted as if for royalty.

Dave Anderson had arrived. His eyes unerringly found Hanlon's over the sea of faces and their glances met. He inclined his head curtly and sat down. The evening was beginning.

Hanlon and Huss watched more punters file into the York Hall – no sign of Hinds yet. There was a cough to one side of Hanlon. It was another of Anderson's shaven-headed associates and a man in his fifties, paunchy, with a flat, almost Aztec face, composed of planes and angles. He was somehow compellingly good-looking and wore a jaunty trilby hat and a loud jacket. Ringlets of dark hair fell down from under the hat.

'You must be Cliff,' said Hanlon. Despite having met him once years ago, she would never have recognized him now.

'You must be psychic,' he said. Despite his comparative age, he was still attractive. Almost literally: there was a cocky, confident swagger about him that exuded an almost tangible pull.

'No, I can read, that's all,' she replied, looking at his knuckles.

His gaze followed her eyes and he suddenly grinned and looked at Huss. 'DI Huss?' She nodded. Marcus Hinds's uncle said, 'Please follow me.'

Clifford Hinds led them with his rolling, swaggering walk, his large, handsome face thrust aggressively forward. They passed through a pair of frosted double doors into the back corridors of the York Hall.

The two women, followed by the silent skull-headed form of Anderson's underling, like the Angel of Death in a Crombie, walked behind Cliff up flights of stairs and down corridors until they came to an office door at the end of a silent, linoed hall. They could hear the muted roar of the boxing downstairs.

A familiar figure stood outside the door, tall and thin, tonight coolly elegant in a three-piece light grey Prince of Wales check suit.

'In here, DI Huss,' said Morris Jones. His eyes were their usual hooded, slightly glazed slits.

Huss nodded and the door closed behind her.

Jones turned his attention to Cliff and the muscle.

'You two can go,' he said dismissively. They nodded and did so. Morris Jones and Hanlon watched them disappear down the corridor.

'Fucking bell-ends,' said Jones dismissively.

He looked down at Hanlon; he was about a head taller. Her cold grey eyes met his. I'm glad I won't have to fight him, she thought. Morris Jones was like Death's emissary.

'So, you never took that money we gave you.' He gave the words a feeling of regret, as if Hanlon had missed some kind of rare opportunity to finally make an intelligent decision.

'You didn't give me any money, Morris,' Hanlon's tone was clipped, annoyed, 'that was for Mark Whiteside's medical expenses. And no, I didn't. It's all in that escrow account. You'll be able to have it back soon.'

'He's still in that coma.'

Hanlon nodded. 'He's being operated on in a couple of weeks. It's on the NHS, I don't need your money now, Anderson can have it back.'

'He thought you'd say that.' Just how did they know about Whiteside's op? thought Hanlon, irritated. Anderson had so much information at his disposal. But who would refuse a request from Anderson? Not if you wanted to live.

'I'll pass the message on,' said Jones.

They fell silent. It wasn't an awkward silence, neither of them liked making small talk, both of them were content saying nothing.

'You did earn it, Hanlon,' he pointed out.

She looked at him in surprise. 'Not really.'

'The *vor*, that Myasnikov, dead. That firm of his, dead and buried. I know, I had to organize the cleaning up.' He sighed and shook his head. 'Dust to dust.'

'I didn't kill anyone, Morris.'

'Of course you didn't, Hanlon.' Spoken in the tone of one humouring a child. Hanlon glared at Morris Jones, her glance taking in his immaculately polished shoes, the razor-sharp creases in his suit. It suddenly occurred to her that when Jones dressed he was probably dressing for death – either his own or someone else's.

Jones's own mortality was a constant companion. Any day, any evening, any night, some rival of Anderson's might decide to remove him from the equation, or a job might go terribly wrong, or simply one day his body might pack it in from the heroin he used. An overdose, a heart attack. Jones was perpetually skating on thin ice.

He didn't care, he lived for the moment. She reflected with a rare stab of humour that that made Jones quite trendy, what with all the current vogue for mindfulness. Perhaps he could set up as a lifestyle coach.

'I don't kill people for money like you, Morris.' Their eyes locked. Mutual dislike but mutual respect.

He looked down at her with genial contempt. 'No, the difference between us is that for me it's an occasional part of my job, but you' – he emphasized the word 'you', it was like being jabbed in the chest by an accusing finger – 'you choose to do it. You just pretend it's self-defence or that you had no choice, which is a load of old bollocks. You're a fucking hypocrite.'

She glared at him, but part of her thought, You can't deny it, it's true. You like hurting people. You've got a problem.

'Anyway,' he said, stretching, 'that's enough small talk, you want to stay and babysit your mate or do you want to come and watch the fights? You're quite handy with your fists, I hear.'

It sounded quite like a challenge. She decided to take it as such. Hanlon felt something snap inside her. It had been the mention of Whiteside, a man that she adored, that had done it. She took a step toward Jones and looked up into his eyes, expressionless as a crocodile's.

'You name the time and place, Jones. I'll be there,' she hissed. Her turn now. She jabbed him hard in the chest with her forefinger. 'Anytime.'

He smiled down at her.

'Well, Hanlon, I'm sure the day will come and when it does,' he adjusted the cufflinks in his shirt and straightened his tie, 'all your troubles will be over.' He turned on his heel and took a pace down the corridor, stopped and turned to look back at her.

'Because you'll be dead.'

CHAPTER THIRTY-SEVEN

Earlier that day, while Huss busied herself with her duties regarding Schneider, Enver concentrated on his: cooking.

RNF (Rhein-Neckar Fernsehen) TV were currently interviewing Schneider in the drawing room of the lodge. Enver found himself making yet another batch of sandwiches and coffee and tea for the media company and for Bayerisches Fernsehen, the big Bavarian TV company, who were patiently waiting their turn.

He sliced and buttered bread, added fillings and garnishes, took tray-bakes that he'd made from the oven. He was doing simple food, a lot of it, but of an exemplary high quality. Ironically he found himself slightly sneering at the low level of expertise needed to do all this in comparison to his pressurized kitchen duties the other day. He caught himself doing that and smiled bitterly at himself – once more, he was falling back into chef's thinking.

Enver spoke serviceable German and as he bustled in and out of the living room he caught snatches of Schneider's interview:

'... I'm not saying all Muslims are bad, not at all, but their values are incompatible with Western democracy. They execute gays, they force women to stay at home and cover their heads, if they're liberal, and their faces and hands if they're conservative...'

Enver, silently seething, put the sandwiches down on a table and went to get the drinks. He came in again:

'... Christiane died protecting not just me but all of you. Can any of you name a single Muslim country that has a free press? Oh, you're happy to criticize me and my policies. But I'm trying to save Germany!'

Schneider paused dramatically, the cameras lingered on his powerful, good-looking face, his expensive haircut. He looked into the lens, his blue eyes moist, and a single tear rolled down his cheek:

'Christiane Hübler died for you all. I will never forget her. Neu Schicksal will never forget her. We must never forget her.'

'*Danke schön*, Herr Schneider, *vielen danke*,' said the visibly moved Bavarian TV interviewer.

'Murdered by Muslim immigrants who want to enslave us and destroy our way of life. *Wir mussen niemals vergessen*!'

Hübler's death, thought Enver, had been a wonderful thing for Schneider. He was energized, the press were clamouring for interviews. He had hundreds of new followers on Twitter. Dr Florian Kellner, his political media adviser, was beside himself with excitement.

And while they work themselves into a lather about killer Muslims, thought Enver, here I am making them cakes and bloody sandwiches.

Enver's day wore on and on. Several times he had to jog up to the hotel to fetch more food. He then cooked a vast amount of chicken and apricot tagine and couscous for the assembled press for their dinner. He was tired, he had a headache and he felt increasingly irritated. Nobody said thank you. Nobody tipped him.

Nearly three million Muslims in the UK and how many of them were involved in terrorism? Just a tiny, tiny percentage and many of them not really British, like Jihadi John, now no more, who had been more Kuwaiti than anything.

Who's trying to keep you alive? he thought, angrily cooking up more couscous for the German film crews and Radio Oxford who had now arrived.

Who's cooking your bloody dinner, ingrates?

Bastards.

Muller had tethered the demon dog up somewhere. It was quite tempting to go and find it, unchain it and watch it go at the media. Really give them something to film.

Five o'clock came up on the kitchen clock in the lodge. Enver went in search of Schneider and found him with the blubbery-lipped, fat-faced Dr Florian Kellner, his number two deputy, who had flown out from Germany to be with him.

Enver momentarily wondered about the wisdom of having leader and deputy leader under the same roof. Eggs in one basket, he thought. Then he yawned; he'd been up since five a.m. and he wouldn't finish until midnight. Typical hours for a Michelin hotel chef. He was almost too tired to care.

'I'm going to take a break now,' he said, 'for an hour. Is there a room you're not using?'

He knew there were four bedrooms upstairs, on the ground floor was the kitchen, dining room, living room and study.

Schneider said, 'You can go back to the hotel if you like.'

Enver shook his head. 'I'd prefer to be here for now,' he said, 'just in case.' With Hübler dead at the hands of Arzu he could hardly afford to be careless. 'Besides, it's hardly worth going back for an hour.'

Kellner said approvingly, 'I applaud your attitude.'

Schneider smiled. 'Go downstairs. In the treatment room down there, there's a bed.' He turned to Florian. 'Go and show him.'

'I'll be back at half six.' Enver turned and wearily walked out of the lounge into the hall and down the stairs to the treatment room.

There was a variety of interesting things to be seen down there. Florian Kellner, who in Enver's eyes looked like a huge baby in a suit with glasses and his pouty, fleshy mouth, pointed them out.

'All this stuff exists up at the hotel but this lodge is for the very rich and they don't like having to share,' he explained. 'Or, I suppose, if they're famous they don't want to be seen with a tube up their ass having a colonic irrigation.'

There was a sauna, a little steam room, a couple of massage couches with Velcro straps for arms and legs.

'Why the restraints?'

Kellner smiled. 'It's those hot stones and cupping and stuff like that where you're supposed to be immobile. I think it's *Quatsch* myself, but rich people like mumbo-jumbo. I suppose if you're strapped down you have to endure it without being able to get up and go.' He looked around him and his eyes alighted on a suitable example of holistic 'medical' nonsense.

'I mean, look at some of this *Scheiss*! Like that.'

He pointed to a large barrel-shaped object, the height of a tall man, like an immersion tank in an airing cupboard.

'It's a cryosauna, like a walk-in deep freeze. You go in there and stand around at minus eighty or whatever. It's supposed to be good for you.' He snorted. 'Complete rubbish. I freely admit I haven't practised medicine for a while but I can't see that working.'

Enver shuddered. He had had enough experience of walk-in deep freezes in restaurants. He hated being inside them. He hated the cold, he was claustrophobic. He looked at the LED display on a panel. It was currently minus forty. There was a keypad to open the door.

'Some woman employee at a wellness centre in the USA got locked in one of these a while ago, died in about twenty minutes,' said Kellner. 'Please don't ring reception for the combination. We don't want you dead as well!'

'I won't,' promised Enver. There was a sofa by the wall, it looked so inviting. 'I'll just sleep on that.'

Kellner nodded. 'See you at half six.'

Enver watched as the fat man padded away up the stairs. There was something innately creepy about him, he thought. At least Schneider wouldn't need to worry about his right-hand man jockeying for power. Nobody would vote for Kellner.

Enver kicked his shoes off and collapsed on the sofa. He was asleep in about two minutes.

CHAPTER THIRTY-EIGHT

'Hello, Melinda,' said Marcus Hinds.

The borrowed office was simple: window, blinds, desk, two chairs and a corkboard on the wall next to a scuffed, gun-metal grey filing cabinet that had seen better days.

Hinds looked good, she thought. Less a journalist, more an edgy male model, the kind who is filmed in black and white, a romantic bad boy. He had the looks, he had the cheekbones. Even the stress on his face looked a little like designer stubble, artfully applied. He was like an actor playing 'man on the run'. It was a look that was fine for a drunken one-night stand, but not for a murder suspect. Huss looked at him coldly.

'DI Huss.' Her voice was flat, cold, official.

'I'm sorry,' he said. This time he sounded like he genuinely meant it.

'So,' Huss said, 'you've got some explaining to do.' She took out her notebook and a pen.

'On the record?' asked Hinds.

'Not really,' said Huss. 'This isn't a statement, but I want to make sure I've got your version of events straight.' She looked him in the eye. Close-up he didn't look so good, he looked unwell, tired, gaunt, twitchy.

'You might as well come back with me, you're going to have to turn yourself in at some stage,' she went on. 'It's absolutely pointless otherwise. How long do you think that you can hide? What are you going to do, relocate to Margate and work in a burger van? Become a rent boy in Mykonos? Get real, Marcus.'

'I know that.' His voice was impatient. 'But I want to make sure that certain people are nicked first, and then at least there's a chance I'll be protected in prison so I can testify against them. If, DI Huss, I go into remand, as I will with two murder charges hanging over me—'

'One murder charge; the CPS aren't sure about Elsa.'

'Whatever, I'll have Al-Akhdaar after me, and the anarchists, not just Eleuthera but any of their affiliates. I must say I am more concerned, though, with the Muslims. So, just for now, I think I'll give jail a miss.' He paused. 'Tempting as your offer is.'

Huss shrugged. 'Your choice. Begin at the beginning.'

It didn't take long.

It had all started with an article he had written for a national daily on the dark web, that part of the internet dedicated to illegality. It had been about the Catalan anarchist hacking community in Calafou in Catalonia in Spain. Then a chance remark overheard in a bar in Las Ramblas in Barcelona had put him on the path of Eleuthera.

'It was exciting stuff, DI Huss. Remember too that these are people who are dedicated to bringing civilization as we know it down. And they have links with some very big tech companies who don't believe they have any obligation to pay tax. In fact, some of them are actively pursuing the idea of creating floating tax havens. I don't need to remind you of how much tax Facebook paid in the UK last year, do I? About the same as you.'

He met old hippies, cyber-punks, disaffected left-wingers. A leaflet given to him in a hipster bar in Shoreditch led to a squat collective in Bristol.

Anyway. A whisper, a rumour in a pub about Eleuthera linking up with Class War and other anarchist groups, united by a love of violence and incentivized by the success of IS.

'They figure if they kill people too, and film it and post it on social media, they'll be heroes to the young, the idealistic and the dispossessed. The greater the violence, the greater the appeal. It's working for them on the continent, it's baby steps here. But all they need are some high attention killings to raise their media profiles; a few thousand people will soon favourite their death porn or like their beheadings.'

Huss nodded, she remembered the sinister Dr Smithfield making the same point.

'So they're in bed with Al-Akhdaar. The Muslims think an Islamic state will fill the void. Eleuthera just want to destroy, smash it all up. Actually, now I come to think of it, maybe they're worse than the Muslims, at least they're idealistic.'

Hinds shook his head. He went nervously to the window, peered out, and then his eyes flickered up and down, as if their agents might have followed him to the York Hall. He drew the blind.

'"My enemy's enemy is my friend." That's the reason they're in bed together. They both hate liberal democracy, they both hate capitalism, they both want to destroy. They would like to turn Britain into Syria, smoking ruins with themselves as warlords. Build mounds of skulls of the heads of their enemies.'

Hinds sighed and pushed his hand through his long black hair.

'I have evidence, recordings of Eleuthera with figures influential in major political parties, meetings with Al-Akhdaar. They have contacts in the police so I have to be careful. A selection of it was on that memory stick that I left you.'

Evan Collins, thought Huss, mournfully. Was it really unreadable or had Evan Collins rendered it so? It was ironic, given that computers were so omnipresent, how few people, herself included, really knew how they worked.

He carried on, Huss mechanically taking detailed notes. It all sounded very plausible, that was for sure.

Then she thought of Hanlon, her sceptical face. She decided to play devil's advocate.

'All of this is just unsubstantiated, though. What you are facing, Marcus, is a bit more concrete than speculation.'

Hinds shifted uncomfortably in his chair. Huss leaned forward over the desk in an intimidating way.

'You say you were framed. Evidence says your prints on the murder weapon. You say you dropped it in a skip and they must have fished it out and placed it next to the body. Well, if they did, no one saw them do it.'

Did Elsa see them do just that? she wondered. Was that why they killed the old woman rather than simply take Hinds's hard drive away? She paused and looked hard at Hinds, his eyes downcast, and continued.

'You say someone tried to kill you. A witness says you attacked them on the stairs. You say that there's a big anarchist conspiracy. Your girlfriend says you're violent and paranoid. Oh, and she says that she's nothing to do with Eleuthera; an anarchist, yes, a terrorist, no.'

She folded her arms intimidatingly on the table and looked hard at Hinds, then she continued, 'You are one of the last people, maybe the last person, to see a murdered woman whom you had specifically gone to visit. Is there anything else? Oh yes, silly me, running away from a crime scene, Marcus. A man who has evaded the police and refuses to hand himself in.'

'I've explained all that,' protested Hinds.

Huss shook her head. 'No, no you haven't. And,' she continued, 'there's more. You have a family with connections to organized crime. In fact, not only that, you're being sheltered by organized crime. Maybe one or two of these could be explained as unfortunate coincidences, but, Marcus, you're doing quite a good job of building up a fairly watertight case against yourself.'

'What do you expect me to do?' His voice was sulky, a petulant child.

Huss stood up.

'I don't expect anything.' She was tired of being jerked around by people. A wave of anger welled up inside her. 'What you will do is provide this proof you say you've got, then I can have something tangible to show my boss who's firmly convinced of your guilt, a feeling I can thoroughly understand, and you'll hand yourself in.'

She stood up and Hinds looked at her miserably.

'If you don't,' she buttoned her coat up, 'I'll turn up at Dave Anderson's properties with warrants for your arrest. All of them. I'm sure Mr Anderson has nothing whatsoever to hide and will be just thrilled to know it's thanks to you that he's got the Old Bill wandering around his gaffs, probably taking selfies of themselves. He's famously tolerant, I believe.'

She walked to the door and turned round.

'Three days.'

Then she stalked out of the office and childishly slammed the door behind her.

My God, she thought, I'm getting like Hanlon.

CHAPTER THIRTY-NINE

'Ladies and gentlemen, we are now starting our descent to Stuttgart airport.'

The BA plane touched down quietly and efficiently in the state capital and Hanlon, carrying only her handbag, was quickly through passport control and immigration. She strode down to the S-Bahn and then she was on her way to a morning meeting that she felt sure would clarify exactly what was happening with Schneider.

Ever since she had taken the phone from the anarchist thug, her view of Eleuthera's role in things had changed. There had been information held in its memory that simply hadn't added up to the narrative as she had perceived it up until now.

She had always felt that there was something missing from the bigger picture and now she was tantalizingly close to putting her finger on it.

This had all started in Germany. She felt sure that the key to it all lay in Germany.

In particular it led her to query Marcus Hinds and his claims of what had been happening. She had also checked again with Forensics. Whilst it was true that Jamie Kettering, the anarchist who had died on the stairs, had died because of a loss of blood, the injuries to his head that he had suffered prior to that would probably have killed him anyway.

The idea that Hinds had been some innocent bystander seemed increasingly unlikely. Hinds was a killer whichever way you looked at it.

She got out at the main station in the centre of the city. The view from the street outside was that of a gigantic building site, traffic and a plethora of Mercedes-Benz stars on top of buildings. Stuttgart is Mercedes-Benz's home and also that of LBBW, the gigantic investment bank, whose logo seemed equally ubiquitous.

Hanlon took a cab to her appointment with Meyer, who had been suggested to her as the best source of information for the Gunther Hart investigation. As the car drove her through the prosperous Stuttgart streets she caught the occasional glimpse of Schneider wearing a sober suit and concerned expression on posters for his Neu S party. The taxi driver spoke good English and she asked him what *Was zu viel ist. Ist zu viel* – which was the slogan on the poster – meant.

'Enough is enough,' he said.

I can go along with that, she thought.

The taxi pulled up outside a formidable-looking building. You could have almost guessed its function. Hanlon walked up to the front desk.

'*Landeskriminalamt* Department, Claudia Meyer,' said Hanlon to the handsome man on reception in the blue uniform as efficient-looking police streamed past.

Five minutes later Hanlon was sitting with Meyer in a

pleasant open-plan office, more or less identical to the ones she was used to, except the ambient background noise was in German and she noticed that the keyboards attached to the monitors were subtly differently configured and had symbols such as the double 's', ß, and umlauts, that didn't feature in English.

Meyer looked at her colleague who she guessed slightly outranked her rank of *Kriminalkommissar*, not that it mattered. Her eyes took in Hanlon's strong face, her easy, graceful, athletic build.

She was impressed with what she saw.

'So how can I help?' Her English was impeccable.

'Wolf Schneider,' said Hanlon. 'Wolf Schneider. Christiane Hübler, Frank Muller.'

'*Ja, stimmt.*' Meyer had thought that would be the case. Over coffee, she explained Schneider's rise from poster boy of AfD, the largest right-wing party, to heading his own breakaway movement which was challenging his former right-wing party for supremacy in the polls.

'AfD's vote, the anti-Muslim vote, had doubled from four *prozent*, sorry, per cent, to eight per cent but Schneider's party is polling at ten to twelve in some places, maybe more. He's the coming man.' She clicked on her PC and Hanlon was looking at Wolf Schneider. There was a slogan underneath.

'Germany needs a real man,' translated Meyer.

'What about Hübler? Are they an item?' Hanlon couldn't think of a reason why it mattered but still, somehow, she felt it did.

Meyer shrugged. 'Christiane Hübler had a record for shoplifting. She claims, claimed, it was a Turkish shopkeeper

208

who had framed her, she hates Turks.' She clicked away at the keyboard, found what she was looking for. 'Yes, here we are: "Filthy, kebab-munching rapists", she described them to *Bild*.'

Unless of course they were good-looking and in her bed.

'Well,' said Hanlon, 'that's fairly clear.'

'It was rumoured she was a member of a swingers' club here in Stuttgart,' said Meyer.

'So for her to look for a one-night stand wouldn't be unusual?' Hanlon asked.

'I wouldn't have thought so,' said Meyer. 'How could it be? Not if you're a member of a sex club.'

'And how about in a relationship with Schneider?'

Meyer scratched her head; a heavily built officer brought them more coffee. He was bald and tough-looking. '*Danke schön*, Lucas. Oh, Lucas, *hier ist* DCI Hanlon, Metropolitan Police.'

'*Angenehm!*' said Lucas gruffly and shook a hairy, leathery hand with Hanlon. He smiled at her and she smiled back with genuine warmth. He was like a German version of Enver. Lucas put the coffee down and moved away. That was another Enver trait – he never felt the need to offer his opinion of what was happening or try and add his presence to encroach on what she was up to. The same could not be said of many of her male colleagues.

'In a relationship with Schneider?' mused Meyer. 'I doubt it. Even if he was, he wouldn't let on. He's a big female following and he's a genius at stage-managing things. He's like a boy band member – girls want them to be single so they can dream that they have a chance.'

'Would Hübler's sex life be a problem politically?' asked Hanlon.

Meyer considered the question. 'If she were involved with ethnic minorities, refugees, say, then yes, it would surely be a problem. It would be a gift to Schneider's enemies.'

Hanlon nodded and asked, 'Muller?'

'A cheap, violent thug. I'm sure you've got lots of them. He's got a record, violent this, violent that. Pretty much what you'd expect, really.'

'Good, I thought so. Now, Al-Akhdaar?'

She cut Meyer short after a couple of minutes; it was plain she had little to add on the shadowy Islamic death cult. A German ISIS. As sinister and as mundane as that.

'Of course,' said Meyer, 'they made their name here with the murder of Gunther Hart.'

She showed Hanlon a photo of Hart. She caught her breath; Hart was stunning. He had a mop of curly hair and the same kind of innocent–depraved face as Robert Mapplethorpe. The Fallen Angel look. He was lying half-naked on a chaise longue, wearing a pair of ripped, skinny jeans. The outline of his cock and balls was high definition.

'I would,' said Claudia Meyer, catching Hanlon's eye, 'wouldn't you? Even Lucas said if he was a bit pissed he might.' She sighed. 'And he did good works, made lots of money in real estate development. He was incredibly popular round here, one of those businessmen who are actually cool, which is such a rarity. His funeral brought Heidelberg to a standstill. After that killing and the YouTube video, Schneider's Neu Schicksal shot up in popularity.'

'He was on the same hit list as Schneider?'

Meyer nodded. 'Yes, the Rhein-Neckar Enemies of Islam.'

'That's a very specific geographical area.' Not just the Enemies of Islam, but the equivalent of the Thames Valley Enemies of Islam. Very German, Hanlon thought, and it seemed Meyer agreed with her.

'Al-Akhdaar are a German *terrorismus* organization. Of course they'd be specific, Germans are. It's a national trait. This is Stuttgart. Gottlieb Daimler and Robert Bosch weren't vague.'

'Fair enough,' said Hanlon.

'Any more questions?' asked Meyer.

'Just one.' Hanlon took her tablet out of her bag. It was really for this that she had come all the way here.

They were almost an afterthought in the photographs section of the phone she had taken, but it was a folder that its owner had seen fit to keep locked, although not safe from Albert Slater's prying fingers.

The fact that they had been so carefully hidden had aroused her attention in the first place.

Three photographs, all colour. The images clear, startling, dreamlike.

The first one a door, darkness, at night, an alley in a city, off a wet street, the black tarmac slick with rain. Puddles reflecting the crimson light. A red and white neon sign over the door. The glare of the neon made all but two of the letters illegible. The last letters were ... *ub*.

Whatever kind of club it was, it certainly wasn't classy or the kind of place you would take your mother.

The second, the same as above except shot at a slight angle to take in the bonnet and number plate of a black

Mercedes E Class containing the letter S, denoting Stuttgart.

It didn't mean that it had to be Stuttgart, of course, but the car was almost posed there as if it had been Photoshopped to indicate the location of the premises. That was, of course, the point of the photos. The premises.

The third. The car was gone now, the door ajar. Open for business.

The picture had a message. Come inside... all earthly delights await you in here... all your erotic dreams can come true, no matter how strange... Nothing, but nothing, is forbidden...

The pictures were tantalizingly close to forming a narrative.

Come inside...

The Something Club, in Stuttgart.

The passage behind the door was womb-red, an almost universal signifier of sexuality. Standing in the half-open doorway was a dwarf girl in a miniskirt and fishnets. She was like a parody of the girls Hanlon had seen the night before in the boxing ring.

She wasn't simply a midget, or short, she had the classically configured dwarf physique. It was this that made Hanlon believe she would be eminently traceable. There couldn't be that many dwarf prostitutes in one town.

'Do you know where this is?' she asked.

Meyer looked at it and shook her head.

'It's obviously the something or other Club and that's a Stuttgart plate on the Merc. I guess it's a brothel. Hang on. Lucas!' she called.

Her colleague wandered over from where he'd been chatting to an attractive policewoman. Meyer spoke to him in German. He looked at the photos and spoke to Meyer who translated, 'He says it's the old Oskar's Klub, in the Bohnenviertel. It closed down years ago. That area has all been sanitized for tourism now.' She looked at Lucas. '*Was habt du sagt? Langsamer, bitte... Ja... genau... ganz schon...* The girl is Lottie, a dwarf prostitute. Oskar's was a club where you could have sex with freaks, like overly pierced whores or really hard-core S&M, golden showers, that kind of thing, and it catered to fetishists too.'

'Is Lottie still around?'

Lucas said something to Meyer who nodded. He got his phone out, spoke to someone. She caught the word *Bahnhof*.

'She's got a place near the station,' said Meyer. 'Do you want to go and see her?'

'Very much,' said Hanlon. 'Lottie's the key to all of this.'

She looked at the photo one more time before she put her phone away. The small dwarf girl. The half-open door of the brothel.

A world of secrets. A world of lies.

Come inside...

Hanlon sat in the back of the police BMW as Lucas drove skilfully through the streets of Stuttgart.

'Tell me more about Oskar's?'

Meyer directed the question at Lucas in an awkward three-way conversation. Hanlon gathered it was a members' club for the experimental or deviant, certainly not for the faint-hearted. It was also exclusive, they had sky-high membership fees, a six-month waiting list, and a reputation for utter discretion.

Those few paparazzi brave or foolish enough to try and get photos of clients had a habit of having their equipment and fingers smashed. The message soon got around.

'Who owned it?' asked Hanlon.

Meyer asked Lucas, who grunted a reply.

'Out-of-towners,' said Meyer.

'*Russisch Mafia,*' elaborated Lucas. There's a surprise, thought Hanlon.

'Is it the kind of place Gunther Hart might have belonged to?'

Meyer said, 'It's *exactly* the sort of place that Hart would have belonged to. He'd have found it funny, he liked to shock.'

Up until now they had been making reasonable progress through the streets of Stuttgart but as they drew near the station, they came to a grinding halt. The station, as Hanlon had realized when she had arrived, was undergoing a major rebuilding programme. Lucas swore irritably as several roads he took or tried to take were closed, sometimes just ending in enormous man-made canyons. The chaos, which one would have expected in London, seemed slightly un-Germanic to Hanlon.

Eventually they hit upon a road that seemed acceptable to Lucas and about five minutes later they parked up outside an anonymous apartment building.

Lucas said something and Meyer translated for Hanlon's benefit.

'He says he'll wait with the car.'

The three of them got out and Lucas leaned against the bonnet and lit a cigarette. Meyer rang the bell marked C. Schwartz and a voice answered. She said something and the door buzzed open.

Hanlon and Meyer walked up the concrete stairs, their footsteps echoing in the well of the building.

On the first floor there was a door open and a sardonic dwarf woman stood regarding them with an unfriendly expression. It was a pose that almost matched the one on the phone, except this was no luridly, explicitly sleazy nightclub. She too smoked, a cigarette was burning between her fingers.

They walked into her apartment. Meyer started making introductions in German and Lottie cut her off. 'I speak English well enough,' she said. 'What do you want?'

She was wearing a housecoat, slippers and an unfriendly expression. Hanlon looked around her apartment, which was studiously anonymous. Everything, floor, walls, furniture, was magnolia, fawn or tan. She suddenly realized that it was almost certainly Lottie's workplace and that she would want to screen her private life from her clients. There had to be another place that Lottie lived, even if it was only a room, rather than this sterile, beige environment.

One patch of brilliant colour did exist in the apartment. On the glass coffee table in front of the sofa was a pack of tarot cards laid out as if for a reading. They were old-fashioned and well-used, the evocative pictures archetypal forms familiar to everyone. Lottie looked at Hanlon almost knowingly.

She pointed at two cards that were turned up. One was

a card of a stern-faced woman sitting between two pillars. There was a large brass-bound book open on her lap, in her hand a quill.

'*The Book of the Law*,' said Lottie touching the card, indicating the open volume. Then she pointed at the twin pillars. 'Jachin and Boaz; Security and Strength.'

'Who is the woman?' asked Hanlon. There was something about the cards that made you want to ask questions. That was partly their function, she supposed.

Lottie looked at Hanlon.

'The High Priestess, I guess that's you.' She paused. 'She represents Love and Hatred.' She closed her eyes and, as if quoting from memory said, 'Furtherance of the ends of destiny.'

'Did the cards tell you why I was here as well?' asked Hanlon with polite scepticism.

'I don't need the tarot for that,' said Lottie, pointing at a MacBook. 'I've got the real news on a variety of feeds.'

The flat was small, just the lounge, bedroom, galley kitchen and bathroom. The bedroom, through the open door, had been fitted up as a kind of sex dungeon.

'Still turning tricks, Lottie?' asked Meyer, as if expressing polite interest.

'I'm moving into tarot readings now,' she said, 'but, yes, I'm still hooking. I'm still very much wanted. Do you find it odd that men want to fuck me, *Kriminalinspektor*, a misshapen hag like me?'

'Takes all sorts, Lottie.' Meyer shrugged.

'I've always been in demand from men, the richer and more successful the better,' said Lottie, proudly. 'Stuttgart's very good for me. I must have fucked the boards of Germany's largest industrial *Konzerne*.' She cupped her generous breasts in her hands. 'God alone knows how much coke they've snorted off my tits and ass. I'm surprised they haven't dropped off.'

Hanlon took the tablet out, the photos.

'Remember these?'

She leaned over for a better look. 'Oh, yes, DCI Hanlon, *natürlich*.' She looked at Meyer. 'My readings are private, you can wait outside.'

Meyer nodded. 'I'll be in the car with Lucas,' she said to Hanlon. She stood up and left the room. They heard the main door close, the echoes dying away in the hallway.

Lottie leaned forward and turned over the rest of the cards.

The Devil. The Lovers. Death, a grinning skeleton mounted upon a horse. The Tower Struck Down and lastly, the vain, gaudily dressed figure walking with carefree steps towards the waiting chasm, the Fool.

'So, would you like to hear about Al-Akhdaar and Wolf Schneider and Gunther Hart?' Lottie's voice was sarcastic and unfriendly, she was about to hurt someone and she had been relishing the prospect of doing so. Whores don't have hearts of gold, or at least not for their clients.

'Oh, yes, Lottie,' said Hanlon. '*Natürlich*.'

Half an hour she left the apartment.

An elaborate web of deceit uncovered by Lottie.

She had just one more thing to do in Stuttgart and then she could go home.

Now she knew for sure that more or less everything that Marcus Hinds had said had been a lie.

CHAPTER FORTY

DI Huss parked her Golf in the staff car park of the Rosemount and went in search of Czerwinski, the hotel manager. The investigative team had finished and the kitchens had now reopened. The hotel had bridged the catering hurdle by transferring all the cooking to a small satellite kitchen in another part of the building that was used to provide food for functions, weddings, business conferences and parties. For the harassed kitchen staff it had been yet another unwanted challenge to get over.

She found Czerwinski in his office looking tired and care-worn. He smiled at her.

'I only ever seem to see you when something bad happens.'

She knew he was referring back to the time that they had last met, in Oxford. Another death.

'Well, Irek, I am the police. We're not normally harbingers of joy.'

He nodded. 'The problem is the clientele, they seem to think it's very unfair a dead person should be inconveniencing them.'

She made a 'me too' gesture. 'That's the public for you. Moan, moan, moan.'

He smiled, picked up a letter. 'Old-fashioned. Not an email. "Dear sir, my husband and I have had our stay ruined by the activities of the police..."'

He put the letter down and looked at her over the desk. 'If Hübler had been famous they wouldn't moan. They'd be taking selfies. "This is me by the murder scene..." He added, 'This has been the worst couple of days of my life. How's the hunt going for Arzu?'

'Nothing as yet,' said Huss, 'but we'll get there.'

Unless he's already fled the country, she thought. The borders of Europe were at the moment in turmoil with hundreds of thousands of refugees. If he had done a runner, they wouldn't see him again. British border police wouldn't have troubled themselves about one person slipping out of the UK.

He could be in Chechnya by now, if he so desired, or equally he could be on his way to joining IS in Syria or Libya or Iraq or Boko Haram in Nigeria. She very much doubted that they would ever see him again.

Czerwinski said, 'Well, at least all of this is coming to an end. Schneider's leaving tomorrow...'

'Really?' said Huss. 'Nobody told me.'

She wasn't unduly concerned. Schneider and his party, Muller and Kellner and that dreadful dog, had nothing to contribute to the Hübler investigation.

'Yeah,' said Czerwinski. 'There's a helicopter coming tomorrow to pick them up from here and fly them to Heathrow.'

'What, and the dog?'

Czerwinski laughed. 'Can you imagine that in a helicopter?

No, that's being driven in Muller's van. Thank God they'll be out of everyone's hair.'

Huss nodded. She very much agreed. And the helicopter ride from one of Schneider's rich sponsors would mean that they needn't find him a car and driver. After the Hübler killing they could hardly entrust him to a limo service or taxi firm.

'Well, Irek,' she said, 'you've got your hotel back. No controversial guests lined up, I trust?'

He stretched in his old leather chair and looked around the crowded cubbyhole that was his office.

'At this level, DI Huss, they're all controversial in one way or another. Rich people, actors, rock stars, you don't usually get money by being nice and this is, after all, a very expensive hotel.'

Huss nodded.

'I suppose so. Anyway, I just came to say goodbye. Enver will leave tomorrow too.'

'Pity,' said Czerwinski. 'Harry Jones was going to make him a job offer. He came to see me earlier, for authorization. I said he was welcome to ask. He genuinely has no idea that he's not a proper chef.'

Huss laughed. Enver would be thoroughly alarmed to hear that. All his adult life had been spent in the quest to avoid working in the family restaurants, and circumstances kept nudging him in that direction.

'I'll tell him,' she said.

'Are you going over to the lodge to say bye to Schneider?' Czerwinski asked.

Huss shook her head. 'No, I've seen plenty of him. I think that I'll just head off home.'

She stood up to go and winced in pain. Supported her weight momentarily on the top of the chair. The painkillers were starting to wear off now and her back was hurting like hell.

Czerwinski noticed.

'You OK?' His voice was concerned.

'Bad back.' Huss thought, To put it mildly. It was excruciating.

'You should use the cryosauna down at the lodge,' he said. 'You can come over tomorrow if you want.' There was a hopeful tone in his voice and a slight look of optimistic determination and pleading in his gaze. 'Seriously, I've tried it. It works.'

Huss shook her head. 'Enver told me about that, it sounds a bit scary, like a walk-in freezer.' I'd hate to get trapped inside, she thought.

'I suppose that is more or less what it is,' said Irek. 'Do come tomorrow, I'll give you lunch.'

Huss smiled. Irek was making a pass at her, she thought.

'I'd take a lot of convincing, Irek.'

'Well,' Czerwinski said, 'obviously you wouldn't want to get locked in, but I get a bad back too, I'm on my feet for hours a day, and it works.' He shrugged. 'Maybe it's just psychological but I think that's what pain is, isn't it? Anyway, the combination's 2222, all the twos.'

'Thanks, but no thanks. Anyway, I'll be off now.'

She left his office, which was on the first floor overlooking the majestic sweep of the drive and the magnificent fountain, everything lit up in brilliant, hallucinatory-clear detail by halogen spotlights. She walked down the magnificent carpeted staircase and across the baronial splendour of the reception area, admiring the fake Gobelin tapestries on the walls, the statues in their recessed niches and the gigantic oil paintings with their pre-Raphaelite allegories of the virtue of industry.

She said goodnight to the attractive girls at the front desk and walked into the cold, November night air.

There was a brilliant moon overhead and an owl hooted nearby.

She toyed with the idea of going down to the lodge to say goodbye to Schneider, despite what she had said to Irek, but another knifelike jab of pain in her lower back made her head round the corner to the dimly lit staff car park.

As she approached her car, a dark figure purposefully made its way towards her. Huss felt a stab of alarm. Arzu was still at large, after all. She wondered what she would do if it was him. She certainly was in no fit state for a struggle.

'Who's that?'

'It's me, DI Huss.'

The figure stepped forward. It was Marcus Hinds.

CHAPTER FORTY-ONE

Hanlon left Lottie's apartment and walked down the stairs, turning over in her mind what she had just been told.

She went up to the unmarked police car and leant in the window. Meyer's sharp, intelligent face turned to Hanlon.

'I'm going to walk back to the *Bahnhof* to get the train back to the airport. Thanks for all your help,' said Hanlon. She wanted time to digest what she had just learned and space, literally, in which to think. Hanlon hated thinking sitting motionless, she wanted to feel the delight of movement, the lithe strength of her body moving.

'Did you get what you came for?' asked Meyer.

'Oh, yes, I most certainly did, 'said Hanlon.

The three of them shook hands and said their goodbyes. The sky was dark and a fine, cold rain started to fall. Hanlon walked slowly along the clean, broad streets of Stuttgart. There were quite a few people about, busy and purposeful. Lights were burning in houses and shops. The cafés were beginning to close. Hanlon thought with surprise, I like this place. Normally she didn't notice places that much, but Stuttgart, with its air of bustle and work ethic, suited Hanlon's slightly dour character. It was a place for the industrious and the hard-working.

On impulse, she walked into one of the cafés, sat down and ordered herself a large espresso and, uncharacteristically, some *Schwarzwald torte*. She hardly ever ate sweet things but it seemed to go with the country she was in.

The café was impeccable, small glass-topped tables, a prosperous clientele of wealthy-looking Stuttgart ladies, the various cakes under glass; Hanlon counted seven different varieties, from the chocolate cake that she was eating to *Apfel Torte*, *Baumkuchen* and *Linzer Torte*. She thought fondly of Enver, how he would agonize about his weight before deciding that actually he probably could get by with a few slices. In fact, the more she thought about it, Enver would be perfectly capable of almost eating his own weight in the various cakes on offer.

And then moving along to the bread stacked neatly above.

Perhaps she ought to lay in a stock of cake to distract the Presa if need be. She smiled grimly to herself. Hanlon had taken steps to neutralize the dog if she had to. Her boyfriend... the term was hardly accurate... The man that she was having a relationship with... again, that was unsatisfactory... Hanlon was involved with a man, a senior officer in another country's security forces, and she had asked him to provide her with a solution to the Presa.

She thought momentarily of Serg and her bleak grey eyes softened. His hard gymnast's build, his eyes, born to command, his almost ethereal good looks with his formidable military skills and easy, sarcastic charm.

She was fonder of Serg than she cared to admit. Had he been based in London she would probably have severed all connection with him. Having him at arm's length somewhere in central Europe suited her.

She could see him when she wanted, and that was very important. The idea that she might have to be at someone else's beck and call was intolerable.

And he was an incredible lover.

Then again, she thought, so am I.

As her strong, white teeth closed down on the cake she put Serg from her mind and thought of what had brought her here. Images of Lottie's tarot cards whirled through her head.

The Devil?

Was that Marcus Hinds, the plausible liar. Suave, good-looking, horribly plausible?

The Lovers, the naked figures smiling at each other with naked lust. Schneider and Hübler?

And who was the Fool, walking thoughtlessly to their death without a care in the world?

She called the waitress over and paid, paused at the counter and, on impulse, bought Enver a selection of home-made chocolates which the smiling efficient woman gift-wrapped for her.

She left the warmth and light of the shop and was immediately consumed by the cold, damp, darkness.

Hanlon noticed the man immediately.

She had first seen him as she'd walked in the café, reflected in the large mirrors that ran along the back of the shop. He hadn't followed her in but had walked on past the door. Here he was again.

He was good-looking, in his mid-fifties, an overall impression of grey, from his full head of grey hair to his grey trousers and shirt, although his jacket and shoes were black. The rain didn't seem to worry him. He wasn't the kind of man who cared about discomfort. He had hard, watchful eyes, a battered nose and deep laughter lines that were at odds with the casual brutality of his features. He reminded her of Corrigan.

Police.

Hanlon's immediate thought. She was one, had been one for rather longer than she cared to think about. She felt she knew one when she saw one.

She sauntered along the shopping street near Schlossplatz, the big square in the centre of the town. Grey Man had a visible paunch and was heavy-set, built for strength, not speed. She crossed the Platz quickly, walked down the entrance to the U-Bahn, and ran through the busy, echoing subterranean place, towards one of the other exits on the far side.

She emerged by an art-nouveau cinema and headed off down a side street. The pavements around here were thronged with people and she thought she must have lost him, he wouldn't have been able to keep up with her. But maybe there was more than one?

Well, we'll soon find out, she thought.

Stuttgart lies in a valley and there are hills on two sides, steep hills. Hanlon had learnt from her Lufthansa in-flight magazine that the former terraced vineyards of the town had long ago been concreted over and built on, but many of the original steps, now staircases, remained, leading straight up the hills.

The hills, her friends. Hanlon did a lot of practice endlessly running up and down thigh-punishing gradients, it was what made her such a good performer, the ability to relish the pain. To recognize the agony and push through it. Pain didn't deter her, it spurred her on.

As if by magic, as she resurfaced several hundred metres away from where she had gone into the underpass with its labyrinth of exits, Grey Man reappeared, unhurried, on the other side of the street. So there was someone else as well as him tailing her then. He had to have been told, tipped off as to where she was. How many followers would she warrant? Six to eight bodies, she guessed. She headed for one of the hills rising up before her. Let's see how fit you are, she thought grimly to herself.

Hanlon was wearing Chelsea boots, far from ideal, but in trainers she could run a marathon in a respectable three hours. Even wearing boots she'd be good for half an hour, she thought. Grey Man looked like he'd have trouble on an escalator. She grinned wolfishly as she increased the pace of her stride. This is going to hurt you.

She strode down the road and then increased her stride to a jog, her hair bouncing in its familiar comforting rhythm. There was a main road with heavy traffic and Hanlon ran across it, weaving through the traffic, the faces of the other pedestrians expressing outrage at the flagrant jaywalking. It would have gone unnoticed in London, but not in Germany where such things are taken seriously.

Horns honked angrily.

From the safety of the other pavement she glanced back. Grey Man had given up the chase. He didn't seem worried

about it. He leant on the railings opposite and lit a cigarette. Their eyes met over the four lanes of traffic and even
from this distance she thought she could see the ghost of a
smile on his face.

Hanlon turned and strode away up a side street. She guessed that she'd still have others on her tail. Then she saw
what she was looking for: steps leading upwards at the end
of a walkway between two buildings, office blocks, glass,
chrome and marble.

The side of the tall hill rose up dauntingly, like a wall,
behind the buildings built along its base. One of the original,
thousand-year-old, stairways built by the original settlers
of Stuttgart cut into the side of the hill, now modernized
with proper steps and handrails, but still as steep and pre-
cipitous as running up an office block fire escape. She ran
for that and two men suddenly broke cover behind her like
pheasants flushed from a covey.

Hanlon hit the steps hard and fast. Head down, arms
pumping.

Who are they? The thought ran through her head as her
legs pistoned up the endless steps. Eleuthera? Or something
to do with what Lottie had just divulged? Had the dwarf
sold her down the river?

She must have run up a couple of hundred steps. Hanlon
glanced back after a couple of minutes. One of the two men
behind her in pursuit was visibly struggling and then he just
gave up, clutched the steel railing and looked up at her with
frustration. She could sense his chest heaving as he tried to
suck air into his burning lungs.

The other was still running, but appreciably slower now.

Hanlon felt great. Her breathing was smooth and regular. Perhaps I ought to go a bit slower, get on a city bike if I can find one when I reach the top, then cycle down to the river and jump in – we could make a triathlon out of this yet. See how fit you are.

She turned and ran ahead, then rounded a corner. She stopped abruptly in dismay.

She thought of Lottie's tarot card, the Fool. The blind idiot sauntering towards the yawning canyon. It hadn't occurred to her that this might refer to her, now it seemed it did. Her with her smug plan of just outrunning them without thinking of this.

Ahead of her, walking unhurriedly in her direction, was Grey Man and a companion. He raised his hand to the brow of his hat in a mock-friendly salute.

God, he's good, she thought. He must have worked out where she was headed and why and had a car on call to drive him up to Panoramastrasse, which was the name of the street at the top of the steps, and then head down to cut her off. From below she could hear the sound of footsteps as the other man made his way towards her.

She was trapped.

Hanlon thought furiously. Ahead was impossible, besides she had conceived a healthy respect for Grey Man. She just knew he'd be a vicious, tough old bastard to deal with. She turned, she'd run down, with any luck with the height and pitch of the steps the face of the man below would be level with her boot. She planned to kick him in the face and continue down.

Not a brilliant plan, but a plan.

The lights of Stuttgart lay spread out in the valley below. She could see the Mercedes star illuminated on top of the art deco railway station, her original destination. It twinkled mockingly at her.

It was almost as if it had been placed there as an ironic reminder of her plight. She took a deep breath.

Then, from behind her, a discreet cough. Hanlon froze and then turned round.

The fight starts here, she thought. There was the figure of a man, shrouded in darkness. He stepped forward so she could see his face. Tall, sardonic, those half-Tartar features that she knew so well.

Relief, anger, disbelief, then she found her voice. 'Serg, you fucking idiot!'

'Hello, Hanlon,' he said, and opened his arms.

Grey Man and his companion rounded the corner.

'*Boss, ti vi poriadke?*' Grey Man called out.

He smiled to himself at the absurdity of the question. His boss, a hard, frightening, driven man, looked more OK than he had ever seen him. Serg lifted his head from where he had buried it in Hanlon's hair.

'*Da, normalno. Vi vse mozhete idte.*' Serg dismissed them with polite indifference.

Grey Man and his companion walked past Serg and Hanlon. Their eyes met and he ran his gaze frankly over her as if evaluating his boss's taste in women. He smiled at her, saluted smartly, turned away and met up with their companion, who groaned as his burning legs straightened and he took another step up this endless stair.

'*A teper vse vimetaytes,*' said Grey Man to his juniors,

barking out the orders in his sonorous Moscow-accented Russian. Serg watched his security team climb slowly down the hill and away into the night.

'Shall we go?' he said to Hanlon, indicating the stairway in front of them.

'*Da*,' she said. It was one of two words of Russian she knew.

Nyet was the other. She wouldn't need that one tonight.

CHAPTER FORTY-TWO

'What the hell are you doing here, Marcus?' said Huss, her breath steaming in the cold, wintery night.

'Trying to get proof that I didn't kill anyone,' Hinds said irritably. He added, plaintively, 'Can we sit in your car, I'm freezing out here.'

Huss shook her head and pressed the key fob. They both got in the VW and she felt a momentary desire to just cuff him to the steering wheel and have done with it. Then call it in. She might well have done if her back hadn't been hurting so much. The last thing she wanted was a struggle in the cramped space of a car. What she really wanted was to go to bed, pull the sheets over her head and sleep.

'Go on then, talk!' Huss switched the heating on and Hinds rubbed his hands theatrically.

'I know that Eleuthera are planning something for tonight. I know a girl there and she's reliable. There's something big scheduled for Schneider. If we go there now, to the lodge, we'll be able to stop it, and I'll be vindicated. I'll get my story and then some.'

'You mean you think the charges against you will be

dropped and you'll make a fortune selling your story.' Huss's tone was sarcastic.

'God, yes!' Hinds's tone was fervent.

'Well, I'd better give Diplomatic Protection a call,' she said. 'They've still got a team up here at the Rosemount, or should have, I'll let them decide what to do.'

Hinds grew agitated. 'Are you crazy! You'll have half a dozen guys in hi-vis clothes waving sub-machine guns, two or three marked police cars, a 'copter with thermal imaging thundering overhead.'

'And a couple of dog handlers, probably,' agreed Huss. 'They love their dogs, Diplomatic Protection. All those woods.'

'Well, Eleuthera aren't going to do anything are they, then,' protested Hinds.

'Good.'

'But what about me?' wailed Hinds. Huss looked at his face, so close to hers in the front of the car. It was certainly not an act. Hinds plainly wanted to establish his innocence.

'It's not all about you,' said Huss. 'Innocent lives are at stake.'

Hinds was growing increasingly agitated. 'Think of Justice! Look, Melinda, I mean DI Huss, this is your big chance to nail the murderers of that old lady, Hübler and that bell-end Kettering. If you catch them here and now, they might well confess to the other killings.' He paused, changing his tack. 'Think how pleased your boss will be.'

Huss thought Templeman would not be pleased at all to be proven wrong. But as the idea sank in that Eleuthera would be put to bed and that smug bitch Georgie Adams would be facing jail time, the bait dangled by Hinds started to gain traction.

'What kind of thing are they planning?'

Hinds shook his head. 'I don't know exactly. I have a source in Eleuthera who has tipped me off.'

'Who?' asked Huss, sceptically.

Hinds shook his head in exasperation. 'A girl called Rowenna, she knew Elsa from the soup kitchen. Mark Spencer strong-armed her into revealing Elsa's whereabouts. She didn't know so she gave Spencer the name of an old boy, Harry someone.' He paused. 'She hasn't seen him since.'

Huss's heat sank. 'That's three days ago, Marcus, maybe four. He could be dead.'

'That's not my fault, is it?' said Marcus, sulkily. 'I've been on the run accused of murders I never committed. Perhaps he's fine, just lying low.'

'I'll deal with it later,' said Huss grimly. 'What did Rowenna tell you is going down?'

Hinds said, 'She doesn't know herself, but she does know it involves Arzu and Georgie. They're the two major players, after all.'

Assassination, presumably, thought Huss. Well, if she could move Schneider and Kellner out, she could move the protection team in via the entrance that Hanlon had used. Frank Muller and Wotan could fend for themselves. She could always, if worst came to the worst, stick the Germans in a cell at Summertown.

Three murders solved, a terrorist cell, maybe two, bust open. Ancillary arrests. Maybe too the chance for someone to take responsibility for the death of Elsa.

She saw Georgie Adams's smug face, gloating in her cleverness. Hinds carrying the can for her activities.

Huss decided to spare Hinds.

'OK, I'm going to go and fetch Schneider, get him out of harm's way. When that's done, I'll sneak the Protection boys in and I'll get a Divisional Support Team Group in. Schneider out, cops in. You stay here but, Marcus, you're coming in with me back to the station, OK? That has to be part of the deal. I can't let you go again. The meeting at the York Hall was off the record, this is very much on the record, have you understood that?'

'Sure, I knew you'd say that, I've come prepared for the nick. Uncle Cliff has arranged a brief for me who'll go out to wherever I'm held. It's all good.'

He was quite resigned now, it seemed, to spend some time locked up on remand.

'Fine.'

She got out of the car and gasped with pain from her back, paused to lean on the bonnet and straighten up. Using her palms to push her spine upright.

Not good.

She walked round to the front of the hotel and made her way step by painful step, walking exaggeratedly straight, as though she was on parade, to the front terrace, the mock Palladian frontage of the hotel lit up brilliantly like the front of the National Gallery transported to the middle of Oxfordshire.

She hobbled down the steps towards the lights of the lodge and followed the path to the main gate.

From behind it she heard savage barking and some curt command in German.

I wonder who that is? thought Huss to herself, sarcastically.

'*Wer ist das*?' Muller's gruff voice.

'It's DI Huss to see Herr Schneider.'

There was silence, then the gate swung open. The Presa, on a choke chain, strained forward, eager to get at her, its massive muscles ridged under the short fur. Its lips were drawn back from its teeth.

Muller leaned back to control the animal, putting his full weight behind restraining it. Huss kept a wary distance. Despite his great bulk, Huss could see he could barely hold back the beast. If it came at me, she thought, I'd be dead.

Muller jerked his head in the direction of the lodge and Huss walked up to the front door and banged on it.

Dr Florian Kellner let her in and closed the door behind her. Huss suddenly felt an enormous sense of relief that the solid oak lay between her and the Presa. The dog was seriously out of order.

Dr Kellner said pleasantly, 'And how may we help you tonight, DI Huss?'

Huss chose her words carefully. 'I have received information, credible information, that an attempt may be made to breach security here at the lodge tonight, and I would like to suggest that you and Herr Schneider come with me and we'll make alternative arrangements for your accommodation.'

Kellner frowned. With his bald head, fat face and rather blubbery lips, he looked a little like a petulant baby. Right now like a petulant baby that was somehow being denied a treat.

'Look, we've got visitors at the moment. Can I take you

downstairs to the treatment room to wait whilst we finish? It really won't take long, but it is confidential.' He smiled. 'That's politics for you, I'm afraid.'

'Of course,' said Huss. 'It's down here, isn't it?' She pointed to where a spiral stair disappeared down to the basement. It was very spa-like, a slim, curved metal handrail with thin metal hawsers running in parallel underneath, like you might get on a ship, and stone and glass steps with recessed lights leading down to the room below.

'I'll come with you,' said Kellner, 'make sure you are comfortable.'

His eyes bulged behind his glasses. God, he's creepy, thought Huss.

He led the way into the treatment room and indicated the sofa that Enver had slept on. 'Please have a seat.' She did so, gasping as she sat down.

'Back problems?' asked Kellner sympathetically. Huss nodded.

'Me too,' he said.

The room was very bright and Huss saw that although it was essentially a reclaimed basement, it had long narrow windows just under its ceiling so it would get some natural light during the day.

'We'll be about twenty minutes,' said Kellner. 'I'll come and fetch you. But don't worry, nobody will get past Frank and Wotan.'

Huss watched him go back up the stairs and closed her eyes, feeling the pain in her lower spine.

The sofa was extraordinarily uncomfortable to sit on. Standing up proved problematic. It was so sore she ended up in a kind of undignified twist with both hands on the sofa's arms, levering herself up, hissing with pain through her clenched teeth as she moved.

She stood there for a moment and took a couple of steps until she was leaning on the treatment bench. For a moment she considered lying on it, but she would have felt ridiculous to be found by Kellner like a crusader on a tomb or a corpse on a slab, and decided against it. Then her eye fell on the cryosauna. The red LED display lights said '-40'. And this was the device that Czerwinski hoped to inveigle her into? He had to be crazy. She walked over to it and tried the handle. It was locked and there to the right of the door she saw the keypad.

I wonder what it's like?

Couldn't hurt to try.

All the twos, thought Huss. She keyed the numbers in and heard a click. There was a red light and it changed to green to indicate occupancy as she opened the door.

She was curious to experience what forty degrees below zero would feel like. Perhaps it would numb the pain in her back. She was already uncomfortably over the recommended dosage of the ibuprofen she had in her handbag. Here was her chance.

The door swung fully open and Huss gasped aloud in shock and disgust at what was inside. It was horrible. She stared for a moment to make sure it was what she thought it was, not that there could be any doubt. And then she closed the door.

She heard a low growl behind her. She turned around slowly.

Muller and the Presa were at the top of the stairs, looking down at her.

'*Du liebe Zeit*!' said Muller softly.

Huss gasped, but it wasn't the bodyguard and the dog that caused it.

Georgie Adams's face appeared from behind Muller's body as she arrogantly emerged from behind her gigantic colleague.

'In English that means, "Dearie, dearie me!"' She shook her head sorrowfully, her eyes narrowed with triumphant dislike. 'Oh dearie, dearie me, DI Huss.'

CHAPTER FORTY-THREE

Hanlon rolled over Serg's naked body and checked her phone. She sat up and pushed her hair back from her face. Serg ran his fingertips down her spine, tracing the beautiful outlines of the muscles on her back.

Sweat was drying on their bodies in the warm air of the FSB's – the Federal Security Service, the KGB's replacement and Serg's employers – safe house.

'So how did you know I'd be in Stuttgart?' she asked.

'I'm in Germany a lot,' said Serg, 'and I work in military intelligence. I know many things. I thought I'd surprise you.'

'Well, you certainly alarmed me.' She stood up and walked to the window on Panoramastrasse. The street was well-named. It lay high above the city and the lights of the centre glittered down in the valley below.

He pushed himself up on one side. He had a long, lean gymnast's body, the muscles sharply defined.

'You have an amazing backside, Hanlon.'

'I know,' she said.

She turned round. 'What the hell did you think you were doing, Serg, following me like that? I was just about to severely hurt one of your men. He was about to lose all his front teeth.'

'I was looking after you.'

'Oh were you? I'm capable of looking after myself.'

Serg propped himself up on one elbow in the rumpled bed. 'I know. But you have powerful enemies, Hanlon. Belanov for one. And now you're mixed up with Neu Schicksal.'

'So you'll know what I'm doing here in Stuttgart?'

'Not precisely, in general terms. Neu Schicksal and Wolf Schneider are obviously of concern to the Kremlin. That's what brought you to my attention when I looked for your name, when I started wondering what you might want that for.' He nodded at the container he'd brought in a plastic bag for her. He grinned. 'Most women want chocolates… Your half-assed English anarchists aren't really my concern.'

'And Al-Akhdaar?'

'I'm more concerned with the growth of IS in Georgia, and its allies in Chechnya and Dagestan, but you could have guessed that, Hanlon.'

'I did.'

She walked over to the bed and sat down by Serg's side. She leaned forward and stroked the fine, almost oriental hair on his head. His mother had been Tartar and Serg's green eyes had a slight Mongolian roundness. He had a kind of half-breed beauty that she found irresistible. Her fingers rested on a patch of scar tissue above his hip about the size of a playing card.

'That must have hurt.'

'A souvenir from Vladikavkaz in Ossetia… Twelve years ago.' Serg propped himself up on one arm. Hanlon ran her hand over the taut biceps. She listened to his sonorous English as he told her of the firefight. The dilapidated dacha near the Tsey Valley. A semi-automatic in his hand, eighteen rounds in the magazine. The brilliant red of blood on pristine white snow. The explosion and the fireball, a running figure, the impact of the round in his side, knocking him over. Sprawled on the ground. Two two-round bursts from his gun. The fleeing man collapsing as if knocked over by a giant invisible hand.

'But did it hurt? Not really, a bit. Now, this is another reason I was following you, to keep you safe from her.'

Serg sat up with easy grace and reached for his laptop.

He entered a password and tapped away then showed Hanlon the screen. She looked at Georgie Adams.

'What's she doing here? I thought you didn't have any interest in half-assed British anarchists.'

'I don't. But she shows up on the files. She has Perm Mafia connections. Belanov has the same friends. Caucasus heroin mainly; that and prostitution. The anarchist stuff is just a front.'

Hanlon frowned. 'How would that help?'

Serg said, 'Your intelligence services regard them as a joke, a bunch of idealistic idiots, and most of them are. So, if they attend a rally abroad they're not going to be checked rigorously or searched because they'll scream it's political persecution, so you can bring in coerced sex slaves to work in London brothels and say they're here for a conference, and you can more easily bring in drugs and money.' He shrugged. 'Adams is the sort of person that officials respect, you know that. She's of the establishment. We know they have links with student bodies in London.'

'So Adams is a criminal, plain and simple?'

'Sure, she's just using Eleuthera. I have no doubt that most of them haven't got a clue how the organization is financed. Or care. She's a very nasty piece of work, though, implicated in several killings and torture and intimidation of women.'

'That lying piece of shit, Hinds,' said Hanlon bitterly.

'Trouble?' asked Serg.

'No, not really,' Hanlon said. 'My colleague will be a bit disappointed, that's all. She was led to believe that Eleuthera were some kind of international conspiracy with connections to major political parties, not some bunch of idealistic idiots being played for fools by a drug smuggler and general gangster. She'll feel let down. I can't have a printout of any of your paperwork, can I, make it official?'

'I'm sorry, no. It is a confidential police document, but now you know it exists you can do a police to police request, it'll just take a couple of weeks. Let me know when the paperwork is sent and I'll take it from there. Without me, you'd never get it, not in today's climate. I'll authorize it, make sure it gets done.'

'Thanks,' said Hanlon. She thought Melinda Huss would be gutted to know that her conspiracy theory was just that, a mere fantasy. That Eleuthera were not connected with the Al-Akhdaar killings at all.

'Anything else I can help you with?'

Hanlon looked at his body, the clock, calculated flight check-in, travel time to the airport. She slid on to the bed. Her mouth covered Serg's as her tongue sought his tongue and her body straddled his.

'There was just one thing,' she breathed.

The laptop screen reflected their sweat-drenched interlocked limbs as Hanlon wrapped her legs round him beneath the inscrutable gaze of Georgie Adams, the sun glinting on her pierced nose ring.

CHAPTER FORTY-FOUR

Huss, under the threat of the Presa and the enormous bulk of Frank Muller, found herself bound to the treatment table. While they had been securing her they kept up a conversation in German of which Huss understood nothing at all. What she did understand, chillingly, was their lack of concern. It was obvious that they felt perfectly capable of being able to deal with her.

The Velcro restraints that were usually used to hold the guests in position whilst their chakras were realigned, healing stones balanced on healing nodes, and to keep them passive during ayahuasca shamanic healing ceremonies so they didn't trip over and hurt themselves whilst tripping on hallucinogens or whatever modish mumbo-jumbo was flavour of the month, held her firm. Adams brutally slapped a piece of gaffer tape over her mouth.

'Hang on a minute,' said Georgie. Muller and the dog halted. Neither he, nor the dog, spoke English but they both understood what was a command, and there was no doubt as to who was in charge. She leaned over Huss and quickly, professionally, patted her down. Then upended her handbag and took Huss's mobile phone and car keys from the assorted things in there.

She turned the phone off, pocketed the keys and swept everything else back into the bag.

She and Muller disappeared up the stairs.

Adams halted at the top and turned and looked down at Huss on the table. 'I'll be back down to deal with you later,' she said, 'once I've moved your car.' Then she turned and left Huss to her thoughts.

I'm going to die, I'm going to die, Please God, don't let me die.

To avoid panic she focused on what she now knew. No more speculation.

Arzu.

The cryosauna was in full view. The mystery of Arzu's hiding place was a mystery no more. It might well have been Arzu's thumbprint that had opened the keypad but that hadn't been Arzu's decision. Arzu's hand and forearm had been detached from his body. They were sitting now in a tray, on a shelf on the other side of the room, defrosting.

So, Arzu hadn't killed Hübler. It had to be Schneider. Or the other two men, but it would have been Schneider's decision. She wondered why. Audio memories of conversations, Hanlon's face frowning as she had said, *'I'm not even sure what her relationship with Schneider was, come to think of it. I thought they were having an affair ...'*

And all that talk of 'loyalty'. Was it a *crime passionel*? Or had he done it to boost his popularity ratings?

Hübler.

Obviously not killed by Al-Akhdaar. For whatever reason, the Germans had done it, obviously aided by Georgie Adams. It very much looked, she thought, as if Eleuthera had been behind all the UK killings, Elsa and Kettering too.

Hinds.

Well, she finally believed that he was, as he claimed, a totally innocent dupe in all of this. That what he had said was true. He was now her only hope of salvation but, of course, as far as he was concerned the Germans were innocent and he would be thinking that right now protection officers would be quietly taking their positions up in the lodge.

Her only hope was Hinds.

Maybe he would get bored waiting for her and come and look for her. It was a slim hope, there was a warrant out for his arrest, after all, and he would be understandably nervous about encountering armed policemen, but it was a hope.

Or he'd meet Adams as she came to move the car and intervene. Would he have the guts to confront her, would he chicken out? If he did tackle her, would he win? Hinds was tough, but she was beginning to suspect that Adams was unstoppable.

She was like Hanlon, serenely self-confident, floating in a bubble of self-belief. An opinion bolstered by those around her.

But Hinds was still a possible source of salvation. When he saw Adams surely he would suspect something had gone wrong, or would he think that to act might be to disrupt Huss's plans? Was he even still there?

He was all she had.

Apart from Hanlon. Where was she right now? In London probably.

Huss lay and looked at the ceiling.

Hopeless.

CHAPTER FORTY-FIVE

Hinds was getting bored in Huss's car, waiting for her to get back from the lodge. He had a half bottle of brandy in his jacket but this was running perilously low. He toyed with the idea of going into the hotel for a drink but felt he simply wasn't dressed for the Rosemount. He was expecting to be arrested and had dressed accordingly: old jeans and a sweater that had seen better days. Uncle Cliff had said he'd find out which nick he was going to be held in and would use contacts to brighten up his life inside.

Hinds was reasonably happy with the way things were going. The truth was, he had been doing very poorly as a freelance journalist. His family contacts, which he'd thought would be useful to differentiate himself from other freelancers, had proved too old-fashioned. The old London gangs were yesterday's news. Readers wanted more relevant stuff. Cyber-crime, people trafficking. His flow of published work had all but dried up.

After he'd found himself in bed with Georgie Adams and got to know her friends, and after he'd seen the wave of revulsion and disgust at the Anonymous protestors in his local pub after some rally or other outside Parliament, he had thought, sod it, why not, and had constructed a conspiracy theory, throwing in references to the hard left and Islamic terrorists.

That's got contemporary relevance, he thought.

He added a few non-actionable hints of contacts between the anarchist hard left and the Labour and Conservative parties (he wanted to be even-handed) of a disturbing nature, just to season the mix.

It was a brilliant and elaborate hoax. Two national daily papers and a Sunday bid for it. He added some photos of Georgie naked to excite them further. Sex, conspiracy, politics, Islamic terrorists, sex texts, pics, it had everything.

Sod the truth, thought Hinds.

He rolled himself a joint on the back of his phone, wound the window down and shook the surplus weed and tobacco away.

He dropped the phone in the passenger door compartment, got out of the car and crouched in the bushes and lit his spliff.

Hiding in the bushes, he reflected on the amazing success of his deception. Finding himself on the run only added to the credibility of the whole outrageous fabrication. But who could gainsay him? Eleuthera could hardly claim they were being misrepresented. They did want violent global revolution.

Let them sue.

Another drag on his joint.

But then it wasn't just the press who believed what he had to say, which was what he wanted, Eleuthera had got wind somehow of what he was writing and they believed it too.

That was the terrible thing.

He had invented a conspiracy involving murder and the complicity of Eleuthera and Al-Akhdaar and it had turned out to be true.

Georgie Adams and Mark Spencer thought he had stumbled upon a secret plan of theirs, God alone knows what that was, and what had turned into a game had now become some form of reality. They really were after him. There really was an Islamic connection. They really were involved in murder.

And he had thought it was just fictional.

His would be another death on their hands, but not a planned one, an incidental one. An incidental death.

He puffed away quickly, the grass fuelling his sense of dissociation from reality.

Georgie Adams had sent Mark Spencer and James Kettering to kill him. He had been attacked, he had defended himself, they had killed that anarchist fool themselves to frame him.

He couldn't believe it had got so out of hand. And Georgie Adams was bloody dangerous.

It was no longer a game.

Footsteps scrunching on the shingle of the car park. He peered round the bush, was it Huss? A figure in combat trousers and a hoodie. The hands gloved. No, Jesus, thought Hinds, it was Georgie Adams. The person he feared most on earth. He had no doubt she would kill him on sight.

Think of the devil, and she'll come.

He watched with a growing sense of dread as the woman got behind the wheel of the Golf and drove off.

Huss, he thought, oh my God!

Things had just got infinitely worse and they were already pretty bad. The only person who actually wanted to help him was in Eleuthera's hands.

Get help? Who would believe him? The police that Huss had mentioned in the hotel would nick him the moment he approached them.

He had to find Huss himself. He wished he wasn't so stoned, it was hard to think straight.

He started to jog down to where he knew the lodge lay, keeping in the darkness of the path behind the shrubbery away from the brilliantly illuminated lawn.

If Eleuthera killed Huss as well as Schneider, his prints would be all over Huss's car. His phone was in it! They wouldn't even need to frame him, he had managed it all by himself. He felt sick to his stomach. He was wanted in connection with two deaths, he had no doubt that absolutely nobody would ever believe him if Huss were dead.

He quickened his pace. There was the lodge, the front gate was open. Had Eleuthera taken the place over already? He had to know what was going on.

Hinds slipped inside and crept up to the window of the living room. There were two men in the room: an enormous, burly giant with a savage black beard like the French rugby player and a bald, fat guy with glasses and a huge, evil-looking attack dog. He could hear that they were speaking German. No sign of Huss.

The fat, bald guy got up and left the room. Hinds stayed where he was, desperately trying to think what to do.

What had happened to her? The Germans were obviously

in no danger, Georgie Adams or that boyfriend of hers must have ambushed Huss. Hinds couldn't think clearly any more.

At least Eleuthera weren't here.

He had to warn the Germans before Adams killed them; the bitch was capable of anything, and doubtless he'd get the blame.

He couldn't just bang on the door, he was wanted by the police. Besides, why would the Germans believe him? They wouldn't have a clue who he was. He could be a terrorist for all they knew.

Where the hell was Huss?

He could feel a metaphorical noose tightening around his neck.

What was he going to do?

CHAPTER FORTY-SIX

Huss heard the sound of the door at the top of the stairs open and craned her head round. Her heart sank.

There, silhouetted against the light of the hall behind, was the sinister form of fat and jolly Dr Kellner, beaming at her with his blubbery lips, his eyes bright behind his thick glasses.

He closed the door behind him and made his way carefully down the stairs, moving slowly and purposefully. Huss could see that his cheeks were flushed and he kept his eyes unnervingly fixed on her tethered form.

He paused at the table by the wall and switched on a desk lamp. Kellner's shadow was thrown monstrously against the wall.

He advanced towards her in the semi-darkness until he was standing looking down at her face. She watched as he licked his thick lips slowly with his fat, pink tongue, and ran his gaze slowly, inch by inch, from her bound ankles to the crown of her head.

She could smell him, a mix of eau de cologne, sweat and cigar smoke, overlaid with the stale fumes of brandy.

He leaned over her and ran the back of his plump hand that smelled of soap over her cheek. Huss gagged.

'Oh, dear, DI Huss,' he said softly, licking his lips again, savouring her helplessness. 'What is it you say in English? "Curiosity killed the cat."'

Huss glared at him with hatred. He smiled at her.

'You really are a very attractive woman, DI Huss, very attractive indeed.'

He licked his lips salaciously, then leaned over her so his face was very close to hers. She could smell his sweat and she could see the thick hairs that sprouted inside his nose as he inhaled her perfume. She felt like throwing up.

'You smell delightful, *meine liebling Frau. Und dein Arsch ist schönsten.*' His hand hovered over her breasts. '*Und deine Brust...*'

Hinds had moved round the side of the house and peered in the narrow, rectangular window at ground level that belonged to the treatment room. My God, he thought, it's Huss.

She was strapped to a table and it was obvious what was about to happen. The Germans had Huss captive? Why? Myriad thoughts whirled through his head. Well, it had to be something to do with Georgie, she had Huss's keys, after all.

He saw the fat guy's trousers fall to his ankles and frantically thought of ways to intervene. He couldn't phone anyone, his own phone was in Huss's car.

He looked around him for inspiration.

Run and get help, he thought. The police would nick him, but at least he knew where Huss was. They'd have to go and check. It'd be too late in one sense, but at least she'd still be alive.

He stood up and crouched down, keeping low, and then heard the crunch of steps on the gravel.

In the lights that illuminated the driveway he could see the huge shape of Muller closing the gate that had been open when he had arrived – there was no sign of the dog.

He was trapped within the precincts of the lodge. The gate was unclimbable, the hedge solid hawthorn, impenetrable.

Hinds realized that Adams had to be in league with Schneider. How or why scarcely mattered. He tried to come up with something. He thought wildly of kicking the window in. That would, at least, distract Kellner. It would also bring Frank, Schneider and the Presa.

His heart sank. There was nothing that he could do, nothing at all.

Miserably he watched through the window as Kellner bent over the bound form of Melinda Huss.

CHAPTER FORTY-SEVEN

The BA flight touched down at Heathrow. Serg had used whatever arcane influence he commanded to get her an utterly pointless upgrade, allowing her to sit in the front row and have her jacket hung up on a coat hanger and her coffee from a china cup instead of a paper one.

An hour and a half between Stuttgart and London. As she sat in her car stuck in heavy traffic between Heathrow and Oxford, it struck her that it was probably going to take nearly as long to drive the forty or so miles down to the Rosemount.

She tried her phone again – would Huss never pick up? Annoyance was giving way to concern. She called Enver. His phone was off too. Maybe that was it, thought Hanlon. She was staying at his place in London.

Traffic started moving and Hanlon drove up the slip road to the M25. She put her hand back into her handbag and touched the small canister that Serg had given her. She had inspected it in the bedroom of the safe house in Berlin, the Cyrillic script meaningless, the skull and crossbones logo, however, needing no translation.

'Does it work?' she said dubiously.

'Yes,' said Serg. 'It even works on bears.'

'How do they know?'

'They got some guy to test it, in Perm, in Siberia. They rounded up a couple of bears, starved them a bit, then put him in with them.'

'That was brave of him.'

'I don't think he had any say in the matter,' said Serg. 'Anyway, it worked. For God's sake, don't inhale any.'

They had kissed goodbye and she had been driven to the airport by Nikolei Gennadyovich Kamenev, the man who'd masterminded her surveillance.

She drove round the M25 and then down the M40. The traffic was light and the Audi felt good on the road. She took the spur road for Oxford and then the main road that led near to the Rosemount.

Hanlon had no clear plan in mind, but she did want to check on the Germans who she knew were scheduled to leave soon. What Lottie had told her was unsubstantiated, but she believed her, and there was photographic evidence held by Georgie Adams. She had a feeling things were coming to a head fairly soon.

She turned off the main road a couple of miles from the hotel and took the B road to where the anarchist campsite had been and pulled over in a lay-by. She got out of her car and changed into more suitable clothing – steel-toed army boots, combat trousers, jacket and a balaclava – and dropped several items into a small rucksack, then she set off up the track to where the caravans had been parked. From there, she would head through the woods, the way that she had come the other day when she had been pursued by Gregory.

She could see a dark car parked up ahead. It was the only vehicle, the anarchists were long gone. She approached it warily, her feet silent on the fallen leaves that littered the track, her body invisible against the dark line of the hawthorn hedge that bounded the rutted way.

A VW Golf, the plates she knew, Huss's car. Hanlon's pulse quickened, this was not good. She walked up to it and looked inside. Huss's bag, her phone visible.

Hanlon started to run up the hill to the lodge. She had run fast with Stevens behind her, armed and dangerous, but not as fast as she was running now.

CHAPTER FORTY-EIGHT

Huss watched Kellner's face moving closer to her own. Nearer and nearer it came, the doctor moving with sadistic slowness. She closed her eyes, flinching, her skin crawling as she waited for his hands to touch her, then, suddenly,

'Florian!'

Schneider's voice was like a whipcrack. Kellner straightened up and Huss opened her eyes. Schneider had appeared at the top of the stairs, interrupting his deputy. There was a furious exchange of German and then Kellner, with a reddened and enraged face, like a scolded adolescent, bent down, pulled up his underpants and trousers, fastening himself with hasty movements, and then stamped heavily away up the stairs.

Outside, Hinds let out a sigh of relief. He started to examine the long window in great detail. He was a Hinds, breaking and entering ran in the family. The window wouldn't pose much of a problem.

Schneider walked up to Huss, his face frowning with anger.

'I must apologize for my colleague. I'll stay with you until

Adams gets back. We are an honourable organization but sometimes I have little say in the choice of my colleagues. I think soon I may have to have a bit of a purge, but that is for another time.'

He started to wander around the room, drumming his fingers on things. Huss could now see he was a man under a great deal of strain. He had a dead body in a freezer and a policewoman bound on a table, a loose-cannon potential rapist and a psychotic minder together with a psychotic dog. And God alone knew where Adams fitted in.

Schneider turned to address her, to explain himself. 'All I wanted to do was save Germany from the niggers and the Muslims and stand up to the Russians. Save us from ourselves really.'

More walking around, more pushing his fingers through his hair. He turned to her and he had tears in his eyes. 'I really respect you, DI Huss, and I hate the fact that you're going to have to die.'

So do I, thought Huss. Part of her, though, was flooded with relief, almost gratitude that he had saved her from Kellner. She thought, It's like Stockholm syndrome, don't be grateful, this man is going to kill you!

Schneider's crocodile tears weren't helping either. If you feel that badly about it, thought Huss, let me go. Lose this nauseating self-pity, this 'now look what you've made me do' attitude.

He sat down on a chair near her head, a man unburdening himself, anxious to explain. I suppose he can afford to tell me everything, thought Huss bitterly, since I'll be taking his secrets with me to the grave.

'Kellner started it,' he said. 'I didn't know at first that he was bankrolling the party by laundering money for the Russian Mafia – that was Georgie Adams's idea. She has political connections in Germany through the international anarchist movement and it was her idea to use us to launder Russian Mafia money. She approached Kellner as a middle man, I mean woman. She got a cut, we got a cut,' said Schneider.

So now it's Kellner's fault, is it? thought Huss. So it was Kellner's idea to accept Georgie Adams's offer of money from the Russian Mafia disguised as party donations, not yours, Schneider. You were too busy formulating policy to worry about the nuts and bolts of party finance.

Schneider continued his self-justifying explanation. 'We'd charge three euros for every one we took from them, put the money they gave us as party donations through our accounts for tax purposes and reinvest the clean money in their legit businesses.' He laughed. 'People assume it's the big *konzerns* behind us, industrial backers, but it's Mafia money. Russian money. And then Hart got wind of it – we were old friends, from when we were· kids, we grew up together, partied together, he knew everything about me – so she killed him and invented the Al-Akhdaar organization, let the Muslims take the heat, and that was genius.'

He poured himself a glass of water.

Huss lay there immobile, silent, the perfect audience for Schneider. She was like a priest in a confessional and soon she would be bound by more than a vow of silence. She would be dead.

It was undeniably clever. Her respect for Adams

grudgingly increased. Who would imagine that a far-right German nationalist party would be financed by Russian organized crime? Who would suspect the anarchists of anything so organized, so capitalist? And then to pin the deaths on the bogeymen of Islam. Even though Al-Akhdaar didn't actually exist, ISIS sources had claimed the executions as theirs.

'So we invented Al-Akhdaar and, as you can see, everyone believes us. Why wouldn't they? And, I'm afraid, DI Huss, that it's Al-Akhdaar that are going to kill you.'

Schneider was right, it was genius.

'And then that idiot Hinds somehow stumbled across a connection. He didn't know Al-Akhdaar were a fiction, but he knew Eleuthera were linked somehow and Georgie was involved. To be honest, we didn't know how much he did know, that's why he had to be discredited. No one would believe him as a paranoid murderer.'

Schneider heard voices upstairs.

'I'm just sorry about you, but at least I can ensure your death will be dignified and painless. I promise I'll make sure of that. I won't ask you to forgive me, but I hope now you can see why I acted as I did. I simply had no choice. I will leave you now.'

He turned and she watched his back disappear up the stairs.

I don't want to die, thought Huss. She could feel tears in her eyes but she refused to shed them.

There was a click as the door shut behind Schneider.

Huss closed her eyes in despair, then shivered as a cold draught blew across her. That was unusual.

She heard a scraping noise. She opened her eyes and turned her head.

Her heart leapt with adrenaline-fuelled excitement. The long, narrow window had opened and as she watched, first she saw a hand, then an arm, then the back of a head as a slim figure of a man squeezed himself through the aperture with agonizing slowness. There was only just enough clearance for his head. Back of head, left arm and shoulder, back and buttocks, leg until he lay along the window ledge. Then he swung round, feet first, still with his back to her. He dropped lithely on to the floor and turned round.

Marcus Hinds. He grinned at her triumphantly.

Thank you, God! thought Huss.

CHAPTER FORTY-NINE

Hanlon ran up the dark silent track that ran through the field and up to the maize strip that shivered mournfully in the cold night air. She rounded a bend and found the footpath that led through the woods to the Rosemount easily enough. There was a sign and a stile by a gap in the hedgerow.

She climbed over the stile and dropped down on to the frozen ground on the other side.

The path would eventually skirt the base of the hotel's large formal gardens and the edge of the lodge. It was narrow but clearly defined, lined on one side with the leafy tracery of dead ferns and low bramble bushes that had a covering of frost, which glinted in the moonlight from above. On both sides stretched the frozen trees of the woods.

It was about ten minutes along the track that she first saw the lodge over the top of the hawthorn. It was a clear night and the roof and upper storey were plainly visible. Lights were on in one of the rooms and there was another blaze of light from the window above the front door.

Her breath steamed as she ran through the frozen leaves. Hanlon clambered through the dead foliage by the side of the path to examine the structure of the hedge. The dead bracken and nettles crunched beneath her army boots and the thorns of the brambles snagged on her camouflage combat trousers. The ground was treacherously uneven under her feet and she could feel the ridges of mud, hard as iron. Iced water shone where puddles had formed and frozen over on the dark ribbon of the track.

She approached the hedge and examined it, anxious to make sure the Presa wasn't going to burst through at some unexpected juncture. The neatly trimmed branches rose silently above her head – she guessed it was about three metres in height. The foliage was dense, impenetrable, with vicious thorns strong enough to pierce leather. There was no way to clamber through that. She moved back to the path and a little way further down found what she was looking for.

Just about visible by day, if you didn't know that the shelter was there, by night you would never have noticed it. It was almost in complete darkness but she didn't want to use her torch for fear of attracting the dog. What was easy to see by day was less so now. Brambles had fallen back over the door and the flight of steps leading to it a couple of metres from the path.

Hanlon descended the concrete steps, feeling the way cautiously with her booted feet for a couple of metres, trampling the foliage underfoot, until she could see the steel door.

She had a lightweight rucksack slung over her shoulder. She unslung the bag and took a torch out, opened the door and went inside.

The first thing she noticed was the absolute darkness and

silence of the place. It was like being inside a tomb. She shone the powerful flashlight around experimentally. She had more time now than when she was last here.

The shelter was empty of everything except a couple of stacks of old metal-framed plastic chairs and some rusting machinery of indeterminate purpose. The air was damp and smelled of mould.

Hanlon walked the length of the shelter, some twenty-five metres, she guessed, to where the dancing beam of the torch had picked out the form of the other door. She also saw the empty window frame through which she had wriggled a few days previously. Now that she had time she thought she'd get the door open. She wasn't sure that she might not need it.

When she reached the door that opened out to the garden, she examined it closely. It was a sheet of old, rusty steel, much thicker than the one she had come through. She tapped it experimentally with the side of her fist. It felt rock solid.

The handle was rusted immobile, there was no give in it at all. She turned her attention to the hinges. These looked far more promising. The door frame was wood with a concrete surround, the wood itself rotten and the concrete cracked. She unslung her small rucksack and took out the cold chisel. There was no need to bring out the small, heavy hammer she'd packed.

She prised the hinges out of their surround, the wood flaking away easily. It had been there for over seventy years and it had turned to powder. She felt the heavy door move. She hooked her fingers around it and pulled it inwards until she had created a gap big enough for her to squeeze through. She looked through the space she had created into the garden of the house.

The moonlight illuminated the lawn that lay outside the shelter as effectively as floodlights. There was virtually no cover between where she was and the silent shape of the lodge before her. There were no lights showing.

She squeezed out of the gap where the door had fallen slightly forward, still attached by the rusted lock. One of the bushes, a rhododendron she guessed by the evergreen foliage, screened her as she stood there thoughtfully.

She was now opposite the front of the lodge. She decided to skirt round the perimeter of the garden till she was at the rear. She could see lights on in the two rooms flanking the front door and two in the upstairs bedrooms. One was a rectangular window over the front door, so she assumed that the hall lights were blazing and the other one had curtains drawn.

She had no particular plan beyond trying to ascertain if Huss was inside.

Hanlon was in her dark clothes, combat trousers, a winter fleece, fingerless gloves, and she now pulled on her balaclava, which she had removed for her run. Only her eyes were visible. Around her left arm she had wrapped a long, very thick weightlifter's belt that belonged to Serg so her forearm was strapped tight. A little like one of those Roman gladiators. She slung the small rucksack over her shoulder and set off parallel to the hedge.

She had reached the side of the house when she saw the

Presa. It must have been sitting outside the back door and now its keen nose had picked up her scent. It didn't bark, it strode arrogantly out to the edge of the lawn and then silently ran towards her, its ears cocked, its tongue lolling and its very white teeth glinting in its open mouth.

Hanlon crouched low, waiting for the animal. The Presa snarled, a deep, vicious noise, and leapt forward, the target for its teeth Hanlon's face and throat.

She braced herself for the impact.

The Presa, almost without slackening pace, its lips drawn back over its white teeth, hurled itself at Hanlon. She crouched down, steadying herself with her back foot, and raised her left arm that was protected by the heavy leather strapping of the weight belt.

The force nearly knocked her over, it was more like being hit by a truck than an animal but she managed to stay upright. The dog bit down on her arm, growling and snarling. Reflected in the moonlight, its eyes were shining, glowing discs. It threw its weight to one side, trying to flip her over so her throat would be exposed. The pressure she could feel through the leather protecting her arm was awesome. She wondered how many psi it was.

Quickly, before the dog relinquished her arm and moved on to her face, she brought up the can of Soviet Union era pepper spray that Serg had given her, which was in her right hand, the stuff that could neutralize a bear, and squirted it in the animal's face from point-blank range.

Ever since she had seen the Presa destroy the Dobermann, she had been wondering how she was going to deal with it should she have to.

The effect of the spray was immediate. The dog let go of her arm and, whimpering, backed away, rubbing its muzzle on the ground in pain and shock from the searing effects of the chemically enhanced capsicum on its sensitive nose and eyes.

It zigzagged along the lawn, leaving a furrow of bent grass as it tried to seek solace and relief from the cold ground for the terrible burning sensation in its face. It had never experienced anything like that in its life, and had no intention whatsoever of going anywhere near Hanlon now. It had decided she was too dangerous.

Keeping a careful eye on the animal, Hanlon resumed her walk to the rear of the house. It didn't follow.

Huss, where the hell are you? she wondered.

CHAPTER FIFTY

Hinds ran over to Huss. She looked at him from the table and he tugged the tape from her mouth.

'You OK?'

'I'm fine, untie me.' Hinds reached down to free the restraints from her wrists when they both heard voices and the door at the top of the stairs opened.

Hinds froze where he was. Huss saw him desperately glance around the room. The steps into the basement were straight down with a solid wall that formed the banister. Unless you actually leaned over and looked down you wouldn't see anyone, your sight line being the room itself as it opened up in front of you. Hinds ran to the wall and flattened himself against it.

Muller appeared, walking slowly down the steps, looking at Huss with a kind of grim smile on his face. He stopped and looked at the open window with a measure of surprise but mentally shrugged and continued down. Huss saw Schneider appear, following him.

As Muller reached the bottom, Hinds sprang at him. It was almost like a flying rugby tackle and the giant German staggered as Hinds crashed into him. He stumbled into the wall and turned his head as Hinds's fist slammed into him.

Huss watched as the two men grappled with each other. Muller was enormous, but Hinds was resourceful and Hinds was strong and Hinds was good in a fight.

He grabbed Muller's wrists and the giant, who was in a kind of half-crouch now on the slippery, modernistic glass and marble tiles underfoot, slipped forward as Hinds heaved again, putting the weight of his back into it. The two of them staggered around as their balance went, collapsing with a muted thud in a heap on the floor. Hinds was up first and he drove his knee into the side of Muller's head, dazing the giant who was knocked backwards, legs and arms sprawling.

Schneider had stayed back from the fight until this moment, but now he acted. He had moved so he was behind Hinds, who had his hands full with Muller. There was a pair of surgical scissors on a shelf, shiny, pointed stainless steel, their tips needle sharp. They glinted in the overhead strip light.

Schneider snatched these up and drove them hard like a dagger into Hinds's unprotected back. The handles of the scissors jutted out from the fabric and a wet patch almost immediately visibly formed through the black fabric.

Hinds gave a kind of hoarse scream. He reached backwards, his hands unable to reach the scissors, fingers ineffectually scrabbling to reach the source of the agony, but by now Muller was on his feet, powerful hands grabbing at him.

Blood, very, very red, poured out of his back on to the whiteness of the tiles and still Muller was on him. Huss watched powerless, Muller standing over Hinds who sank to his knees as the giant's hands circled his throat, choking the life out of him.

It seemed to take a very long time. An agonizing death for Marcus Hinds.

Huss watched as Hinds's body relaxed, his arms, which had been clawing at Muller's, dropped to the floor and his head fell forward.

From above they heard a woman's voice. 'Jesus Christ, what a fucking mess! What the hell have you been up to?'

Georgie Adams was back.

CHAPTER FIFTY-ONE

'That's much better,' said Georgie Adams approvingly.

Kellner had appeared behind Adams with his arms full of cleaning materials and the three men and Adams had set to work.

The body of Marcus Hinds had been wrapped in bin bags, the floor and all the other surfaces were being meticulously cleaned.

Adams had taken over control of the situation, to the obvious relief of all concerned. She paused after a few minutes and spoke to Schneider.

'Tell Muller to get upstairs and check on the perimeters and the house security. I closed the gate behind me, and I can't see any reason why we should be disturbed, but I want to know that everything's OK up there.'

Schneider nodded and relayed her instructions to Muller, who put down his mop with relief. He disappeared up the stairs.

Now Schneider and Kellner looked up at her expectantly.

'Get that lot,' she said, pointing to the bin bags containing Hinds's body, 'into Muller's van. I want Arzu in there too. Leave the hand. We'll need that for later, add the finishing touches.'

Schneider and Kellner nodded. Within ten minutes the basement at the lodge was spotless.

Schneider said, 'Won't there still be traces of blood around?'

Adams nodded. 'Probably, but there's four litres or so in her,' she said, pointing at Huss. 'We'll spread it around a bit, a few of Arzu's fingerprints here and there. Another victim of Al-Akhdaar.'

'*Sehr schön*,' said Schneider admiringly.

'Shall we kill her now?' asked Kellner.

Adams shook her head. 'No, last minute. I want us to be able to access this room if necessary without getting blood anywhere it shouldn't be.' She looked at Huss in an evaluating way. 'Also, if anything goes wrong, we've always got a hostage.'

Huss lay miserably on her table with her eyes open but unseeing. She hadn't cried until the death of Hinds. Now she felt nothing. She guessed she was in a state of shock.

No help would be forthcoming. The protection team up at the hotel would have no cause to come here. Presumably Schneider, Kellner and Muller would all decamp later. She'd be found in the morning, why wouldn't anyone assume that Al-Akhdaar had done it? She probably would if she were in their shoes. They all believed so strongly now in ISIS's potent reputation that of course everyone would think they did it. Murdering an attractive, young blonde British policewoman, what could be more ISIS? Arzu's prints everywhere. They certainly wouldn't imagine that Schneider would have had a hand in it – what could he possibly gain?

And even Templeman would probably put her death down to her own impetuousness, her own desire to have her conspiracy theories proved right, hiding in the lodge hoping to arrest some imaginary anarchists, who, irony of ironies, were imaginary.

Hinds's other woman, his other source, if she ever came forward, would back up the Al-Akhdaar theory and Marcus Hinds would forever remain a suspect in two murders, maybe even her own, if there were a stray piece of forensic evidence that hadn't been tidied up.

She opened her eyes and looked into the eyes of Georgie Adams. They were slightly almond shaped and her round face with its small nose and slight dusting of freckles and a very full, very cruel-looking mouth was extraordinarily attractive.

Adams leaned forward. 'Don't go away,' she said. She left the room, turning out the light as she went.

CHAPTER FIFTY-TWO

Hanlon looked up at the tall walls above her. Apart from one room, the lodge was in darkness. She was at the rear of the house. She heard voices and moved away into the darkness of the garden. Muffled instructions, the noise of the front door being opened, footsteps on the gravel of the drive and then the crash of the rear doors of the van being slammed. She waited a few minutes for things to settle down and then crept forward, back towards the house. She quickly moved to the lighted window that was next to the back door and looked in.

It was the kitchen where Enver had spent his time working. He had naturally left it scrupulously clean. It was a large, square room with a large, square steel table in the centre. It was very much a part-time kitchen that saw occasional use. Most of the guests would choose to eat at the hotel in Michelin-starred luxury. There was none of the signs of use of a kitchen in which someone actually cooks a lot. There were no bottles of oil or pans and dishes left out, no sign of disorder, no scrunched-up tea towels. It was quietly, forensically tidy.

The big work table in the centre was a gleaming, blank surface. In the far corner an expensive gas range with a section that she guessed was a built-in griddle. There was still a prep list in Enver's handwriting on the shelf containing spices and herbs. No wonder the kitchen looked so tidy with Enver fussing over it, she thought. God, if anything happens to Huss he'll never forgive me.

She did note with wry amusement that he, or more likely the kitchen porter, had forgotten to switch off the griddle plate of the stove. The icon under it was glowing bright red.

There was a double sink and various machines, white goods, dishwasher, fridge, freezer under the expensive work surfaces. It was very sleek and minimal, the walls bare apart from a metal shelf with cartons and containers of spices over by the stove in the corner.

She noticed outside the back door, near where she was standing, was a mat with two dog bowls, one for food, which was empty, and one for water. There was a kennel behind them. The Presa's lair.

She tried the handle to the back door and to her relief it was open. She'd be able to get in easily if necessary. She closed it again. Somewhere in this house she expected to find Huss or some sign of Huss. She resumed her circumnavigation of the outside walls.

The next window along proved to be the living room. She peered in. There were four people in there: Schneider, Muller, a third man that she hadn't met but recognized as Florian Kellner, and Georgie Adams, looking very much coolly in charge.

They were all sitting down, deep in discussion. Hanlon thought briefly. She was weighing up the odds if it came to a fight. Kellner could be discounted as a physical threat, too old, too flabby. Adams, she felt perfectly capable of flattening. Schneider she likewise discounted. He was a politician rather than a fighter. That only left Muller. If he were taken out of the equation she knew who she would put the money on if it came to a fight.

Huss would be somewhere in the lodge, where else could she be?

Muller was a risk she was able to accept. Nobody could possibly imagine there might be someone prowling around, not with the dog securing the outside perimeter.

Hanlon moved back the way she had come to the front of the lodge and studied the van that was parked outside.

It was a large white Mercedes with German plates. She guessed it was Muller's, that inside there would be a cage for the Presa. It was unlocked and she opened the passenger door and climbed inside. Sure enough, there was a massive barred structure in the rear of the van to contain the dog, with two thick rolls of carpeting inside.

She heard a whining and a scrabbling at the van door. She looked out, the Presa was outside, wanting to get in.

Hanlon looked around her. The car key was in the ignition. She took it out and put it in her pocket, then, holding the can of pepper spray at the ready, she opened the passenger door a fraction, then pushed it open with her foot.

The gigantic dog barely paid her any attention. It recognized her as the pain-dealing woman to avoid but it didn't want her anyway. It was the stuff in the back that it wanted to get at, the stuff with the meaty smell. It leapt into the front seat and then disappeared over the top of that into the back of the van. It pressed its muzzle up against the mesh of the cage, sniffing and growling.

Hanlon looked at the rolled-up carpeting with new eyes. Not one, but two rolls, six-foot lengths.

The dog's sinister interest aroused her suspicions. God, I hope that's not Huss in there, she thought. She held her torch between her teeth and reached a couple of fingers through one of the gaps in the square mesh and tore open a gap in the bin bag that poked out from the carpeting like the filling in a wrap. She wriggled her fingers inside, and felt. Hair. She shone the torch down, dark hair.

Hanlon repeated the performance with the other roll, this time it was boots, boots too big to be worn by Huss.

Two bodies, neither of them Huss's.

Hanlon toyed with the idea of getting help, instantly rejected it. There was no way of knowing what would happen to Huss if she did. Personally she thought it more than likely that Georgie Adams would kill her at the first signs of police intervention. Serg had translated the police report for her on Adams's history and crime involvement and it made grim reading. And who knew what Schneider would do.

What she had learned from Lottie would be enough to destroy him, two more bodies would be the final straw. The end of his political career, the end of his existence. He might well decide to go out in a blaze of glory.

Götterdämmerung.

The twilight of the gods.

Hanlon jumped out of the van and slammed the door shut. She locked it with the remote and moved away to the bonnet where she would be hidden from the view of anyone coming out of the front door.

Time to take out Muller, her biggest obstacle to finding Huss. She thought of Huss in Adams's hands and allowed her rage to build up inside her.

Come on, Muller, she thought.

For a few seconds, nothing happened, then the movements of the Presa triggered the internal sensors of the van and the alarm started its two-tone wailing, in time with the lights flashing.

The front door of the lodge opened and then slammed shut as Muller stood there, swearing in German. Hanlon unlocked the door with the control.

Hanlon heard '*Scheisse*' and '*Hund*' and then the scrunch of his feet on the gravel as he went up to the driver's door and went to yank it open, or tried to.

As he did, Hanlon materialized alongside him. He blinked in surprise as in one smooth, ultra-fast movement she turned side on to Muller, minimizing herself as a target, right hand shielding her face, left ready to jab. Moving off her back foot, she straightened up and leapt forward.

Hanlon's fist thudded into his face. Her mind went back to when she'd been in the ring with a comparable-sized man, God, she thought, it was only just over a week ago that she'd been sparring with Chris Campbell in the Bermondsey gym.

This was so different. Muller was his size, but he didn't know how to fight. He had no guard. As she sprang towards him he had blinked in surprise, his hands held at shoulder height. Her knuckles had powered through his lack of defence.

It was her left fist that had smashed into his eye socket, fracturing the bone, and as he recoiled from the force, her other hand, her right, driven by the force of her hips and legs, had crashed into the mass of hair that was his face. Blood poured from his smashed nose, splashing down his T-shirt.

A look of pained surprise, then anger crossed his face.

The force of the punch was immense and he staggered back, his hands flailed at Hanlon but he was woefully slow. She side-slipped one wild throw of his huge fist and ducked, crouching low, as another passed over her head. Then she turned and ran.

Muller was slow on his feet. She ran just fast enough so he couldn't catch her. She sped away from the house in the direction of the shelter, Muller panting after her. She slipped through the bunker's open door, giving him time to grab a hold of her jacket. He was almost twice her weight, nearly twenty stone, but momentum was on her side and as his fingers dug in she dived forward, pulling him off balance, twisted like an eel and sprayed the last of the Russian pepper spray into his eyes.

He immediately let go of her and clasped both hands to his head, a hissed litany of curses escaping his lips. Now Hanlon really went to town.

Muller was blind and in agony.

Another combination of punches from Hanlon, a left hook into the side of his head, another right hand, and now he had both hands in front of his face, trying to shield his head whilst he tried to work out what was going so terribly wrong.

His head was ringing with concussion and pain. His eyes were burning, acid, he thought, I'm blind, and on top of that hard blows, massive punches were raining down on him. Nobody had ever hit him like this. How can this be happening? he thought. It can't be happening.

But it was.

Suddenly she saw his legs go, she had knocked him practically unconscious.

Hanlon closed in on him. Her left hook had opened the skin at the end of his eyebrow, and blood was trickling into his eye, blinding him. She had no need to pace herself, the important thing was not to let up for a second. His body was straight on before her, she had the whole pick of him for a brief moment as a target. She danced up to him and kicked him straight between his legs with her steel-toed boots.

All her force. All her strength. Slamming into his balls.

His core exploded with pain.

There was no referee to stop her, no rules. Muller gave a grunt of agony and folded up, his body dropping down. As he did so, her hands, left and right, hooked into the side of his head.

I'M GOING TO PUT YOU TO BED sang through her head, sang through her brain.

Explosive, sweet punches. Harder than she'd ever hit anyone before. Into his temples. Right and left.

BANG!

BANG!

The force of the blows rocked his head to one side and then the other, he was completely disoriented, black shapes swirled in front of his eyes and he thought he was going to throw up. He could no longer stand or lift his arms.

He fell to his knees and, barely conscious, crawled across the dirt floor of the shelter. As if kicking a rugby ball she booted her steel-toe cap as viciously and hard as she could into his right kidney. His body sagged down and he roared with pain and she did it again, in the same place.

She could see his eyes close and his body go limp as he finally lost consciousness.

She stood there looking down at him in the semi-darkness. She pulled off her constrictive balaclava and shoved it in her bag, shaking her wiry, dark hair free.

She felt slightly dazed. For her the world had contracted to just the space where she was and the bloodied body on the floor in front of her. She had forgotten where she was.

A male voice she had heard before said, 'I don't think he's going to make the count, DCI Hanlon.'

Schneider stood there behind her, a torch snapped on and she could see he was not alone. The .22 that Spencer had used the other day, its muzzle unmovingly trained on her, was held by Georgie Adams.

CHAPTER FIFTY-THREE

Huss lay in the darkness of the lodge's wellness centre. She had heard selective noises filtering down from above: the sound of the car alarm; footsteps from running feet; the banging of the front door.

In her state of heightened awareness where every sound could have vital significance, she felt almost psychically attuned to what was going on. Whether or not this was simply imagination or reality, her five senses keyed to a pitch they never normally had to work at, she didn't know. Maybe it was like the sensation when you have a car crash, that everything is happening in slow motion.

She thought with excitement, It has to be Hanlon. If it were her colleagues there would be an awful lot more activity, not least calls for the occupants of the lodge to emerge. None of that. She sensed disturbance, urgency, and then she heard voices, calm now, measured tones, and her heart sank.

She thought sadly of Marcus Hinds, his handsome face and tousled dark hair casually shrouded in a bin bag, and she remembered too the sadistic glee in Georgie Adams's eyes.

She had no doubt now that Adams was involved in this not for any money – her wealthy Scottish family were more than capable of buying her anything she could have wanted. In an idle moment, back at the station, she had googled her father who was, as Templeman had said, a prominent lawyer in the corporate world and non-exec director of several firms.

Georgie Adams was doing this because she liked hurting people; more than that, thought Huss. She liked killing them.

She thought of Adams, going to Russia as part of her university studies, getting drawn into the shady Russian *bizniss* world where crime and capitalism and politics meet. No, that was wrong, Adams wasn't the sort of person who would be drawn in, she had gone there to deliberately find the kind of lawless, amoral thrills that she craved. Sex, power, money, crime.

It was all there to be had.

And what a find for the Russian Mafia, what an envoy. Posh, rich, British student, no suspicion attaching to her. And studying politics, of course she could meet people like Kellner, she had perfect cover.

And she had brains and organizational ability and, with a face and a body like that, the most amazing hold over men.

And the awful thing was she would probably get away with it. Muller would spirit the bodies of poor Arzu and Hinds away. Both of them killed to take the blame for murders that they hadn't committed.

She would die and the non-existent Al-Akhdaar would take the blame and Schneider's popularity would rise another few percentage points.

She lay in the darkness and thought that in a way it was significant that Adams had stage-managed the crucial killings of Gunther Hart, Christiane Hübler – both of whom had been on the verge of exposing Schneider – to look like the work of an IS splinter group. She was a kind of Jihadi John figure for whom the main attraction was not ideology, but death.

And death would come to her soon.

That much she knew.

CHAPTER FIFTY-FOUR

The rifle in Georgie Adams's hands was ominously steady. The three of them, Schneider, herself and Hanlon, marched back to the lodge. Muller had been left where he lay. Kellner opened the door to them blinking in surprise, his reward a torrent of German from Schneider, and they went through into the kitchen.

'Go and stand in the corner over there,' ordered Adams. Hanlon did so. Her back was against the stove. Under the table she noticed a bucket of dirty water with a couple of tea towels in that had been left there by Enver's lazy kitchen porter earlier.

'You might as well give yourselves up,' Hanlon said.

The three others stood looking at her from across the broad kitchen table that lay between them.

Hanlon spoke again. 'There are two bodies in that van, Huss is here, I'm here and Frank Muller will need hospital. What are you going to do? You're screwed.'

Adams said, 'Muller's not going anywhere.'

Adams had obviously decided that Muller was not going to live. Hanlon realized that the dynamics of the situation had changed and that it wasn't Schneider now who was in charge. Georgie Adams called the shots.

Now, as Adams looked contemptuously at Schneider, as she turned her head and Kellner was polishing his glasses, Hanlon moved her hands behind her back and closed them around the tub of chilli powder that she had seen earlier.

'Get rid of her now,' said Kellner.

'No, I want the bitch to know we'll get away with it,' replied Adams. 'And, Florian, shut the fuck up and never, I said never, try and tell me what to do.'

There was a smile on her face, but her voice was cold. Kellner's not going to last, thought Hanlon suddenly.

'Sorry, Georgie,' said the chastened deputy leader.

Now, as the two of them discussed her, glaring at each other, she, hardly daring to breathe, flipped the lid off the spice and tipped the container's contents into her hands. She now had two handfuls of chilli powder. Hanlon imperceptibly moved closer to the red heat of the hotplate on the stove.

Adams looked at Hanlon, the rifle cradled in her arms.

'After you're dead, you'll join the others in the back of that van. I'll take it on the ferry over to Calais.' She smiled. 'As you may know, there's an anarchist camp down in the refugee area they call "the jungle". I've spent time there. The police down there are overwhelmed, not just with rioters and people trying to jump lorries but there are also quite a few murders, Afghanis killing Africans, Iraqis killing Syrians. Lot of unsolved crime.'

Kellner replaced his glasses. Adams addressed him, raising the rifle to her shoulder now. The muzzle pointing unwaveringly at the centre of Hanlon's body.

'Crime that goes unreported, crime that the French police have no intention of solving.'

She turned to Kellner.

'Florian, you can go downstairs now and kill that woman.'

Kellner's fat, baby lips twitched with pleasure. 'How?'

'I want as much blood as possible in the room, none on you, I want her to bleed out, slowly but surely. I'm sure you'll cope, you're a doctor.'

'Oh, Florian,' Schneider's voice was gentle, 'I told her it wouldn't hurt, give her a local anaesthetic or something, do it gently...'

Kellner looked at Adams for confirmation.

'Fine, I don't care, I'll cut her head off later.'

You bitch, thought Hanlon. Their eyes met across the room, Hanlon's grey eyes gleaming with hatred.

Kellner smiled and left the room. Schneider stood trying to look impassive. In fact, he looked distinctly ill at ease.

'Arzu and Hinds will be found in the fields. They'll be put down as dead refugees. Nobody will investigate them. I'll let the dog alone with your body for a bit.'

She paused to let the message sink in. 'We don't want identifiable hands and face.'

Schneider added, more, Hanlon guessed, from a politician's dislike of being sidelined than anything else, 'You'll just have disappeared, Hanlon. Huss and Muller will be found dead in the morning, killed by Al-Akhdaar. Kellner and I will leave in about half an hour, Muller staying behind to settle our bill and then catch the eleven o'clock flight to Stuttgart, and all of this will all be over.'

Georgie Adams raised her rifle.

CHAPTER FIFTY-FIVE

The light flickered on in the treatment room and Huss turned her head slightly to see who was coming in.

She had been hoping against hope that some form of rescue might come. It was always Hanlon that she thought would deliver her, if anyone. Thoughts of rescue filled her mind, visions of an armed response team clattering down the stairs to her rescue, hopefully after some heavy small-arms fire upstairs.

But now all hope faded as she saw Kellner with his blubbery, creepy grin and a small medical bag.

He put his bag down on the desk, took out a hypodermic syringe and inserted the needle into a small glass bottle, which he dropped back into his bag. He held the hypodermic up to the light and did an air shot to make sure there was just liquid in the barrel of the syringe.

He stood next to her as she lay bound and immobile on the table, then reached down and pulled her shirt up so he was looking at the expanse of flesh between her waistband and her ribs. Then he gently inserted the needle and injected her with whatever was in the syringe.

It was painful, but not unduly so.

'It's a local anaesthetic,' he explained. 'I don't want to hurt you, DI Huss.'

He waited a minute or so, then dropped the syringe into his bag and took out a skewer-like implement.

He pushed the end into Huss's side. She felt the skin part and then a dull pain as it made its way into her body, but most of the pain was countered by the local. The probe disappeared inside her, then there was a feeling of resistance and she felt – she couldn't have heard, could she? – a slight pop and Kellner's features, on which had been a frown of concentration, relaxed.

He swiftly pulled the instrument out and almost immediately a thin trickle of Huss's blood followed.

Kellner stroked her cheek. 'I've made a small nick in your liver, DI Huss, and you'll just slowly bleed away. It won't hurt at all. You'll feel a bit faint, that's your blood pressure dropping. In about a quarter of an hour you'll lose consciousness, but I'll be down to see you before that... We have unfinished business to attend to, my darling. We were interrupted last time...'

His hand stroked her with greater urgency, he leered at her.

'... then, after I've finished, in about another quarter of an hour, you'll be dead. *Das ist nicht so schlimm*. But don't worry, it'll be painless, like going to sleep.'

He stood up and straightened his tie.

'See you soon, *meine liebling*! *Tschüss*.'

She watched as he walked away up the stairs. She hoped she would be unconscious before he returned.

She lay there still and silent.

What else could she do?

I'm dying now, she thought.

She wasn't in any pain, the local anaesthetic in her side had taken care of that, all she could feel as the blood trickled out from her right side was a faint tickling sensation as it flowed down her skin and a spreading warmth as it pooled underneath her body.

She could see the redness of her blood if she raised her head off the table and she could hear it dripping on to the floor. It was almost beautiful. Other people's blood, and she had seen a fair amount, made her feel sick, but she didn't mind the sight of her own. She could smell it too, heavy and warm.

She was still feeling quite calm, tranquil almost, but she could feel herself becoming light-headed. She wondered how much blood she had actually lost. She felt another warm trickle down her body. It seemed to be leaving her body in irregular bursts. It wasn't unpleasant. In fact, if you had to choose a way to die, bleeding out like this was not a bad way to go at all.

She thought of Enver Demirel, her fiancé. He would miss her. Poor Enver. She thought of Hanlon.

Hanlon would avenge her, she thought.

Nothing would stop Hanlon.

She closed her eyes and her breathing slowed.

CHAPTER FIFTY-SIX

Kellner reappeared in the kitchen.

'All done?' asked Adams.

'Yes,' said Kellner.

'*Tot?*' asked Schneider.

He nodded. '*Sie stirbt.*' He looked at Adams. 'She's dying.'

Hanlon was waiting coldly for her moment. Huss was dead. She had failed to rescue her, but she might be able to avenge her. Melinda Huss would want that.

'And now it's your turn,' smiled Georgie Adams.

The rifle barrel centred on Hanlon's face. She took a deep breath, inhaling as much as she could till her lungs were full, and tipped the contents of both hands on to the burning metal.

As she felt the chilli powder spill from her fingers, she instantly closed her eyes.

The fumes released as the fine spice hit the red-hot metal of the griddle were invisible, more of a gas than a cloud of smoke. With unbelievable speed it filled the kitchen. It was like the heat of a chilli but squirted into the soft tissue of the eyes and nose. Incandescently painful. And totally immediate. No real warning.

One instant Adams had Hanlon's face squarely in the sights of the rifle while she tried to think of a more discreet way of killing her that would avoid spilling blood. The next her eyes were in absolute agony and her nose and mouth on fire.

Adams had no idea what was happening. She automatically opened her mouth, gasping in shock, and in her panic sucked in a lungful of the searing gas. She bent double with the pain. Uncontrollable tears blinded her – it was more or less the same effect as the pepper spray had on the dog and Muller.

The two men were similarly affected. It was the same ingredient, capsaicin, as in the spray, the sort that's used in mace and crowd control agents, and to Adams, Schneider and Kellner it felt like acid had been rubbed into their eyes and tipped into their lungs.

Hanlon heard the gasps, shouts, choked swear words and coughs from the three of them. She heard the noise of the table squealing as its legs pushed against the tiles of the kitchen. She heard a crash as Kellner blundered into the tall steel bin by the back door.

Adams's rifle was useless. She was blinded by the gas. She had no idea where Hanlon was. She was in too much pain to think. She couldn't see.

Hanlon, her eyes still firmly closed, dropped down to her knees. Her foot had been resting against the bucket of water with the cloths in, and now she plunged her hands into the bucket, grabbed three wet tea towels and swathed her head in them.

The soaking wet cloth over her face, mouth and lungs

protected her from the main effects of the gas, as far as breathing was concerned, but she knew that her eyes would be affected the moment that she opened them. She at least knew what was causing the pain, she knew what was coming.

She jumped to her feet, parting the wet cloth that obscured her face so it looked like she was peering out from a veil, niqab-style. Kellner had his back to her, his eyes firmly closed, and was fumbling for the door into the garden, escape foremost on his mind.

Adams had both hands over her face, the rifle lay on the table and Schneider, coughing and choking, hands and arms outstretched like a man playing blind man's buff, was heading to the door of the kitchen.

Hanlon leaned across the table and grabbed the rifle by the tip of its barrel and pulled it towards her, but now her own eyes were streaming uncontrollably. Still, she had the gun now. Triumph and relief flooded her.

Then she thought, Huss?

CHAPTER FIFTY-SEVEN

Bent over, coughing and wheezing, barely able to see, Schneider ran into the hall and kept going.

Still in the kitchen, Hanlon was not in much better shape than the three others. She couldn't believe how much the stuff hurt. She had the rifle, she felt along it until she located the safety and checked it was off. The gun felt heavy and reassuring, but she doubted she could hit anything except a wall. Her eyes were on fire. Coughing and crying, bent double, tears streaming from her eyes, she staggered into the hall after Schneider.

Practically blind, Schneider tripped over Kellner's medical bag that he had left in the hall. As he stood up after his stumble, Hanlon was on him. She dropped the rifle. She wanted him in her hands, she wanted to tear him limb from limb. All rational thought had disappeared in a wave of bloodlust.

She slammed a straight right into his face and as he fell back from the force of the punch, hit him with a flawless left hook. Schneider staggered back in the direction of the steep stairs leading down to the treatment room and Hanlon pushed him hard so he fell backwards step after step after step in a whirl of arms and legs.

Now Hanlon grabbed the .22 and ran down after Schneider. He moved backwards into the treatment room. He cowered away from her as Hanlon stared at Huss, like a body on a morgue table, covered in a blood-sodden sheet, her eyes open.

For a second, Hanlon thought that she was dead, then she noticed a slight movement of the crimson fabric. Huss was still breathing.

'Shit,' said Hanlon. Ignoring Schneider, she ran over to where Huss was lying and pulled the sheet back. She grabbed a towel and pressed it to Huss's side, trying to make a pressure bandage to stop the bleeding.

'Get up off your ass, you piece of shit, and hold this bandage,' barked Hanlon.

Schneider did so while Hanlon dialled emergency services on the landline, then the hotel reception to get a medical team down.

CHAPTER FIFTY-EIGHT

Kellner found the handle and yanked open the back door. A rush of cold air billowed in. He stumbled outside coughing and choking and Adams, aware the rifle was gone, followed him. She had seen what Hanlon had done to Frank Muller, she didn't want a similar fate. She had noticed the look in her eyes when she had learned Huss was dead. She knew exactly what would happen to her if she fell into Hanlon's hands. No mercy.

Outside the back door, Kellner and Adams looked at each other. Adams stared at him with contempt. He was so useless, she thought.

'*Mein Gott*, what are we going to do?' wailed Kellner.

Adams was already moving.

'The van,' she commanded.

Kellner panted after her. He was overweight and hadn't run anywhere since he'd been at school. His feet slipped on the wet grass. Hanlon would be phoning the police. Disgrace, prison, ridicule, ruin, all of these lent him speed. He wanted to get back home to Germany as soon as possible, see his lawyer. Get his side of the story in first. His brain slipped into gear. None of this was his fault. He was just easily led, too nice for his own good.

Schneider, it was all Schneider.

He was frightened of Adams too, but more frightened she would leave him behind. Drive off without him. It's just the sort of thing she would do. He gasped with the physical effort, he had a terrible stitch, and put a spurt on but she overtook him as they reached the van, heading for the driver's door.

Still sobbing with the unaccustomed exertion, he flung open the rear doors of the van.

The Presa was angry and still in pain. It was also furious at being cooped up in this van and the smell of blood from the two inaccessible bodies was infuriating. It had been shut in the van now for a long time and it was enraged. Anger made it violent. Never a rational dog, its small mind was full of the need to sink its teeth into something and tear and tear and tear… Then suddenly the doors of its prison were thrown wide.

It seized its opportunity. It sprang into action.

Adams, in the driver's seat of the van, felt the vehicle rock as the dog sprang forward. She heard a tearing, high-pitched scream from Kellner as sixty-five kilos of muscle and teeth slammed into him. She risked a quick look back and almost wished she hadn't. Kellner was down on the ground with the dog standing over him, its jaws clamped on the man's calf.

The Presa shook its head vigorously, tearing at Kellner's flesh. He howled and screamed in pain, the leg of his trousers darkening in colour, his fat arms beating ineffectually at the Presa. His struggles and blood excited the dog even more and its powerful jaws suddenly left its leg and then, cobra quick, fastened on to his arm.

Adams put the van into first and drove away. Kellner's glasses lay smashed by his side, his eyes bulged with agony. He screamed continually now and the dog's eyes stared at his naked throat with interest. It let go of Kellner's arm and transferred its grip to his soft, yielding windpipe.

After a while Kellner ceased to move and the Presa dragged him into the shadows by the shed where he could finish what he was doing uninterrupted.

That was where the police found them later.

CHAPTER FIFTY-NINE

It was the hotel doctor and assistant with plasma who beat the ambulance by three or four minutes. As they got a line into Huss's vein, her eyes opened and alighted on Hanlon. A small smile flickered across her lips and then her eyes closed.

The Diplomatic Protection sergeant and two of his men clattered down the stairs. Hanlon recognized him from Claridge's. She pointed at Schneider, sitting sullen and defeated on the floor.

'Nick him,' she said.

Schneider's wrists were cuffed. 'Charge?' said the sergeant.

'Attempted murder of two police officers,' said Hanlon, curtly. That'd do for now. 'Oh, by the way, you'd better follow me with a medical team,' she said, remembering Muller.

Another protection officer, firearms she assumed from the badges on his uniform, appeared. They had found Florian Kellner, or what was left of him.

'Sorry, sir,' he said. 'You're going to need to come and look at this.'

The sergeant looked around the bloodstained room, the stretcher containing Huss being carried up the stairs, the German MP with the badly beaten-up face. There was a severed wrist with hand attached in a bowl on one of the worktops. Idly, the sergeant wondered who that had belonged to. He stared at the woman in front of him. He had heard rumours about her that he had refused to believe as being too far-fetched. Well, he thought, time to re-evaluate.

If anything, they had wildly underestimated her.

She was looking at him belligerently. He said, conversationally, 'Well, DCI Hanlon, you certainly know how to throw a party.'

CHAPTER SIXTY

Two days later Hanlon visited Huss at the Radcliffe Hospital. She reversed her Audi neatly into a bay in the car park and sat for a while behind the wheel.

She was glad that Huss had survived, not least because the following week was Mark Whiteside's surgery. The survival of Huss seemed like the best omen she could have for the operation.

She was not remotely religious but she found herself at times like this praying for a successful outcome for Whiteside's operation. She desperately wanted him back. Being with Serg had reminded her of the depth of feeling that she was capable of, but had refused to allow herself ever since Whiteside had been shot. It was like a part of her was in a coma too. In a deep freeze.

She shook her head briskly. When, when, not if, Mark Whiteside recovered, then she would allow herself to live again.

Briskly, she got out of her car, slammed the door behind her and strode across the hospital car park.

*

Huss was sitting up in bed attached to two IV lines, propped up on pillows and her hands outstretched, like she'd been crucified.

'How are you feeling?' asked Hanlon.

'Oh, fine,' said Huss. 'Thank you for—'

'Don't mention it,' said Hanlon curtly. She didn't want to be thanked and Huss knew that she wouldn't want to be, that it would embarrass her.

'Thank the Lord Enver didn't see me like that,' said Huss.

'Indeed.' Hanlon had seen Enver just after Huss had been taken away to hospital. Enver had been back on his duties in the main kitchen as junior sous. None of the kitchen staff had any idea of the drama that was unfolding just a couple of hundred metres away and of them, only Enver was all that interested.

The food was the primary concern. The kitchen was all that mattered. Their whole world. Nobody knew who Schneider was, or cared.

Now the police had left and everything was back to normality.

Enver was due to officially leave the Rosemount that day at noon, on the excuse he had been recalled back to the agency.

'I have made the cover of *Bild*, though,' said Huss with amusement. She showed Hanlon the German tabloid with a photo of her on a stretcher, paramedics on each side. Huss's blouse was open and she was showing a lot of cleavage. It was really the main focus of the image. There was a smaller photo of Schneider being pushed into a police car, looking grim.

'What does it say?'

'*Die Schöne und das Biest*. Beauty and the Beast.' It carried the byline Jurgen Flur. Huss continued, 'I've been in the *Oxford Mail* but never a red top. Especially a German one.' She raised her honey-coloured eyebrows. 'Excitement.'

Hanlon smiled, Huss put the paper down.

Huss decided to change the subject. 'So it was all a big con.'

'In a way, but slightly odder than you think.' Hanlon told Huss about her trip to Germany, her visit to the dwarf prostitute.

'Schneider had threesomes with Lottie and Gunther Hart at Oskar's. Almost certainly Hübler joined in. He may even have met Hübler there. Perhaps *Bild* will run an exposé. That's why he got Adams to kill Hart, because Hart had threatened to expose him. Hart knew nothing about money-laundering for the Russian mafia. People will put up with a lot from a right-wing politician, but they don't expect kinky sex. Especially gay, three-way kinky sex. He'd have been a laughing stock. You can't be a successful hard-right politician if people are laughing at you.'

'It's strange,' said Huss. 'He confessed everything to me, but not the gay sex. Killing people, Mafia connections, he was fine with that, the money laundering, but not the sex. It's not like I could have told anyone, isn't it odd?'

'Very.' Hanlon's mind flashed back to the transparently pale Huss and the huge amount of blood that had come out of her, the doctor who had saved her practically hysterical with relief that she was still alive. By all accounts it was Kellner's lust, wanting a still-living Huss to slake his desires on, that had kept her alive. A slightly deeper thrust into her body, another half-millimetre, and she would have been dead.

'And Christiane Hübler was going to go public?' asked Huss.

Hanlon nodded. 'She had photos, recordings, Lottie made them for her. That's why she seemed to have that odd hold over Schneider. She also guessed he'd arranged to have Hart killed by Adams, her and the lovely Dr Kellner. She got Lottie to send her the cream of the crop to her phone in England. That's when Schneider decided she had to die. She was like an unexploded bomb about to go off. One text to *Bild*, one attachment, end of Schneider.' She sat down in the chair for visitors. 'It had to be done quickly but, of course, he had Georgie available.'

'But why kill her in England?'

'Lottie gave me the date that she sent Hübler the photos of the three of them, Lottie, Hart and Schneider, having sex. Including Hart and Schneider coupling. It was the afternoon of when she was murdered. I don't know what she wanted, marriage maybe? Money? It scarcely mattered. She was untrustworthy. My guess is that she threatened him with the photos and he felt he had to act. He was one phone call away from ruin. Remember, he had Georgie – who better to entrust that to? She's by far the most competent of the lot of them.'

'So that's why he had her killed at the hotel?'

Hanlon nodded. 'Adams coerced Arzu into texting Hübler to meet him for sex in the kitchen. They'd had sex before when he showed her around the lodge. She killed Arzu, the hand was removed either by her or Kellner so his thumb would activate the lock on the kitchen door, and when Christiane turned up, she, or maybe her and Spencer, killed her. The lock gave the time of death, more or less, and the Germans all had an alibi, all present at that video conference.' She pushed her hand through her thick, wiry dark hair. 'It was very well planned. We all thought that Arzu was part of Al-Akhdaar and that he was the killer, just as Adams planned.'

'And Marcus Hinds managed to stumble on the truth?'

Hanlon shook her head. 'He invented a truth by mistake. He thought it was just a good story and that nobody would be able to prove otherwise. Even in his wildest dreams he could never have imagined that Adams had any links with Schneider.'

She got out of the chair and moved restlessly around Huss's room.

'He invented a non-existent connection between Eleuthera and Al-Akhdaar. Just to sell a story, just to make money. How was he to know that Georgie Adams was involved in money laundering and murder? How was he to know she had invented Al-Akhdaar as a strawman to pin a murder on? So when he said that he had proof, which of course he didn't, that Eleuthera were involved with Al-Akhdaar, she believed him. She thought he was on to her, and that meant he had to die and that his evidence, like that hard drive that Elsa had, had to be destroyed. We all kind of believed him, he fooled everyone.'

'So it all boiled down to sex and money,' said Huss.

Hanlon nodded. 'Islamic terrorism was never there, just

paid-for sex and dirty money. Arzu, Elsa, Hinds, Hart, Hübler, and the others, all dead just to feed Schneider's ego and Georgie Adams's desire for God knows what.'

'I wonder where Adams is now?' said Huss.

'God alone knows, but I'm sure she'll turn up again. She's probably at some anarchist camp somewhere. She's got great IT skills, seemingly, she's ex-Anonymous. I'm sure she's busy creating a new identity for herself. We'll doubtless hear from her at some time in the future. Spencer is on the run too.'

'And what about you?' asked Huss.

'I'm handing my notice in,' said Hanlon. 'Mark's got his op coming soon, he'll need me.' She sighed. 'I wasn't there for him before, I can at least be there for him now.'

CHAPTER SIXTY-ONE

It was his last day at the Rosemount. Enver finished plating the last of the breakfasts for a table of three – kedgeree, an omelette and eggs Benedict on a warm brioche – and yawned.

'Service,' he called. 'Table twelve, Bryony, off you go.'

'Thank you, Chef,' said Bryony. She hoped he'd be staying, all the waitresses did, he was so nice, so calm, and, my God, those muscles!

'Is there a problem?' he asked. She was suddenly aware that she'd been ogling him through the pass instead of doing her job. Such a nice face! Was it too soon to invite him out for a drink? Something told her he'd be shy. Well, she could cope with that. She was well aware of how attractive she was. She expertly took the plates in her long, elegant fingers and, smiling bashfully at Enver, swept out of the kitchen into the dining room.

Enver, oblivious of Bryony and unaware of her interest in him, checked his phone – no message from Huss. Twelve o'clock and he'd be out of here for good.

He wondered vaguely what had got into Bryony. She was behaving very oddly.

He looked at the prep list on the wall:

Harissa sauce, gin and tonic jellies, langues du chat, *turned potatoes (DESIREE NOT KING EDWARDS!!!!!!)*...
it went on and on.

He ran his finger down the list, fifty-one items.

No longer his problem. He started work on the harissa.

'Hi, Enver, can I see you in my office...'

It was Harry Jones, the sous.

He followed him into the office.

'Czerwinski's told me the agency want you back and they're sending me a replacement,' said Jones, leaning forward in his chair and taking a mouthful of coffee.

'Yes, Chef, I'll be sorry to leave,' said Enver, waving an apologetic hand, 'but you know the decision's not mine. I go where I'm sent.'

'Oh, sure,' said Harry, 'but, well, I'm very impressed with your work, Enver, you're a sodding good chef and I was wondering if you'd like to come and work for me full time. The salary will be good, and we're going places, Enver, this could be your big chance...'

Enver sighed and leaned over Harry's desk...

And in London, in a rented room in Kilburn under another name, Georgie Adams had dyed her hair a mousy blonde and coloured her eyebrows to match. With her new glasses she didn't look much like her old self at all.

She had plenty of money and plenty of confidence in her ability to build a new life. But first something for Hanlon to remember her by. Hübler had told Schneider the story of Hanlon and the man she loved and Schneider had told Adams.

Such touching loyalty, she thought. It really should be rewarded.

Not many London hospitals have ITUs dealing with long-stay head injury patients and it hadn't taken Adams that long to locate Whiteside. Neither did it take long to find the name of the company that had the cleaning contract for the hospital.

Cleaners are always needed and Adams, with her forged CV and backstory, a history of learning difficulties, was hired immediately. It didn't take her very long either, using a brute force algorithm, to hack into the cleaning company's systems. Access to company rotas had her transferred to the company cleaning team allocated to the hospital.

It wasn't hard at all.

Enver's feet scrunched in the car park as he hefted his bag into the back of his old Volvo and slammed the tailgate down.

He looked at the Gothic pile of the Rosemount and the enormous extractor vent like a ship's funnel that rose out of the roof of the kitchen.

I'm waiting for you, whispered the Rosemount kitchen, speaking for all kitchens worldwide. *You can run, but not forever.*

He felt his phone vibrate and took it out. He opened the message and the image attachment. It was Kelly Reeves, naked from the waist up, the date written in felt tip across her heavy breasts, each bearing a produce and day sticker, 'left' and 'right' in the appropriate place.

The message ran, *Dated and labelled, Chef! Just as you like it!! ;) Call me if you get lonely! xxx Kells*.

He shook his head as he clambered into the car and started to laugh.

Mark Whiteside shared a room with a man called Paul Bentley. There was a nurses' station just inside the ward's double doors, a ward with half a dozen beds, two single rooms and the double one Whiteside was in.

The room was cleaned every day at eleven a.m. Nobody notices cleaners. They're an anonymous part of the furniture. Adams carefully wheeled her cleaning trolley in and methodically locked the brakes as she'd been shown. The room was bright and airy with a view over the rooftops in the direction of the Seven Sisters Road.

The two men lay in their respective beds, various tubes attached to them and monitors for their vital signs displaying red electronic digits. Each man had a whiteboard on the wall near their heads for spur-of-the-moment notes from the nursing staff. Bentley's board said, *Does not like salmon*. As Bentley was perpetually unconscious Adams wondered momentarily what it could mean. He was hardly in a position to complain.

She looked down at the handsome, bearded face of Mark Whiteside asleep in his bed. So this was Hanlon's former colleague, here thanks to Hanlon's sticking her nose into other people's business. She wondered if he had been Hanlon's lover.

Adams thought, I don't need to leave a note, she'll know who this was from, and why.

She glanced through the circular porthole-type window of the room. The doors, skirting and woodwork was pale pine veneer. Presumably to keep everyone relaxed although the patients, at this end of the hospital, could be scarcely more so. The nursing station was empty, no one was around. There was an air of somnolence, of relaxed quiet about this ward, that was almost hypnotic. It was so peaceful apart from the faint noise of the machinery.

Adams took a hypodermic syringe out of her pocket. Heroin is very easy to come by, if you know where to look on the net. And Adams did.

'Sweet dreams, Mark,' said Georgie Adams, leaning over him. 'This is for you, Hanlon.' She put the needle into one of the veins in Whiteside's powerful forearm, drew back the plunger a fraction and watched Whiteside's blood swirl into the chamber. Satisfied she had the needle in the vein, she pushed the plunger in all the way.

Whiteside stiffened and then relaxed and sighed. It was done. That simple. That quick. Adams dropped the syringe into the mouth of his black bin bag attached to her trolley and pushed it swiftly out of the room and into the corridor.

As she walked away he could hear the noise of an alarm and of feet urgently rushing to Whiteside's assistance.

She smiled to himself. This is the way the world ends for Mark Whiteside. The sound of a medical emergency in a hospital, hurried footsteps on lino.

And in a hospital in the Oxfordshire countryside, DCI Hanlon said quietly to Huss, 'I think it's time for a new beginning.'

A letter from the publisher

We hope you enjoyed this book. We are an independent
publisher dedicated to discovering brilliant books,
new authors and great storytelling. Please join us at
www.headofzeus.com and become part of our
community of book-lovers.

We will keep you up to date with our latest books, author
blogs, special previews, tempting offers, chances to win
signed editions and much more.

If you have any questions, feedback or just want to say hi,
please drop us a line on hello@headofzeus.com

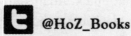 @HoZ_Books

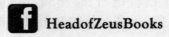 HeadofZeusBooks

www.headofzeus.com

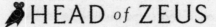

The story starts here